SKADI
AND THE
GEATS

STEVEN GRIER WILLIAMS

MILFORD
HOUSE

an imprint of Sunbury Press, Inc.
Mechanicsburg, PA USA

MILFORD HOUSE

an imprint of Sunbury Press, Inc.
Mechanicsburg, PA USA

For information about special discounts for bulk purchases, please contact Sunbury Press Orders Dept. at (855) 338-8359 or orders@sunburypress.com.

To request one of our authors for speaking engagements or book signings, please contact Sunbury Press Publicity Dept. at publicity@sunburypress.com.

FIRST MILFORD HOUSE PRESS EDITION: March 2024

Set in Adobe Garamond | Interior design by Crystal Devine | Cover by Derek Thornton/Notch Design | Edited by Gabrielle Kirk.

Publisher's Cataloging-in-Publication Data
Names: Williams, Steven Grier, author.
Title: Skadi and the Geats / Steven Grier Williams.
Description: First trade paperback edition. | Mechanicsburg, PA : Milford House Press, 2024.
Summary: Hrothgar, the Earl of Lejre, has staked his claim as ruler of Midgard, but only under the threat of physical harm. Children have been ripped from their parents. Communities have been destroyed. Hopelessness grips the weak and strong alike. But there are still those willing to fight for their home. Skadi is a skilled Viking warrior who, for the first time, will have to trust others to win the day.
Identifiers: ISBN : 979-8-88819-184-2 (softcover).
Subjects: FICTION / Fantasy / General | FICTION / Fantasy / Action & Adventure | FICTION / Fairy Tales, Folk Tales, Legends & Mythology.

Designed in the USA
0 1 1 2 3 5 8 13 21 34 55

For the Love of Books!

This book is dedicated to James R. Thompson. He is kind, thoughtful and forward-thinking. James represents all that we hope for in a public servant. He is also a wonderful friend and mentor.

ACKNOWLEDGMENTS

Thank you to the family and friends who continue to support my writing. I am so appreciative of you!

PROLOGUE

"I told you, Mother, I did not want to move. I had friends back home," said Hrothgar.

"Destin is with us. And you will make new friends."

"Yes, don't forget about me," Destin said.

"I just want to stay on the mainland."

"Our new home will be on the mainland," his mother said.

"Then why are we at sea?"

"Because it is the quickest route. We have discussed this. Listen, son, I know change is hard, but sometimes it is necessary. Be patient with your father and me. It is going to be ok."

Hrothgar reluctantly nodded and wandered to the starboard side of the longship. The sea spray washed over him as he stared out at the waters of Midgard. The sea was calm, and there was not a single cloud in the sky above. It was the kind of day that sailors dreamed of.

He and his parents had only left Borgarnes a few hours prior, but already he was homesick.

"What are you writing?" said Hrothgar, noticing Destin jotting down something on a scroll.

"It is something my first mentor would do so I started doing it too. I am reflecting on my thoughts and writing them down."

"What thoughts are you writing now?" Hrothgar said.

"They're private actually."

"What do you do with them then?"

"I keep them," said Destin. "You should consider writing down your thoughts like I do. I have moved before, and this helped."

"Your parents moved so you could study alchemy. My parents are moving for them," Hrothgar complained.

"They're moving for you too."

"Easy for you to say."

"Adjustment is not easy, my friend. But you will be ok. Trust me."

"You better end up the best alchemist in all the realms."

"It will be hard to surpass Gullveig. But I will give it my best effort."

Hrothgar looked out at the sea. Destin put down his scroll.

"I learned of an interesting alchemy skill."

"You know I do not understand how this alchemy works. Why do you bother telling me everything you learn?"

"Because it is interesting."

"I'm not interested."

"Hrothgar, just humor me."

The boy turned his attention away from the sea and towards his friend.

"Are you going to show me or just tell me about it?"

"Well, it would be a bit difficult considering where we are, but I can describe it."

Hrothgar rolled his eyes.

"I'm listening," he said.

"It's called sentient transmutation."

"That sentence had four words in it, and I was familiar with two of them," Hrothgar said.

"It is when . . ."

"Hold that thought," Hrothgar said.

Against the serene water, something in the distance caught the boy's eye. He turned to his parents.

"Mother and Father, do you see that what I see?" he asked.

The adults came to his side, and he pointed way off into the distance.

"It's a ship," said his father.

As it neared, the longship came clearer into focus.

"It does not look like a karvi longship like ours," said Hrothgar.

"It isn't," said his mother. "That's a skeid longship."

"Vikings," said Destin.

Hrothgar broke his gaze on the ship and looked up at his parents. He saw the terror on their faces.

"You two get below the deck boards in the storage, now," said Hrothgar's mother.

"But . . ."

"Now," she shouted.

Hrothgar and Destin ran away from Hrothgar's parents towards a hatch that led below deck. The boys found refuge in a corner. Their surroundings were mostly dark, save for rays of light that came through the breaks in the panels above. Hrothgar could hear his parents scrambling to turn their ship so they could flee, but he knew they were caught – the Viking vessel was moving too quickly.

"Get below with the boys," Hrothgar heard his father say.

"I won't leave you."

"Don't leave them."

Moments later the hatch opened, and Hrothgar's mother joined him and Destin.

"Mother, what is happening?"

"Quiet," she whispered. "They are here."

He shifted his attention to the panels above him and saw the shadows of multiple men walking across the deck of their longship.

"What do you want?" said the boy's father, his voice carrying below deck with ease.

There was no response, but the boy heard more and more footsteps as more and more men boarded.

"I don't have much."

"We know this ship. We know you are wealthy miners from Borgarnes. We have been tracking you since you left port. There are others aboard this ship somewhere. Find them."

Hrothgar heard this and his heart started to race even faster. He wondered, what did these men want? – he was afraid he knew the answer but did not want to admit it to himself.

"Mother what do we do?" he whispered.

She put her fingers to her lips. He scrambled to move closer to her and she rested a hand on her shoulder.

"Destin get over here," she whispered. "It is going to be ok."

"I don't have much. Just take what you want and leave," said the boy's father.

"Open that hatch over there," said one of the Vikings. "These merchant vessels always have special compartments with treasure to be had."

"Please, there is nothing here," pleaded the father. "You are correct – I am wealthy, but I keep my wealth on the mainland. Let me come with you and I can show you where it is."

"I said open the hatch."

Hrothgar grabbed his mother's arm and moved her and Destin away from the hatch. His father overhead ran to guard the entrance of the hatch.

"Get him out of the way."

Hrothgar then heard his father's guttural yelp and saw blood seeping through the cracks in the deck above. He put his hand to his mouth to keep from screaming and felt his mother's embrace tighten.

"Be brave son," she whispered. "You too, Destin."

Light flooded the storage compartment and Hrothgar, his mother, and Destin were dragged onto the deck of the longship. He saw his father lying dead on the deck in a pool of his own blood.

"Father," he shouted. "I'll kill you."

He felt his mother embrace him. He looked up and saw tears streaming down her face.

"Mother," he said softly.

"This must be the most pathetic crew I have ever seen," said the Viking who had stolen them from below deck. "It was foolish of you to think you could traverse these waters safely."

"We aren't afraid of you," said Hrothgar as defiantly as he could muster.

"You should be," said the Viking.

"Take the mother. Kill the boys."

Hrothgar turned back to his mother and shouted, "No."

Beyond her, he saw the sky darkening at a frightening pace from grey to black. The sea started to churn, rocking the ship in its growing waves. Then a lightning bolt flashed across the sky.

Hrothgar was not the only one to notice the change. Destin, the Vikings, and his mother all looked skyward as heavy raindrops began to fall. All parties were confused since only moments ago there was no sign of a storm.

While the rest looked up, Hrothgar shifted his gaze out to sea and saw the crest of a massive wave moving towards them.

He patted his mother's arm and said, "Mother, something is coming."

She looked in the direction he was staring, as did the Vikings and Destin. The wave grew bigger and bigger, and everyone save for Hrothgar, his mother, and Destin started to panic. The Vikings scrambled to get back to their ship and as they did the wave broke, sending water hundreds of feet into the sky.

Hrothgar grabbed his mother and closed his eyes as the water splashed down on the longship and the folks aboard. When he opened his eyes again, everyone on the ship was engulfed in a massive shadow. He looked up and nearly fell at the sight of the creature looming over them.

"What is . . . that?" he stuttered.

"Jörmungandr. The World Serpent," his mother whispered.

Hrothgar stared at the giant sea serpent and quickly noticed that the massive creature was not looking at them. It did not appear that Jörmungandr was even aware of them. Hrothgar looked in the direction that the serpent was facing and saw the tiny silhouette of a man hovering high in the sky.

A flash of lightning lit up the sky and even from far away, the boy saw that the floating man had red hair, a red beard, and a hammer in his right hand.

"Thor," shouted one of the Vikings.

The World Serpent started to move and the waves it created rocked the longship with such force that everyone was thrown off balance. Some of the Vikings were flung overboard.

Thor spun his hammer and hit Jörmungandr's massive jaw. The serpent crashed into the sea, capsizing the longship.

Hrothgar felt an arm wrap around him and pull him to the surface. His mother was holding onto a large piece of wood that broke from the ship.

"I have you, son," she said. "But I do not have Destin."

Above, chaos and violence reigned supreme as Thor and Jörmungandr battled. But below, fear and hopelessness pervaded amongst the humans caught in the middle of the struggle.

"Stay close," said Hrothgar's mother, pulling him as tightly as possible as she held on to the plank.

"Destin where are you?" shouted Hrothgar.

"I am here," shouted Destin reaching out beyond the darkness.

Hrothgar grabbed his hand and pulled him close to share the plank with him and his mother.

Turbulent waters made it nearly impossible to hold onto the plank, but the three did their best to cling to their only lifesaver. The Vikings who had attacked were not so fortunate and were all drifting away at sea. Most of them had already drowned, and the remaining few were actively drowning.

"Mother, we aren't going to make it," shouted Hrothgar.

"We will," she replied.

"I am scared," said Hrothgar.

As soon as he spoke, an oar that had gone under with the capsized longship, popped up from the sea, knocking Hrothgar and Destin free from the plank.

"Boys," shouted his mother.

Although he was separated from his mother, adrift at sea, Hrothgar looked up and through the sea spray and heavy rain drops he saw the mighty Thor bring his hammer, Mjolnir, down upon the head of the World Serpent. Massive bolts of lightning shot forth from the devastating blow, and the creature sank back into the black Midgardian waters.

The violent waves subsided, and a calm quickly returned. The clouds began to part, and Hrothgar knew Thor and the serpent were gone. His whole body shook with fear but he tried to match the surroundings and slow down.

"Son," said Hrothgar's mother, whose voice was noticeably weaker.

Hrothgar righted himself as best he could and turned his attention to his mother. Her body, or what was left of it, smoldered on the plank – the result of one of the lightning bolts from Thor's hammer.

He swam with all his might to be at her side.

"Mother," he shouted.

"Your father . . . and I . . . we . . ."

"Mother," Hrothgar gently shook her. "Please do not go."

Her body slumped onto the wooden plank, then drifted into the sea. He held her, but she was dead weight, and her soaked pelt dragged her down. He went under with her, attempting to bring her to the surface. He kicked with all his might to keep her with him, but his need for air eventually forced him to let her go. He rushed to the surface to gulp in some deep breaths.

"Hrothgar," Destin said, swimming to his side. "What happened?"

"They are gone," Hrothgar said solemnly. "I'm . . . alone."

ONE

A LESSON IN POWER

Twenty Years Later

For any passerby, the sound of footsteps and hooves marching down the moonlit road were all that would be heard. The men were silent, and the horses did not neigh. It had been many days since their last raid. Food sources were dwindling, and frustration was rising. The cold night air of Midgard was piercing. The wind wafted the smell of fresh bread, and an inn came into view. The leader of the group raised his hand, and all stopped.

The man next to him whispered, "Not here. This inn is too full."

"Which is why it shall be this one."

"There will be others."

"Hovard, I want to see what they have inside the inn."

Hovard paused for a moment, then looked back at the caravan of rugged men on horseback. The air was silent except for their clinking swords being unsheathed.

"Fell, inns were to be off limits," whispered Hovard. "You know that."

"That was then, my friend. Now there are no rules. It was their mistake for setting up an inn so far from any town," Fell said as he unsheathed a massive broadsword. "Stray from the pack and your fate is sealed. It's a cold night. I could go for a fire."

Hertha tended to the fire, heating the caldron which provided hot water to all the guests at her inn. Twelve families stayed with her—travelers

1

from all over Midgard. She was thankful to the Aesir and the Vanir for sending so many people her way.

"Love of my life," said Keld, her husband. "The family in the first room is asking if we carry mead from the Island of Erlend. They are also asking for more bread."

Hertha looked beyond the caldron she was tending toward the stove a few feet away.

"The bread is soon to be finished and we have just a few flagons left of the Erlend mead. It is not as easy to come by as of late, so be sparing. It is stored behind the flour on the top shelf," she said.

Keld nodded and proceeded to grab the fermented elixir. Hertha watched the man she loved for ten years pour the family a few cups of the drink and then disappear up the stairs.

She got up from the caldron to go check on the bread more closely and as she did, glanced out the window by the stove. Something in the shadows caught her eye, but she could not quite make out what it was. Hertha inspected the grounds from afar, then got closer. She poked her head through the window, did not see anything, then proceeded to check the bread.

The warmth of the stove calmed her nerves, and the smell of the bread gave her peace.

"Just a few more moments," she whispered before shutting the stove door.

"Is there enough to share?" said a mysterious man behind her.

Hertha turned around, startled. She knew she had sensed something or someone nearby. But she was not granted a chance to look upon the intruder. The hilt of a sword knocked her unconscious. Her body fell to the ground in a heap.

When she awoke, Hertha immediately realized she was bound to a chair and gagged. She struggled with all the might in her small body to get free, but it was to no avail. To her left, she heard mumbling. Keld was bound and gagged beside her. She looked forward as a man stepped into view and squatted in front of her. He grabbed the bonds around her wrists and tugged on them.

"Innkeeper, your establishment will serve as a decent respite from the cold for my men. The pace at which this realm grows bleaker seems to be increasing," he said.

"Mmmmmmmmmm," she mumbled through the gag in her mouth.

"Calm yourself," said the man as he reached up to pull the gag free. "You are tied quite tightly. You are more likely to hurt yourself than me."

"Who are you?" she shouted. "What do you want?"

The man put his pointer finger to his lips, then looked behind him. Hertha followed his eyes to where he was looking and saw the families staying at the inn all huddled together in the primary dining hall of the inn. They were surrounded by fearsome men with long beards and even longer swords.

"What do you want?" Hertha said as calmly as she could manage.

The man smiled and said, "From what I can tell, this is one of Midgard's more valuable establishments. All these families must mean you earn your fair share in gold, even in these desperate times."

Hertha looked at the man, then her husband, and then the captive families.

The man grabbed Hertha's cheeks and turned her attention back to him. "Am I wrong in my assessment?"

Hertha started breathing heavily and her eyes got red.

"Do you speak?" shouted the man.

"No," answered Hertha. "You are not wrong. The gods have looked favorably upon us."

The man stood up and looked over at another man in the corner.

"You see," he said. "What did I say? I told you this was the inn for us."

"Please take what you want and let us be," Hertha said.

"We intend to take everything."

"And you will let us be?"

"Give us no trouble and I will not kill you," said the man, stroking Hertha's face and wiping the tears from her cheeks.

She pulled back as best she could.

The man smirked and then pointed at one of the fathers in the room. A sword strike took the man's head and it rolled to a stop at Hertha's feet. The entire room erupted in hysteria, but the threat of further beheadings brought the families under control, save for the wife and the son of the man who was killed. They whimpered in the corner.

The man grabbed Hertha's chin and held her head steady. He finished wiping the tears from her red cheeks.

"Please let these people go. I'll give you whatever you want but let them go."

The man laughed.

"You came here for treasure. We have plenty, but it is safely hidden. If you hurt them, you'll get nothing," Hertha said.

"Defiant. How long have you and this one been wed?" said the man looking towards Keld. "Innkeepers are often husband and wife. Do you break from tradition?"

"Please do not hurt him."

The man placed his sword under the Keld's chin and lifted his head, so they looked at one another. Keld shook all over.

"Untie me and I'll take you to where we keep our gold."

"It seems tradition is alive and well here."

The man sheathed his sword before untying Hertha. He grabbed her under the shoulder and pulled her to her feet. His hands were rough to the touch and scarred.

"Lead the way," he said.

She looked back at her husband. He shook his head at her, and she silently responded, "I must."

Hertha led the man out of the main hall towards a hatch in the floor twenty feet away. She unhooked a chain and lifted the hatch, revealing a staircase that descended underground.

"Don't raiders raid villages and towns? I thought inns were off-limits. Even people such as yourselves need places to stay while . . . raiding."

"Keep going."

She didn't press it any further, grabbed a torch off the wall, and led the man underground.

"This is all we have," she said as she lit a torch along the nearest wall, lighting up the entire underground storage room.

Two large chests sat in the middle of the room. Both were locked, but Hertha pulled a key out from her pelt. She attempted to hand it to the man, but he waved his hand at her.

"You do it," he said.

Hovard waited as Fell and the innkeeper made their way underground to collect their prize. He stood with the men, over the captive families and the one beheaded father dead at his feet. The whimpering of the dead man's family and the cracking of burning torches filled the room. He looked at the woman and her child and though he did not say it, he wished to apologize.

"Why are you doing this to us?" said the woman.

One of Hovard's men struck her and she fell to the ground. The man moved to cut her throat, but Hovard grabbed him and pulled him back.

"That will not be necessary," he said.

"Mother," shouted the woman's son as he scrambled to cover her.

"We are going to kill them all. You know that?" said the man.

Hovard pulled back.

"Bite your tongue," Hovard snapped.

"When have we ever let anyone live? Fell wants to set an example for the girl you dragged with us."

Hovard looked down at the boy and his mother who hugged one another and cried.

"There must be another way," he whispered.

"We have it," shouted Fell, who returned from his trip to the inn's basement with the innkeeper.

Hovard saw the innkeeper carrying a large treasure chest.

"There is another in the basement. Hovard, go grab it for her."

He looked back at the man who struck the mother, then headed for the basement hatch. He saw the treasure chest Fell referenced and picked it up. It was extremely heavy. This inn must have truly been a popular location. As he was ascending the stairs with the treasure chest in hand, he heard the mother scream and then the shouts of the other captives. Hovard dropped the chest and ran back to the main hall to find all the hostages being hogtied one by one.

"What is the meaning of this?" shouted Hovard.

"Where is the treasure chest?" Fell said.

"We don't have to do this," said Hovard. "We can let them live."

"Bring the treasure chest to me, Hovard," said Fell. "And make sure you collect all that was dropped.

Hovard observed the room. He looked at the terrified family members, the terrified innkeeper, and her husband who was still bound to the chair. He looked at Fell and his men who stood around the captives with their hands on their swords. Hovard let out a sigh and then proceeded to collect the chest which he dropped on the stairs.

Some gold had scattered about, so he picked it up before returning to the main hall. When he returned, the last of the captives was bound and immobile. Only the innkeeper remained free.

"Take the chest out to the horse and bring the girl in," said Fell.

"No," said Hovard. "At least spare her from seeing this. She is still young."

"Take the chest outside. And bring the girl in."

"Please, Fell," said Hovard, panic creeping into his voice. "She is only a child."

"She is old enough to know what this life entails. Collect her."

Hovard took a deep breath then relented and exited the inn.

"What are you going to do?" said Hertha standing behind Fell but in front of his men.

"Bring your husband over here."

"Tell me what you are planning."

Hertha heard him strike her before she felt it. She grabbed her cheek as blood dribbled over her bottom lip.

"Bring him to me now."

Hertha looked at her husband who just as before shook his head. But she had no choice. Hertha walked over, grabbed the chair he was bound to, and pulled it to Fell.

"That's close enough," Fell said. "Now step back."

As she moved away from Fell and her husband, she heard the footsteps of a small child. She looked back and saw a young girl.

"Who is she?" said Hertha.

"She is not of your concern."

Hertha watched as Fell picked up a canister. It took a moment for her to recognize what it was and just as she did, she was too late to stop Fell from dumping the contents of the canister onto her husband. Hertha scrambled to intervene but was apprehended by two of Fell's men.

"Stop," she screamed as the oil flowed over Keld. "Please stop this. Stop."

Fell gestured for one of his men to hand him a torch.

"I will do anything. Please just don't do this. Please I am begging you. Let him live. Please."

The whole room was chaos. The families all screamed as Fell held the torch over the panicking Keld. Hertha struggled but could not free herself from the two men who held her. Her face was red, and tears streamed over her cheeks.

"Step back men. This is it where the fun begins," said Fell.

"No. No. No. No," shouted Hertha. "Please."

The torch touched Keld's thigh, and the flames immediately consumed him. His screams pierced the ears of every person in the room but for Hertha, they pierced her heart. She was near uncontrollable and almost broke free of her bondage but Fell struck her on the forehead with the hilt of his broadsword. The two men holding her let her go.

She touched her forehead and stumbled backward. Blood flowed freely from the gash as her vision blurred. Hertha dropped to her knees and the last thing she saw before falling unconscious was the fire that consumed her husband, spreading to the floor of her inn.

Hovard watched Fell hit the innkeeper, then shifted his attention to the innkeeper's husband who had long stopped screaming and was engulfed in flames. The fire was spreading to the floor and the bound captive families were doing their best to evade the flames with their bound wrists and ankles.

He looked down at the young girl by his side who watched the fearful families with eyes wide open. Hovard turned his attention back to the families as the flames reached the first of them.

"Help us," shouted the mother of the boy. "Let my boy go at least. Please just let him go."

"Let us get the boy," shouted Hovard to Fell.

Fell looked back at Hovard and shook his head.

"We have no room for another stray."

Hovard put his hand on the young girl's shoulder. He could feel her breathing heavy. The screams of the family members filled the inn as the flames took them.

"Let's go," said Hovard to the girl. "You don't need to see this."

"She stays."

The fire erupted over the hogtied captives and their screams dwindled. Only the boy and his mother who shuffled to the back remained. The rope that bound the mother's wrists caught fire and she was able to break free. She went to untie her son but was quickly cut down by one of the men nearest her. She fell atop her son and the flames caught her pelt.

Hovard put his hand over the young girl's eyes.

"What did I say?" said Fell.

"She has seen enough," Hovard said.

"Put your hand down."

Hovard hesitated then did as he was told.

The flames reached the boy. Hovard looked away. He glanced down at the young girl and unlike him, she did not turn away.

The fire by this point was climbing the walls of the inn and reaching into the rafters.

"That's enough," said Fell. "Hovard, grab the innkeeper. She lost a husband and I need a wife. I wouldn't want such a skilled bread maker to go to waste."

Hovard sighed and threw the woman over his shoulder. He then touched the young girl on the shoulder.

"Let us leave this place," he said.

She looked up at him and nodded.

Hovard took her hand and pulled her out of the inn. Once outside, he let her go only to throw the innkeeper over the back of Fell's horse. Fell joined him and the girl by his horse. He tied the innkeeper in place then looked down at the small girl.

"Do you understand what you saw?" Fell said.

Hovard watched but remained quiet.

The girl shook her head.

Fell looked up at Hovard.

"Tell her," said Fell before mounting his horse.

She turned her attention to Hovard.

He knelt to be at eye level with her as the flames burst through the roof of the inn behind him.

"The people in that inn were . . ."

The girl did not speak. She just looked at him blankly.

Hovard looked back at Fell. He made a motion with his hand to encourage Hovard to speed it up. Hovard turned back to the girl.

"Midgard has no place for weakness," said Hovard. "We are strong. They were not."

She didn't respond. Embers floated through the night sky, dancing around Hovard and the girl.

"Fell is a savage, but he is right," said Hovard. "These people were killing themselves for setting up an inn so far from a town. The strong do what they will and the weak suffer what they must. Do you understand that?"

She nodded.

"Your own strength is all you have in Midgard. Don't ever forget this lesson, Skadi."

TWO

THE VARGR

Twenty-Three Years Later

Bard pulled out a piece of dried fungi from his sack and used it to start a fire. The sun was setting. The quiet was unsettling, but once the fire started to roar, he sat back and looked up at the night sky. He oddly did not feel so alone with so many stars overhead and the full moon.

He grabbed the map he was making and checked to make sure he marked his location. Upon doing so, it struck him just how far he had gone. His home, in the town of Lejre, was as far away west as it could possibly be, meaning he was as far east as any human had ever traveled—deep into the uncharted territory of mainland Midgard. It astounded him he had come across such little resistance. It was a good thing the Age of the Vikings had ended, otherwise he might not have been able to travel so freely. Animals though . . . they were still out there. Luck must have been on his side, he thought.

The sound of leaves crunching caught his attention. It came from behind him, so he sat the map back in his sack and grabbed his sword. Bard inspected the nearby tree line but did not see anything.

"Who is there?" he said. "I have a sword and I know how to use it. If you try to harm me, I will surely kill you."

He got to his feet and unsheathed his sword. His eyes darted back and forth, in search of any sort of movement. He did not see anything, but he heard it again. Someone or something was just beyond the tree line and just out of sight.

"Show yourself or risk being cut down," he said confidently. "I know you are there."

No one responded and yet the sound grew louder, and it seemed there was more than one entity out there.

"Are you a coward? Be seen."

It was then he heard the sound that sent a shiver down his spine. In all his journeying he was fortunate enough to avoid what he now faced so far from home. The growling came from multiple directions. Bard knew what was just beyond the tree line—a pack of wolves. A cool breeze swept across the land.

The first menacing creature stuck its head into the clearing. The growling wolf's deadly teeth shimmered in the firelight. Bard's knuckles turned white gripping the hilt of his sword. Thick beads of sweat formed on his brow as his breathing sped up.

"Stay back," he shouted. "I am warning you. Stay back."

But the wolf continued to advance and as its body exited the tree line, the heads of three others emerged. Four wolves in total advanced towards Bard. He hesitated but tried to remember his training. He started to shout and demonstrate aggression. He stepped toward the wolves, trying to show he was the alpha, but the wolves continued to advance and thanks to him stepping forward, the gap was even tighter than before.

"This isn't working," he said rhetorically.

He stepped back again, but now all four wolves were beyond the tree line. In the full light of the fire, they were bigger and even more fearsome than he originally thought.

"Begone human," said the largest and nearest of the four wolves.

"You speak?" said Bard, not believing his ears.

"You have trespassed into the Ironwood. We are the Vargr, children of Angrboda and kin to Fenrir. We are giving you one warning. Go home if you don't want to die."

Bard was terrified, but he was still an adventurer. He worked up the little courage he had remaining to speak.

"I have traveled a great distance. May I ask you a question?"

"It is true you have traveled quite some way. There are no human settlements anywhere near here and we are not without heart. Ask your question and then go."

"Is the witch truly real?"

"You hear me speaking do you not? Go human before we tear you limb from limb."

Not wanting to press his luck, Bard nodded and proceeded to snuff out the fire. He mounted his horse and turned away from the wolves. They watched him ride off.

Moments later, Bard found himself traveling by moonlight, thinking about the Vargr and the witch known as Angrboda who no one had ever laid eyes on. He questioned what he should do. He was on a mission, but he knew those wolves would not give him a second chance.

It was then he saw something shimmer on the ground. He looked back at the clearing where he encountered the wolves. It was barely visible, and Bard felt comfortable stopping to inspect the shiny object. He hopped down from his horse and walked over to the object. It sparkled and even glowed a smidge.

"What is this?" Bard whispered.

He picked it up and inspected it. Then as realization took him, his eyes widened. He stuffed the object in his satchel and made for his home in Lejre with haste.

One Year Later

"We have reached the edge of the forest," said Bard. "Stay vigilant, the Vargr could be anywhere."

He looked back at the forty warriors that accompanied him on his trek from Lejre to the Ironwood.

"You just lead the way, and we will worry about the four wolves," said the man nearest him.

Bard nodded and continued.

Just like the night one year ago, it was again a full moon. Bard kept his eyes on the ground while feeling out the route he had taken before.

"It is around here," he said. "We are close."

A young woman dressed in a pelt covered in runic markings walked up alongside Bard. He looked her way. He was feeling uneasy and assumed perhaps she was the source of his unease.

"This is the place?" she said.

"I found it here in the Ironwood," he said. "A shimmering ore that permeates the ground."

Bard continued to scan the ground. As did the woman.

"The Earl will reward you greatly for this discovery. You are the only one to show promise of what we seek."

"I am humbled."

"But that is only if it is truly here."

"It is. I swear it on my unborn child's life."

A flicker of light caught his eye. It was off to the left just beyond some bushes. He ran to it and just as he was about to pick it up, the massive paw of one of the Vargr covered the glowing metal. Bard fell backwards.

"We told you to go, human," said the wolf. "This land is not for you."

"They're here," shouted Bard.

He scrambled backwards as quickly as he could while the men he was traveling with rushed to his side. They all drew their swords. Some were armed with bows.

"You all think you can take the Ironwood and exploit its resources. Your kind is more like the Aesir than any other race in the nine realms."

Bard jumped to his feet as additional wolves lined up beside the alpha. It was the four he had encountered a year earlier. They were just as fearsome as before, but Bard was alone the first time. This time he was not. He was still afraid but also curious as to what the outcome would be now that he had been granted some of the Earl's guards. And then there was the mysterious woman who was with him. He was not fully aware of who she was and why she journeyed with him, but he imagined she was plenty capable since this was uncharted Midgard they had ventured into, and she wielded no blade. Either she was a fool or incredibly capable.

Feeling a bit emboldened, Bard said, "You four may be massive creatures and kin to the mighty Fenrir, but that means nothing now."

"We will rip you apart and eat you," The alpha Vargr said flatly.

Ten more wolves emerged from the tree line to stand alongside the initial four. Bard's eyes got wide, and he took a step back. He looked at the men he brought with him.

"You are the Earl's most skilled with a blade. Are we going to be ok?" he asked the guard nearest him.

The man simply put a hand on Bard's shoulder and stepped in front.

"Let's hope that means yes," Bard whispered.

He fell back as the men engaged the fourteen Vargr. Bard stopped beside the woman who traveled with them.

"These are the Earl's best, right?" he asked.

"The Earl said they received training in the Geatland. Hopefully that was enough. But then again, the Vargr are supposedly the children of the Witch of the Ironwood. Fearsome beasts known to most only in legend," said the woman.

"Is the witch real? Are we going to die?" said Bard.

The woman shrugged her shoulders.

"We'll find out soon won't we," she said.

As Bard watched the clash sweat raced down his forehead. Sure, these men were skilled warriors who could wield a sword or bow better than he could ever hope to, but these animals were fast, strong, and winning. Bard squirmed when he saw the first man take a claw to the face. He almost retched when he saw another man get his abdomen ripped open. And he did throw up when he saw a third man get his head taken off. He had once been a warrior himself, but never had he seen a battle like this. It made him long for the old days.

"They are being slaughtered," he said wiping the crud from his mouth. "We have to get out of here."

The woman sighed and picked up a torch that one of the men had set when he engaged the wolves. Its light had dimmed but, in her hands, it lit right up—brighter than before. Bard noticed the instant reaction and took a step back.

"How did . . ."

The woman smirked at him.

"Are you a rune writer?"

"I am not, my friend."

The fire erupted into a blaze and projected across the battlefield washing over the nearest Vargr. The creature burst into flames and died in seconds as it was quickly turned to ash. The warmth was fierce, and Bard stumbled backward to keep from ending up like the wolf.

Every combatant, human or wolf, turned their attention towards this mysterious woman. There was a stillness in the air. Bard recognized the fear that had swept over all parties. He remembered that same feeling when the Vargr revealed themselves to him a year ago. But now he saw the same look in them as well. Bard shifted his attention to the woman, and it seemed she was counting. Then the fires exploded again. They were controlled and each Vargr disintegrated. Only a few of the men caught her deadly blaze. For the most part, from what Bard could tell, her aim was dead on. In moments, the battle was won. Only the alpha Vargr remained.

"Humans are an abomination. We know of how you pillage to build your towns. You slaughter each other for fun and some of you think of yourselves as gods on Midgard. This land is unspoiled. It is clean and free. Your kind will ruin it."

"You think so low of us," said the woman.

"Why should we not? Look at what you have done. My brothers and sisters are gone. We were at peace here. Away from man's machinations and Odin's schemes. Our mother will mourn, and you will pay."

"The witch . . ." Bard shouted. "She is real?"

"I think we have heard enough," said the woman.

Bard covered his eyes. The final flash from the torch was brighter than all the rest. Absolutely nothing remained of the alpha. The woman's sleeve caught fire and she dropped the torch to pat it out.

Bard ran to her to help and to ask, "How did you do that?"

"I am a . . ." said the woman.

An unaccounted-for wolf jumped from just out of Bard's line of sight. It caught him by the shoulder and dragged him to the ground. It bit into his neck and tore out a massive piece of flesh. In a moment Bard was dead—ripped apart and eaten.

A few men struggled with the final wolf, but it wasn't until a slender warrior put his blade through the creature's skull. He flicked the blood off his sword and sheathed it.

"Egil?" said the woman.

"It would seem I arrived just in time, Solveig."

"We had this under control," she said.

Egil looked around at the scarred land and burned bodies of humans and wolves.

"Trust me. We were soon to be finished with this battle," said the woman.

"There was a time when I wanted a wolf for a pet," said Egil.

"I could always make you one."

"Wouldn't that be nice," Egil said.

"What are you doing here?"

"I have been tailing the caravan. When I heard my father say you would be joining these men, I had to make sure you were ok."

"I can take of myself. I did more to stop the Vargr than your father's guards."

"I saw."

"Why are you really here?"

"Is this the place?" said Egil.

"It would appear to be. The scout saw some of the ore right over there before the wolves attacked."

Egil moved to where Solveig pointed. The glowing ore was stained in blood. Egil couldn't tell if it was human or wolf. He picked up the metal and wiped it down on his pelt.

"This is what my father sent his men to die for," he whispered. "Iron ore?"

"This ore has seidr magic properties. It is the same core element that Mjölnir is made from or, so we are told. It is rare for any realm but especially ours. However, if my suspicions are correct, then we are standing on the largest deposit ever discovered in Midgard."

"And that means what?" Egil said.

Solveig took the ore from Egil's hands.

"It means everything," she said. "And it means we will need laborers."

One Year Later

Egil arrived on horseback with Solveig to the small fishing town of Höfn. It was the furthest town from Lejre and the last human settlement before

16

the uncharted territory of eastern mainland Midgard. He saw an elderly woman hanging cod in a hjell and two children playing only a few feet away. In the distance was the coastline.

"It is beautiful here," he whispered.

"And it is rightfully placed between home and our growing mine," said Solveig.

Egil looked at Solveig.

"The work will be backbreaking. The people here won't be the same," Egil said.

"This is the role they must play," replied Solveig.

"This is wrong."

"Their lives will have meaning . . . purpose. That's something so few have."

"Then let them make the choice to help on their own," said Egil.

"If you do not have the stomach for this then go back to Lejre, Egil. I do not need you here."

"This is not what your father would have wanted, and you know that."

"But it is what your father wants, and it is what our realm needs. Do things differently when you are the Earl. For now, this is the way," said Solveig sharply.

Egil eyed Solveig. He saw the conviction in her eyes and though he wanted to debate her further, he knew he was lost. He reluctantly nodded.

"I still love you," he said.

"I love you too."

He then watched as she dismounted and proceeded to go door to door of the small town, inviting the families of each household outside. It took a few minutes but not before long over 100 people were surrounding Egil in the village green. He gave them a moment to settle before speaking up.

"Quiet now," he said.

"What is going on?" shouted one man.

"My name is Egil Hrothgarson. I have come to you on behalf of the Earl Hrothgar of Lejre. A mine is being constructed in the Ironwood Forest. The contents of that mine will reshape Midgard for the better."

17

He paused, thinking about what he said. Egil looked at Solveig who gestured for him to continue.

"But the contents of this mine will need to be transported safely to Lejre. The men and women of this town between the ages of 13 and 60 shall be road builders."

There was a rumbling through the crowd.

"Quiet now," shouted Solveig.

"This is a fishing village. We fish. We are people of the sea. What if we refuse?" shouted a woman from the crowd.

"Refusal will be met with swift and severe punishment," said Solveig standing next to Egil.

"Swift and severe?" the woman said.

"Henceforth you shall no longer be fishermen. My fa . . . the Earl demands compliance. You will receive formal assignments in the morning," Egil said, attempting to temper the potential for unrest.

As soon as Egil spoke those words, fifty men on horseback entered the gates of the town.

"Rest well tonight. Work begins tomorrow," added Solveig.

"You can't do this to us. Hrothgar has no authority here," shouted the same woman.

Egil looked at Solveig.

"She'll come around," he whispered.

"Show weakness now," said Solveig. "And they'll pick you apart later."

"Show mercy now and they will work with you later."

Solveig shook her head.

"Has my father gotten so deeply inside your head? You study magic Solveig. You're an alchemist. You're not a brute."

"Your father and I see a Midgard transformed by this work. It frustrates me that you choose to be blind to the future we seek to create."

"I just do not see your path as the only one."

Egil and Solveig shared eye contact for a moment and did not say a word, then Solveig pulled on the reins of her horse and rode towards the woman who had spoken out. Two of the men on horseback joined Solveig. The woman and her family erupted into a frenzy as she was dragged away. Egil wished he could turn away, but he did not.

His stomach churned as he watched one of the men draw a whip from his satchel. The crowd screamed, but the fervor quickly dampened when the flogging stopped.

"Work begins in the morning," shouted Solveig, who returned to Egil's side after the deed was done.

Egil looked at the woman he loved, but also, if he was being honest with himself, deeply feared.

"Your father put me in charge of this project. I won't let him down. And until the time comes when you are the Earl, I would suggest you not let him down either. The work is going to get uglier before we see the benefits of the mine."

Five Years Later – Present

Hege was cold and her body ached. She had worked for far too long, with far too little rest. They all had. But despite this truth, she still knelt by an elderly man to treat the burst blisters on his hands. She poured water from her flagon that she needed to quench her thirst over the open wounds, washing away some of the blood, pus, and dirt.

"Thank you," said the man, his voice incredibly feeble.

Hege bandaged his hands and then left the man with the remainder of her water to drink. She stood up and assessed the work left to be done where she and many others were stationed.

"No breaks," said a man on horseback. "You. Get back to work."

Hege turned to face him.

"When will this end? My parents brought me to the mainland for a better life. Not whatever this is."

"What did I just say? No breaks."

"The road from Lejre to Bard Mine is almost complete. What more is there to do?"

"But it is not complete. Get back to work."

"And if I refuse," she said.

"Why do you consistently try to push your luck, Hege? You know what will happen. You'll be whipped. Then you will go back to work."

"I have been whipped before," said Hege. "I was whipped when they first came to my village. Those scars are still the ugliest."

"Then you will be hanged and the old man you just spent too much time mending will take over your responsibilities."

At that moment a loud crash caught her attention as well as the attention of the guard. The elderly man had dropped a crate of tools off the back of a cart. The guard on horseback rode over to the man and struck him with the whip. Hege ran after him and stepped between the man and the guard just in time to take the second hit on his behalf.

"It was an accident," she shouted through the pain of the whip striking her back.

"Get back to work both of you," shouted the guard before returning to his post.

Hege helped the man to his feet.

"Thank you, child," he said. "Are you ok?"

"I'll be fine," she said looking back at the guard.

"You should not risk your well-being for me. I am old. You are young. You have much life to live and much to care for."

"He is right," said Hege's friend, Carr, who had appeared near next to her. "Think of your children before acting against the Earl. It is only a matter of time before these madmen get more creative with how they punish you."

"But this cannot go on," she said. "If we work together."

"These people may not turn their sword on you if you keep acting against them. You might not fear death for yourself, but what about others?" Carr added.

20

RETURN TO FENSALIR

"I have said this already—this way is off limits," said the man. "The ground here is sacred, and we ask that you respect that."

Skadi stepped toward the man. She towered over him.

"You are in the way," Skadi said, frustration building in her tone.

"It is believed Odin rested here once many moons ago."

"Odin has surely rested many places," Skadi said.

"But here we have proof," said the man pointing to what looked like the remains of a campfire.

"Anybody could have prepared that campfire," said Skadi, patience slipping even further.

"But we know it was made by the Allfather. The legend has passed down through the ages."

"Move out of my way."

"I'm sorry but I cannot let you through here," the man said putting his hand up to block Skadi. "We have rules."

She reached out, grabbed the man's shoulder, and squeezed ever so gently, and the man winced.

"I could remove your arm. We have been in this town for two days and on the road much longer than that. This is the last place we need to search. Let us get through. Now."

The man's face grimaced at the pain in his shoulder but despite that, he still said, "No."

Skadi squeezed a bit tighter.

"Mother," said Bjorn.

Skadi glanced at her son, sighed, and released her grip. The man backed away and massaged his arm.

"We are sorry," Bjorn said to the man.

"It's not here," Mimir said. "My body is elsewhere. I can sense it."

Skadi looked back at the man. She debated apologizing, but shame had taken her.

She pivoted and walked away.

"What was that back there?" Mimir said.

Skadi hardly responded and only grumbled.

"We have been on the road long enough. I think we should head back to Fensalir for a bit."

"We have not yet found your body," Skadi said.

"It is ok. We should rest."

Hours Later

The gates of Fensalir parted as Skadi, Bjorn, and Mimir approached the runic-covered doors at the end of the road upon which they traveled.

"Welcome home Skadi the Jötunn-Breaker, young Bjorn the Brave, and Mimir the Bodiless," said the guard at the gate as they passed through the entrance of Fensalir.

Once the three were outside of earshot, Bjorn said, "When did we get these titles?"

"Must have been while we were on the road," said Skadi.

"I like both of yours," said Mimir, "but mine feels a little . . . too on the nose."

"Bjorn the Brave," noted Skadi, smiling at her son out of his view.

Skadi led the trio through Fensalir to the site of the battle with the Jötunn from months ago. It was a massive exhumation site, as the cave of the jötunn was explored to give grieving parents a chance for closure. The half-human, half-Valkyrie, Eirdóttir was charged with overseeing the exhumation.

"Eirdóttir," Skadi said as they approached the cottage at the edge of the exhumation site.

There was no reply. Skadi opened the door of the cottage and peered inside.

"Eirdóttir?"

She circled the cottage. There was no sign of her.

"Mother, where is she?" Bjorn asked.

"Elfr is gone too," Skadi replied.

"But she was watching him," said Bjorn.

"Something is amiss," said Mimir.

"Skadi," shouted Eluf, Fensalir's newly elected council leader as he sprinted to her location.

She turned when she heard her name. Eluf was the first person to step up in the wake up of the previous council's treachery. He was an honest person, who Skadi felt appreciated the weight of what he was responsible for but was not yet prepared to handle. Because of that, she was quick to assist him when he asked, even though it was frequent.

"Skadi," he repeated her name, panting from his run. "I'm glad you're back. Something terrible happened. And I have this."

"What is it?" said Skadi.

"A message," said Eluf holding out a scroll. "It's from the would-be king of Midgard, Earl Hrothgar of Lejre. He is requesting your presence at his great hall, Heorot."

Skadi took the scroll from Eluf.

"Who is Hrothgar?" said Bjorn.

"A powerful human warlord and as the Earl of Lejre, he is the leader of the largest human settlement in mainland Midgard," said Mimir. "Maybe even all of Midgard."

"What could he want?" Bjorn said.

"The scroll says he may know the location of Mimir's body," said Skadi.

"How would he know of that?" said Bjorn.

"This is odd," Skadi said. "We have not announced our journey."

"Word has still spread of your exploits Jötunn-Breaker," said Eluf. "The people talk of your battle and that you seek the body of the wisest man alive. I'm not surprised word has reached Hrothgar. If anyone has the resources to know what is happening in Midgard, it would be him."

Skadi put the scroll to her side and looked around Fensalir.

"What terrible thing occurred here?" Skadi said to Eluf.

"While you three were journeying, a mysterious man arrived in Fensalir. I am afraid to accept what some of have said as truth, but it is believed that this man was Loki."

"The Trickster," whispered Mimir.

"Some saw him talking to Eirdóttir. I do not know about what. But then he was gone, so was she. Elfr, too. They're all gone."

"He took them?" said Skadi.

"Eirdóttir and Elfr have been absent for days and we have no clue where they could be."

"If this Hrothgar person knows where Mimir's body could be, perhaps he knows where Eirdóttir and Elfr might be as well," said Bjorn.

"It is possible. If any human is suited to know the ins and outs of Midgard, it would be the Earl of Lejre," said Eluf.

"Let's go. I'm ready," said Bjorn.

Skadi looked at her son. It still bewildered her how much older he looked having consumed the roots of Yggdrasil.

"What?" he said, recognizing *that* look on his mother's face.

"Without Eirdóttir, Fensalir has no protector. I need you to stay here."

"But . . . mother I want to be with you."

"This town needs you. Understand?"

Bjorn sighed but said, "But mother, I think you need me too."

"I will always need you. That will never change," said Skadi before turning to Eluf. "Mimir and I should go now. The longer we wait, the longer it will take to find Eirdóttir and Elfr."

"You don't want to rest?" said Mimir. "It's been weeks since we were last here."

"We are no closer to finding your body, and now our friend is missing. We shouldn't wait. There is also Lofn who is still unaccounted for. Or have we forgotten the draugr maker?"

"My body can wait, and I am hungry," said Mimir. "Taking a moment to rest won't hamper finding Eirdóttir or Elfr or Lofn."

"How can you be hungry without a stomach?" Eluf asked.

"Mother, Mimir is right. Take a moment," Bjorn added.

"Go eat and then we leave," said Skadi before handing Mimir to Bjorn.

She turned her back to them and walked away.

"Is everything ok with her?" said Eluf.

"I don't know," said Bjorn. "I'll go talk with her. "Here you take Mimir."

He handed the living head to Eluf.

"She has been on a mission ever since the battle with the jötunn. There is something not at rest within her," said Mimir.

Bjorn found his mother sitting behind their home, looking up at Himinbjorg Mountain with her sword leaning against the hjell to her right.

"Halvar I cannot do this alone," she whispered.

"Mother, are you ok?"

"I wonder if Heimdall knows where she is."

Bjorn grabbed a stool and took a seat in front of Skadi, so she was forced to look at him.

"Mother, what is wrong?"

She shifted her attention and met his gaze.

"Don't worry about me. I'm fine."

Bjorn reached out and took her hand.

"It is ok to not be fine," he whispered.

The two met each other's eye contact.

"What's the matter?"

"Have I failed Frija? She died for what she believed in and I . . ."

The sounds of children laughing floated through the air.

"Do you hear that?" Bjorn said. "That is because of what we did."

She smiled.

"I wish one good deed could erase a lifetime of wickedness," she whispered.

"Mother we are who we choose to be, and you do not have to do this all alone."

Bjorn stood up and proceeded to hug his mother.

"Child you are . . . incredibly wise," Skadi said.

"Mother, can I tell you something?"

"Of course. Anything."

"I miss father."

"I do as well son," she whispered.

"Are you actually hungry or did you just say that to get Skadi to take a break?" said Eluf to Mimir as he carried him to his cottage. "And where does the food go?"

"I'm still connected to my body. If I do eat, it ends up in my stomach. But the seidr magic that is keeping me alive negates the need for me to eat. I just enjoy the taste of a good meal. I was deprived of them for so long, sitting by the well."

"What do you want then?" said Eluf. "My hjell is full of cod."

"I wouldn't mind some plums and hazelnuts. Maybe a chicken as well."

"Let's see what I can muster up."

Eluf sat Mimir on the table near his stove then proceeded to rummage through the cabinets looking for what Mimir requested.

"I know I have some hazelnuts but plums . . ."

"It's ok if you don't have it all. I really just want the chicken," said Mimir.

"One moment then," said Eluf before heading outside.

When he returned, chicken in hand, he saw Bjorn and Skadi standing by Mimir.

"Did you come to eat too?" Eluf said.

"Don't waste the chicken on Mimir," Skadi said.

"Hey," shouted Mimir.

"You and your family need it more than him. We are going to go now and meet Hrothgar."

"What about the hazelnuts? Let me get some of those at least. For the road."

Eluf released the chicken through the open door, grabbed a handful of nuts, and placed them in a small container. He handed the container to Skadi.

"Thank you," Mimir said.

"Bjorn will stay here to watch over Fensalir while we are gone."

"Be careful," said Eluf. "I know you have all the power of the World Tree inside of you, but Hrothgar is known for his cunning and there is a rumor that he has a skilled alchemist at his disposal."

Skadi nodded, then turned to her son.

"Listen to Eluf but if trouble arises, I trust you to make the right decisions."

"I will."

Skadi picked up Mimir and situated him in a holster on her back that she kept fastened to her person. Moments later, the two were beyond the gates of Fensalir.

"Lejre is far from here but if you run, we'll be there quickly," said Mimir.

"I know, I just want to talk to you about this Hrothgar for a moment. I've heard of him before."

"He is known," said Mimir. "There are not a lot of humans who catch the attention of the gods, but I have heard some of the Aesir mention his name. They say he is ambitious. Maybe too ambitious."

"Do they fear him?"

"Do the Aesir fear a human? Is that what you're asking?"

"Yes."

"That I don't know. But anyone who earns the attention of the gods should not be taken lightly. And Eluf was right. Hrothgar does employ a powerful alchemist."

"What is alchemy?"

"It is the ability to transmute one material into another. Alchemists are rare. Most folks only know of rune writers, those who draw runic symbols on the walls of towns to keep out jötnar. Alchemists can manipulate that which is otherwise not malleable."

"Like what?"

"Metals. Rocks. Energy. In some extreme cases, living creatures as well."

"Do the gods not have that power?"

"It is a learned skill. Not one that most have bothered to acquire, however, there is a dark elf that is particularly capable. As well as a light elf."

27

"A jötunn terrorized Fensalir for decades but while I traveled, it was humans I saw enact the greatest evils."

"That my friend is a statement I cannot dispute. Your kind does have a special knack for heinous behavior. Humans and the Aesir are a lot alike in that regard."

"Let us find out what this Hrothgar wants and try to change human behavior later," said Skadi. "If he leads us to your body or any of our missing enemies or Eirdóttir, this trip will prove worthwhile."

"Agreed," said Mimir.

FOUR

DREAMS DASHED

Egil rode along in quiet, surveying the work being made on the road that connected Lejre to Bard Mine. Solveig hung back a few feet, trotting along behind him. He stole a glance back at her, locked eyes, and turned away.

"What is it?" she said.

He did not answer.

The sun was out, but it was still cool. Winter had long since arrived in Midgard, and not even a cloudless sky could warm up the travelers.

Egil observed some poor soul toiling away at a sign on the side of the road. A man on horseback was standing over him with a whip in hand. Egil could see the scars on the man's arms and legs.

"My father sent a raven to bring me home. Does this mean what I suspect it means?"

"It may."

Egil looked back at the man with the scars. He looked so frail and was doing the work of at least two, maybe three people.

"Let us return to Heorot Hall," said Egil.

Hours Later

Under a cloudless sky, Egil and Solveig arrived in Lejre. The massive gates that guarded the entry to the human town parted as they neared, and as they entered, a few nearby guards stood at attention.

"I shall join you after," said Solveig.

"You're not going to come with me?"

Solveig shook her head.

"This is a conversation for a father and son."

"Solveig, I need you with me. My father and I . . . we see Midgard very differently."

"And your father and I see it more similarly than you and I."

"But you and I are to be wed."

"I'll be here for you. But have this conversation on your own first."

Egil watched Solveig ride off before shifting his attention to his father's hall atop the highest hill in Lejre. He breathed in deep and let out a long sigh.

"Here we go," he whispered, pulling on the reins of his horse.

Moments later, he dismounted and tied his horse to a post outside of the hall. His heart raced. He thought he was ready for this moment, but here he was, probably the most nervous he had ever been in his life.

Egil pushed open the doors and sitting at a raised table was a man reading a scroll as various men and women moved about the hall.

The man sat the scroll down and said, "Everyone out."

Egil observed the room full of people erupt into a frenzy as they scampered out of the hall. The man waited until the hall was clear before speaking up again.

"Come here, boy," he said gesturing for Egil to approach him.

Egil stepped forward through the empty hall.

"What is this?" said Egil.

"Are we making good progress?"

"The road is nearly complete."

The man didn't respond.

"Father, why am I here?"

Hrothgar breathed out deeply and stood up. Egil observed his aging father. He saw how his pelt barely clung to his slender frame and how his face looked hollow and weathered.

"Do you remember your mother well? You were so young when she passed."

"And yet I could never forget her."

"She has been on my mind lately."

"I always think about her."

Hrothgar stared at Egil. Egil struggled to read his expression.

"Age has crept up on me. I feel it more so than I see it when I look at my reflection. When we are young, we think this day will never come and when it does, you are seldom prepared for it."

"You have lived a long-life father. Longer than most in Midgard and your legacy will persist through the ages."

"What is legacy—a memory of someone long ago?"

"Legacy is . . ."

"The question was rhetorical," Hrothgar said harshly.

Egil recoiled mildly at his father's tone.

Hrothgar turned his attention to the window that looked out over Lejre. Egil followed his father's gaze to the same viewpoint.

"You see the town. You see the walls that protect it. You see the thousands of people moving about, living their lives without concern for the violent creatures of Midgard. Before I arrived here, there was none of that. Lejre was just another human outpost clinging to life in the cold."

"What you have done here is impressive father," Egil said.

"And yet you still do not see the larger picture," Hrothgar said, shifting his attention back to his son.

"Excuse me?" Egil said.

"I have been thinking about how your mother sought to raise you and how she sought to undermine me. She was too kind, and I fear that rubbed off on you."

"Mother was generous and empathetic."

"She was soft. She failed to see the big picture."

"Enlighten me."

Hrothgar gave a half-smile.

"I sent a raven because I want to tell this in person. I will continue to serve as the Earl of this town."

Egil stepped towards his father. His already racing heart sped up even faster. His palms were clammy, and he wanted to scream. But he did his best to keep his composure.

"What?" he said.

"I changed my mind."

"Father you can't do this. The plan was for me to succeed you."

"The plan was for you to continue my legacy."

"I thought legacy did not matter?"

"Legacy is all that matters. What are our lives if not an opportunity to leave our impression on the nine realms? You would see my work stamped out of existence because of the bleeding heart you got from your mother."

"Father, you act as if you will live forever despite knocking on the door of Helheim. I see how frail you have become. We all do."

"I'm the Earl. I say when I step down. And when . . . if you take over."

"This is a mistake."

"The only mistake was letting Wealhtheow keep you at her tit for too long."

"How much longer then?"

"Ten years."

"Father, ten years?"

"Twenty."

"Father!"

"This is my town, and that road is my road and Bard Mine is my mine. You think you can come in and strip that from me? Deprive Midgard of what I am building? No. You will not have that opportunity."

"The people suffer because of the mine. Because of the road. Because of your rule. I have seen it with my own two eyes."

"That putrid weakness that your mother displayed is all over you. You are incapable of doing that which is most necessary."

"And you are cruel, old, and petty. You spend all your time here in your hall. Do you know what the people think of you?"

"A wolf cares little of what the sheep thinks."

"So, the people are sheep?"

"Son, you have only known prosperity and ease. I blame myself for that. I gave you too much. That changes today."

"And you revel in hardship and suffering. Father, we are not at war. The monster is dead. It's been dead for decades."

Hrothgar stood up from his table and stepped down to Egil's level. The two men stood eye to eye.

"It was never about the monster."

"What is it about?"

Hrothgar put a hand on Egil's shoulder. Egil wanted to pull away but did not want to appear weak.

"You think you are a man of the people but you're not. You're above the people and you know as soon as you become the Earl everyone else will know it too, and that scares you."

"There is nothing wrong with seeing those with lesser means as equals."

"Is that what you are doing?" The Earl asked dismissively.

"Do you know what happens to our people at the mine and on the road? Your guards torture and kill for the fun of it. Countless men, women, and children have died just so you can transport some rare iron ore to this town."

Hrothgar dropped his hand from his son's shoulder and turned to face the window. Egil did not stop observing his father. He looked at this one-time giant of a man and could not imagine that he ever looked up to him.

"The fact that you do not see why we need the ore is precisely why I am making this decision. You do not have the stomach to lead, boy. Dark times are coming, and I would rather myself be at the helm than you."

"I just don't see why people must suffer to get the ore."

"Enough. I am done debating this with you."

Egil clenched his right hand into a tight fist. Hrothgar looked down and smiled.

"Are you going to hit me?"

Egil stood firm for a moment then unclenched his fist.

"I pulled this town out of the dark place it was in when that ogre attacked. It was my leadership that got us to where we are today, and I am not about to hand over all my hard work to a child who just wants to be liked. Get out."

A door to the left of Hrothgar opened and a large man cloaked in a dark pelt with one hand entered.

"Why is he still here?" said Egil.

"We have matters to discuss. It is time for you to leave."

Egil observed the man who just entered the room and then shifted his attention to his father. He looked at Hrothgar and the two didn't break each other's gaze.

"This isn't over."

"Yes, it is, son."

Egil exited his father's hall and made his way across town to Solveig's home. He found her brewing a pot of tea and preparing some bread.

"Are you the Earl?" she asked without turning around.

Egil closed the door and stepped further into the cottage.

"Did you know this was how things would go?" he said.

She put down the bread and turned to face him.

"You did, didn't you?" Egil said.

"I had my suspicions."

"All these years you have been saying I can do things differently when I lead and now my opportunity to lead was stolen from me."

"A gift that has not been given cannot be stolen," Solveig said.

"What does that mean?"

"You weren't the Earl yet. Your father stole nothing from you. He just didn't give you anything."

"Is there a difference?"

"A big one."

Egil rolled his eyes and grabbed the bread. He ripped off a piece and put it in his mouth.

"You should have let that cool longer."

"I am hungry now."

Solveig shrugged her shoulders.

"It's good."

"I know."

Egil put the bread down and stepped closer to Solveig.

"Do you know why that one-handed man is still here? Why he has my father's ear?"

Solveig looked at Egil curiously, then shook her head.

"He should be gone now."

"My love. Consider for a moment that perhaps your father has your best interests at heart."

Egil looked at Solveig suspiciously.

"You did know this would happen."

"I am your father's alchemist."

"And you are to be my wife."

"You would make me choose between the two of you?" Solveig asked.

"What is there to choose? You love me do you not?"

"Of course," said Solveig cupping Egil's face. "But your father . . . his intentions are . . . necessary. Lejre . . . no . . . Midgard needs his leadership now so you must wait."

Egil grabbed Solveig's hands and removed them from his face.

"This is a betrayal," he whispered.

"I am loyal to the best interest of our kind."

"And what my father is doing is in the best interest of people?"

"I do not love to see the conditions of those who toil away at the road or in the mine, but I can keep an eye on the future."

"Future—has my father so thoroughly entangled his fingers in your head? What would your own father think of your allegiance to a madman?"

"My father died because we had no defense against the Aesir. You know that."

"Your father, like my mother, was a man of peace. He liked to write and study alchemy. I remember this from when we were children. Why can't you?"

"It is because I do remember that I must stand with your father now. What Thor took from me can never be forgiven."

"Solveig, you're making a mistake. A big one. If you continue down this path, I cannot stand with you."

"Then perhaps it is best you leave," she responded.

Egil stared at the woman he grew up with and was soon to marry, and now did not recognize. He reached for her, and she pulled away.

"Solveig don't," he whispered.

"Get out," she said.

Egil hesitated for a moment then, heartbroken, he exited Solveig's cottage.

FIVE

MEN ARE MONSTERS TOO

Skadi's sword, Ridill, was sheathed and attached to her waist. Since consuming the roots of the World Tree, riding a horse was now a slower form of transportation, so Skadi simply ran along the path leading to Lejre. On occasion, she and Mimir would pass a traveler who would look at them strangely but there was never someone brave enough to question them.

As they approached the massive road, known all throughout Midgard, Skadi opted to slow down and eventually stopped running altogether.

"This is it," said Mimir. "The road that Hrothgar has been building for years."

"It has been some time since I traveled along it," said Skadi. "It has come a long way."

"You were here before?" said Mimir.

"We traveled along it when Bjorn was young. It was far from complete. It appeared to be more of just a large clearing of trees and less of an actual road. Bjorn's father often encouraged us to avoid it altogether. He thought the way Hrothgar's men treated the laborers was sickening."

"What did you think?"

"I was different back then."

"It is an impressive feat for humans. The level of coordination required to build something like this is rarely seen in any realm, let alone Midgard."

"Undertakings like this have a high cost."

"And not one of gold and silver," said Mimir.

"Even the Aesir, who often rely on seidr magic for building, are not without the occasional casualty. But this road and the mine it connects to are said to be soaked in blood."

The cold was biting, and Skadi pulled her pelt tighter around her.

"How are you feeling Mimir?" she asked.

"The cold does not affect me the way it does humans but perhaps we can speed things up."

The shrill of a woman screaming stopped Skadi dead in her tracks.

"That sounds unsettling," said Mimir.

Skadi turned her attention in the direction of the screaming and quickly ran off the road. She passed through thick brush and felled trees and came upon a woman on her knees who was nearly inconsolable.

"What happened?" Skadi shouted as she approached the woman.

"They were innocent," said the woman.

Skadi knelt in front of the woman and put her hands on her shoulder. The woman was staring at the ground weeping.

"Look at me," said Skadi. "What happened?"

"Skadi," said Mimir in a subdued tone. "Turn around."

She slowly turned her head and saw nothing.

"Up," said Mimir.

She shifted her gaze skyward and what she saw disturbed her deeply.

"No," she whispered.

"They were my babies," the woman said. "Why would they do this?"

Hanging from a large branch were a boy and a girl, no older than thirteen. Their bodies were bruised and worn from exposure. Skadi leapt to the branch and undid the rope, then gently carried the two down to the ground.

The sound of leaves crunching alerted Skadi to another's presence.

"We warned you," said a man on horseback, approaching from behind the woman.

Skadi made sure the two children's bodies were situated and then unsheathed her sword.

"Who are you?" said the man.

"Did you do this?" Skadi said.

She gripped the sword hilt a bit tighter.

"Be mindful not to do anything you may regret," said the man. "Put that sword away."

"Did you . . . do this?"

The man caught a glimpse of Mimir and said "Is that a head attached to your back? Are you the Jötunn-Breaker?"

"If you know of me then you know what I am capable of."

"I do not want any trouble with you. This was a private matter. You should leave," said the man in a noticeably timid tone.

Skadi looked back at the bodies of the two children.

"The jötunn killed children," said Skadi.

The man pulled on the reins of his horse, so it stepped backward a bit.

"This was different," he said. "The woman refused . . ."

He was not able to finish his sentence. In an instant, his head was detached from his body and rolling along the forest floor.

Skadi flicked the blood from Ridill and sheathed the sword. She turned around and saw the woman scrambling to her slain children. Skadi walked over and reached for her, but she pulled away.

"Please go," she said.

"Who was that man?" said Skadi.

"Just go please."

The woman was trembling and hugging her children. Skadi paused, then retracted her hand.

"Come on. We should let her be," Mimir whispered.

Moments later, Skadi was back on the road to Lejre. For a while, she and Mimir moved in silence. But after a few moments, it was Skadi who ended the quiet.

"I see nothing has changed since I last traveled this road. This was what my husband spoke of."

"Hrothgar's reach touches families in the worst way," said Mimir.

"No parent wishes to outlive their children."

The conversation lulled and the two continued for a while longer in quiet. But Mimir decided to break the silence this time.

"Skadi, are you ok?"

Skadi did not immediately answer.

"I know Bjorn spoke with you before we left Fensalir, but I just wanted to ask also."

"Everything is fine, Mimir."

"I am willing to bet that you are indeed not fine."

Skadi looked down at Mimir.

"That was without a doubt, one of the greatest of tragedies, but you . . ."

"You have seen me kill before Mimir . . ."

"I'm not talking about killing, although I have been considering what the life of a pacifist might be like."

"Then what is it you are referring to?"

"Fate. Purpose. . . . You decided that man's fate, Skadi. Without question."

"Without question? The markings on that woman's children indicated they were tortured before they were hanged."

"He was a monster. That part is not in question."

"And I slay monsters."

"Skadi, you help others."

Skadi paused before responding, "An interesting interpretation of me killing the jötunn."

The two continued for a little while longer in silence. But then it was Skadi who once again ended the quiet.

"All that happens on this road is at the behest of Hrothgar. Even if he knows the whereabouts of your body and has insights into where Eirdóttir and the two council members might be, it will be difficult to work with him."

"If Loki took Eirdóttir, the resources of Hrothgar might be the only way to track her down."

"He gets to do as he pleases and people like that woman back there have no recourse simply because he has everything," said Skadi.

"The strong do what they will and the weak suffer what they must."

"Something I wished never to hear again and yet feels truer than ever."

"There is something else we should discuss," said Mimir.

"Loki."

"Yes."

"What is on your mind?" said Skadi.

"Loki will want revenge against you."

"What makes you so sure?"

"Though the Trickster God may live amongst the Aesir in Asgard, his parentage is not of that realm."

"The jötunn was Loki's father?"

"His name was Farbauti. I was not sure, but I am now. How would the jötunn of Fensalir know of the end of times if not told by one of the most cunning gods in all the realms?"

"How dangerous is Loki?"

Mimir paused, searching for an answer.

"Your silence is telling."

"He is not to be trifled with. But he is obsessed with Ragnarök. There may be a chance he ignores you but . . ."

"But it is unlikely?"

"Again, if I could only nod. Loki was once visited by a god not of these realms and ever since he has been different. He has been vengeful."

"Perhaps I need to return to Fensalir."

"Think about Eirdóttir. Loki took her. There is no doubting that. Hrothgar may be the only one capable of leading you to her."

"The same Hrothgar who is to blame for the deaths of that woman's children," said Skadi.

"There is much to be mindful of. I have never been less certain of the future that lays before us."

"We best not waste any more time then. Are you ready?"

Mimir breathed in deep and sighed.

"I'm ready."

Skadi leaned over a smidge then shot off in the direction of Lejre, leaving a cloud of debris in her wake.

Hege wiped the tears from her eyes and kissed each of her children on their foreheads. She then proceeded to dig a grave for each child. Though the dirt was soft and moved easily, this was the hardest work she had ever engaged in. Every shovel full of soil felt a thousand times heavier than the one before it. Every movement strained all her muscles. Her brain was still in a fog and yet she willed herself to do the terrifying job of burying her own children.

"Lo there do I see my father. Lo there do I see my mother and my sisters and my brothers. Lo there do I see the line of my people back to the beginning. Lo, do they call to me, they bid me take my place among them in the halls of Valhalla, where thine enemies have been vanquished, where the brave shall live forever. Nor shall we mourn but rejoice for those that have died the glorious death."

She laid each child in their respective grave and then covered them. Hege wiped tears from her eyes so she could see what she was doing. She knew if she stopped, she would find a way to join them.

"I am so sorry," she whispered. "You paid for my decisions."

When neither body could be seen and were both sufficiently covered in Midgardian soil, Hege crossed through some bushes where she had stored the headless body and the head of the guard who killed her children. She spat on the head and removed the sword from the dead man's waist. After attaching the sword to her person, she reached out to soothe the horse tied to a tree.

"Easy," she said as she grabbed the reins and hopped onto the back of the creature.

Hege wiped away the last of her tears.

"Hrothgar will pay for what he's done. I swear on my life and all the realms he will pay," she said, before squeezing her hips around the horse and pulling on the reins.

SIX

LEJRE

Skadi saw the wall of Lejre as she and Mimir approached. She was immediately taken aback by how tall it was—by her estimation, it easily reached 150 feet in the air. Instead of being made from wood, like the more modest walls that surrounded Fensalir, it was made from stone and appeared to be interlaced with some sort of glowing metal. Additionally, the runic symbols that all human towns used were larger to match the scale of the wall.

Skadi stopped running as she neared and walked the final way, taking in the spectacle of the wall that surrounded what was known to be the largest town in Midgard.

"Lejre," whispered Mimir. "I have never seen it up close like this. The only wall larger may be that of the one the Builder constructed for the Aesir. This really is an impressive testament to what humans can achieve."

"If we destroy each other," added Skadi.

She walked up to the gate and was greeted by two guards on horseback.

"You travel with the bodiless man. You must be the Jötunn-Breaker," said one of the guards.

"Yes?" said Skadi, accepting her new title.

"We have been instructed to ask you to wait here until Hrothgar's alchemist arrives."

Skadi looked at each of the men. They were dressed similarly to the man who killed the two children a way back.

"Do you patrol the entire road?" said Skadi.

"We are the Guards of Lejre. We serve at the pleasure of the Earl all the way to the mine," said the man.

A small door behind the two on horseback opened and from it appeared a robed woman. Skadi looked past the guards blocking her from entering Lejre.

"I shall take it from here," she said stepping between the two men.

The guards dispersed.

"Skadi Hervor, known throughout Midgard as the Jötunn-Breaker. Born in Thrymheim. Parents dead at a young age. Viking wanderer turned hero. My name is Solveig Destindóttir," said Solveig, extending her hand.

Skadi observed the mysterious woman. She was unlike anyone she had ever seen before. Her robe was covered in runic symbols and Skadi sensed a power within her that was almost godly. However, though she may have been oddly impressed with this woman, she did not meet her hand for an embrace.

"You know a lot about me," said Skadi. "I feel at a disadvantage. I know nothing of you."

Solveig retracted her land.

"We like to be well-informed in Lejre. It is dangerous in Midgard beyond these walls. We like to be careful lest we end up like the pour souls in Fensalir."

"I see," said Skadi.

"You are the alchemist," said Mimir, attempting to break the tension.

"I am."

Skadi eyed the woman some more. Alchemists were new to her.

"Your lot is rare," Mimir said.

"It is a difficult art to master during a human lifetime."

"And yet you are so young," Mimir said.

Skadi lifted Mimir to face her.

"Enough fawning," she said.

"The Earl wants me to bring you to him. Please follow me . . . he would like to meet you."

Skadi hesitated. She had all the power of Yggdrasil coursing through her veins and yet this woman gave her pause.

"I assure you. We mean you no harm."

"Your assurances mean very little," Skadi said. "Would an Earl normally send an alchemist as a greeter?"

"For someone like yourself, who absorbed the power of Yggdrasil, he would. One can never be too careful."

Skadi scanned the woman before her then said, "Lead the way."

On the other side of the massive 150-foot wall that protected the town of Lejre, Skadi followed Solveig through the bustling streets. Some who were familiar with Skadi's legend would stop and stare, but most ignored her and Mimir. One man, however, caught Skadi's attention—the way he stared at her stood out compared to others. She locked eyes with him and did not break his gaze.

"Have you ever been to Lejre before?" Solveig asked as the threesome maneuvered through a crowded market.

Solveig's question recaptured Skadi's attention.

"I have not," said Skadi.

"Did you know it is the largest town in Midgard?"

"I did."

"Over 50,000 souls populate this town by my estimation. Much larger than your hometown of Thrymheim and your adopted home of Fensalir with its modest 5,000. I believe there are more people here than there are dark elves anywhere."

"How is it that such a town was able to grow so large?" Mimir said. "When I still had a body, I would travel the realms, and even beyond Midgard, you rarely see towns this big."

"Many came here from Fensalir when your children started dying at the hands of the monster."

"Those who could make the journey and afford to change their lives, you mean," said Skadi.

Solveig looked back at Skadi and smiled.

"There are people here from every status."

"But it is not the wealthy who are dying to build the Earl's road is it?"

"You feel strongly about the road. The Earl will be more than happy to talk about your feelings and the road as much as you like once we arrive at his hall. Until then, perhaps we keep the conversation light. How was your journey here?"

"Gruesome," Mimir answered.

Solveig nodded and turned around.

"I'll be quiet then."

Skadi followed Solveig and not a word was shared between her, Mimir, and Solveig. Skadi made sure to keep an eye on Solveig as she led them.

"How is it an alchemist came to serve the Earl of this town?" said Skadi.

"My father was an alchemist and friend of the Earl."

"And does your father serve him too?" Skadi asked.

"My father passed many years ago."

"I'm sorry," Mimir said.

Once they were past the main part of the town, the trio reached a steep incline. Skadi awed at the large hall at the peak.

"That is Heorot Hall. It is the birthplace of this town."

"The birthplace of this town?" Skadi said.

"A story for another time," Solveig said. "Let's go. It is a lengthy climb to the top."

"It is not that far of a climb. I can just leap to the top."

"Before perhaps, but no longer."

"What sort of cryptic statement is that?" Mimir asked.

But Skadi knew instantly that something was different. Her body felt drained and tired in a way she had never felt before. Whereas before her pelt and sword felt weightless, she now felt them clinging to her body. The cold too—she felt it fiercely.

"We have been deceived," said Skadi.

"The power of the World Tree is a power that should be shared," said Solveig, holding up a small glowing orb, that fit snugly in her palm. "That which is easily gained can be easily taken."

Skadi went for her sword.

"I wouldn't," said Solveig before pointing at ten men approaching on horseback. "These aren't just your lowly raiders. These men are the Guards of Lejre. Trained warriors who have been charged with keeping the peace in this town."

Skadi kept her hand on the hilt of her sword as she eyed each of the men before returning her gaze to Solveig.

"Do not fret. You have the wisest man alive with you and he didn't see this coming. Hrothgar does want to meet you, but we did not want your gift from Yggdrasil to be the cause for any harm to come to our Earl."

Skadi reached for her Bifrost key.

"Hand it over," Solveig said. "It'll do you no good anyway."

Skadi reluctantly gave her key to Solveig.

"Let's keep going."

Skadi sheathed Ridill.

"This is just a setback," Mimir whispered.

"And if it isn't?" Skadi asked.

"When we get to the hall, it is likely we'll be separated. We must be extremely careful going forward. This is not a town. This is a fortress."

"Not a fortress . . . a haven," said Solveig.

Surrounded by men on horseback, Skadi, Mimir, and Solveig ascended the rest of the hill in silence. At its peak, they were high enough to see all Lejre. They reached a flat surface and then some stairs. Upon reaching the final stair, they arrived at Heorot Hall, the home and seat of power of the Earl Hrothgar.

"The Earl wants to meet you. He has known only one other human to defeat a powerful creature the way you did. I will be standing nearby. If you try anything, you will be killed. Do you understand?" Solveig said.

Skadi looked at Solveig for a moment then nodded.

"I'm going to need Mimir too," Solveig said.

"No."

"It is ok," Mimir said.

"If you hurt him, I will kill you," said Skadi.

Solveig simply smiled.

The cold air at the top of the small mountain where they stood was especially chilly. Snowflakes danced around them.

Skadi removed Mimir from her back and looked at him.

"It will be ok," he said.

"We still have to find your body," said Skadi.

"We will."

Solveig cleared her throat.

Skadi handed Mimir over.

One of the men on horseback hopped down and proceeded to open the door of Heorot Hall.

"After you," Solveig said to Skadi.

Skadi stepped across the threshold. The interior of the hall was brightly lit with torches lining the walls. Between the torches were massive murals, each depicting one of the nine realms. At the end of the hall was a raised landing with a large table. And sitting behind that table was an elderly man cloaked in a dark brown pelt. He looked up as Skadi entered.

"An invincible Viking, who ushered in a new era of peace for the people of Fensalir. The Jötunn-Breaker. Welcome to Heorot Hall. I am honored to meet you."

Skadi observed the man stand up from his desk and step down from the raised landing. He strode through the hall with a confidence that only a ruler could exude. He stood before Skadi. She was tall, but he was taller. However, his face was weathered and his body frail.

"You came here because I might have knowledge of the whereabouts of Mimir's body."

"And because we are looking for a friend as well as foes," Skadi said.

Hrothgar smiled.

"When I heard of what you did, I was immediately transported back to my youth, when I was new to ruling this town. We had a similar problem. A powerful creature terrorized the people here. It was a creature of darkness, exiled from happiness. The destroyer and devourer of humankind. We suffered this monster's wrath for twelve years. And unlike your jötunn, this beast did not just consume children but whole men and women. It was a fearsome foe. But we bested the creature in time. I learned a lesson though. I learned that the people of Midgard are woefully underprepared to deal with the different beasts and gods that populate the nine realms. Have you heard of the Nyköping Massacre?"

"It was a human town that was destroyed centuries ago during the Great War between the Aesir and Vanir."

"Roaming gods took pleasure in torturing beings they found to be lesser. All manner of atrocities were committed against the humans of that town. The people who died immediately were the lucky ones. You might have noticed the walls that surround Lejre."

"I have."

"Safety. That is what we offer here. The people of Midgard need it. And they need hope. I wanted to meet you because you provided that for the people of Fensalir."

Skadi looked around the hall. She took in the murals and landed on the Earl.

"Why are your men killing children on the road?"

"Do I condone the measures my men take to ensure the work gets done? Not always. But necessary measures must be taken to ensure our survival when Odin can wipe out settlements by barely lifting a finger, or the Jötunn father of Loki decides to make a small human town his home so he can feed on the weak," said Hrothgar. "The power you were gifted from the World Tree will go a long way towards securing our people's future."

"What does that mean?" Skadi said.

But before the Earl answered, Skadi felt herself apprehended and her sword cut from her pelt. She struggled and threw one of the men from her. He crashed into a nearby wall.

"Still quite strong I see," said Hrothgar.

Skadi put the second man in a chokehold and was about to break his neck but immediately stopped resisting when she saw Solveig hold up Mimir.

"There is someone else here who wants to see you. He will meet you in your cell."

"Skadi," Mimir said as calmly as he could muster.

She looked back at him as she was ushered from the main room of the hall.

"It will be ok," Mimir said.

"Use the tunnel. Get her out of here," Hrothgar shouted at his men.

Hege lurked in the bushes just outside of the light of the campfire where four guards drank mead and told stories. She observed them for a while and once she was sure they were drunk, shifted her attention to the cottage to their rear.

Hege stuck to the shadows and walked as delicately as she could. The door was locked from the outside. She removed it and quietly, but quickly, entered the cottage. All but three of the beds were occupied by people sleeping.

Hers was one of the unoccupied beds. The other two were her children's.

Hege maneuvered beside the occupied bed across from her empty bed. The man in it was fast asleep. She placed her hands on his shoulders and nudged him slightly.

"Wake up," she whispered.

He stirred but didn't wake. She shook him again with a bit more force.

"We only get so much sleep. What is it?" he said.

"Carr, we must talk."

His eyes opened and she stepped back.

"Something terrible has happened."

He looked beyond her at the empty beds of her two children. He sat up.

"No," he said with worry in his tone.

Hege's eyes started to water.

He embraced her, knowing exactly what had happened. She wrapped her arms around him.

"Will you help me now?" she said.

"I'm sorry I didn't earlier."

"The guards outside are drunk and the door is unlocked. We can get these people out of here."

"Where are we going?"

"I've been storing supplies not far from here. We can go there and then we can go anywhere."

"What about the others on this road who are not free," said Carr.

"We can free them too."

Carr looked at the empty beds once more and nodded.

"We are wasting time speaking."

A STRAINED
RELATIONSHIP

Skadi paced in her dungeon cell, considering her and Mimir's predica-
ment. She thought about the woman she met on the road and her children. She racked her brain for everything she knew about Hrothgar. For
someone who governed the largest town in Midgard, she had heard very
little of him during her travels. Perhaps that was a testament to the fear
he commanded.

Skadi stopped pacing and took a seat on the single bench. Over her
head was a window too small for anyone to fit through but large enough to
torture someone with hope of freedom. She pulled herself up to the window and the light that shone through was just a torch on a wall opposite
her. She dropped to the ground disappointed and started to pace again.

Skadi thought about Bjorn and Fensalir. Never had she considered
a life there until Halvar died. He had often spoke fondly of his place of
birth, but she had ignored it, preferring the freedom of life on horseback.
But now all she could think of was home in Fensalir with her son. Skadi
did not fear dying in Lejre, only never seeing Bjorn again.

She tried pulling on the door of the cell and it hardly budged.

"I need leverage," she thought, looking at door of the cell.

Skadi inspected the hinges. There was no top to them.

Skadi turned around and saw the bench was not bolted to the floor.
With a bit of force, she proceeded to pull it away from the wall.

"If I can just . . ."

"Just what?" said a familiar voice.

A chill ran down her spine. Skadi spun around slowly and saw standing on the other side of the cell door her Uncle Hovard.

"Somehow I knew you played a role in whatever this is," she said.

Hovard approached the bars of the cell. Skadi advanced from the opposite side.

"I should never have threatened Bjorn."

"No, you should not have."

"Your boy had nothing to do with your actions. I was angry, but I can see more clearly now."

"What is Hrothgar doing? What is he planning?" Skadi asked.

"No way of knowing. He has an inner circle, and I am not part of it."

"Then what are you doing here?"

Hovard looked away for a moment as if he were regretting something.

"Speak, Uncle," Skadi insisted.

"I knew the gift Yggdrasil granted you would intrigue him."

"Uncle, you are a fool."

"It got me what I wanted."

"Uncle, are you so blinded by your need for revenge that you would partner with another monster?"

"My clan is gone. My son is dead. And even the power the jötunn granted me is starting to fade. If there is a way to find peace, I will find it."

"Revenge will not bring you peace. It only poisons your mind and clouds your judgment."

"Revenge is all I have. And unfortunately for you, you are trapped behind a cell in this dungeon."

Skadi noticed his hand starting to glow.

"You would kill me in my cell? Where is the honor in that?"

"I abandoned my honor the moment I threatened Bjorn. All I want is right before me and I will not let this moment slip by."

Skadi took a step back from the door.

"Uncle, think back to when we first met. My mother, your sister. She trusted you to keep me safe. I thought you wanted to be better than Fell."

"You were like a daughter to me," Hovard said raising his glowing hand in the direction of Skadi. "Until I had a son. The strong do what they will and the weak suffer what they must."

The heat from Hovard's palm washed over Skadi. It was greater than she remembered it being.

"You do not have to do this," shouted Skadi.

"This is all I have left."

Skadi might not have had the speed or strength she did when the power of Yggdrasil flowed through her, but she was still a warrior, and her senses were just as keen as they always were. She dropped to the ground as a wave of fire filled the space. She grabbed the bench she was attempting to move and jammed it against the cell door and pushed down, applying leverage so the hinges loosened. The blast of fire from Hovard pushed the unhinged door into the cell, smashing against the wall to Skadi's rear. She evaded being trapped beneath the door and as quickly as possible jumped to her feet and ran out of the cell past Hovard. He turned so the flames emanating from his palm followed her, but Skadi ducked around a corner just out of sight. She was breathing heavily, her heart was racing, but she was unscathed. Although, she did have to pat her pelt where some flames caught her.

"What is going on here?" A guard standing in the hallway shouted.

The guard went for his sword, but Skadi caught him in the chin with a closed fist. He was shaken but did not fall. Then, around the corner Hovard approached with his fire. Skadi grabbed the guard she stunned and put him between her and Hovard. The fires engulfed the guard, giving Skadi just enough time to escape through a nearby door.

She continued running until she felt there was sufficient distance between her and Hovard. She put her hands on her knees and took a few deep breaths. She had almost forgotten what it was like to face real danger. Since consuming the roots of Yggdrasil, little had threatened her. Skadi stood up and wiped the sweat from her brow while looking back. She heard footsteps coming down the hall.

"Why can he not let this go?" she murmured.

Skadi spied another door which she passed through. It opened onto a busy market street. A few people looked at her strangely, but most ignored her. She looked back and saw Hovard turning the corner into the room she just exited. They locked eyes for a moment, and then Skadi disappeared into the crowd of people.

One Hour Earlier

Egil observed from the shadows as the Jötunn-Breaker was escorted from Heorot Hall by multiple guards. He thought she looked fearsome but knew she was doomed. He waited a little longer until it was just Solveig and Hrothgar who remained in the hall, and then he stepped from the darkness.

"Father," he said, hand on the hilt of his sword.

Hrothgar and Solveig turned their attention to him.

"I am imploring you to reconsider your decision, Father."

"My love, you are making a mistake," Solveig said calmly. "Take your hand off your sword."

Egil's heart was racing. Never had he challenged his father so directly. His palms were clammy and his whole body was shaking. He thought his heart might burst out of his chest.

"Solveig, the mistake was yours," he said.

Solveig stepped between Egil and Hrothgar.

"It's ok, Solveig," Hrothgar said. "Let the boy speak."

"Father, I have traveled the road from Bard Mine to Lejre an innumerable number of times. The people you have forced to serve in the mine and build the road face living conditions not fit even for animals."

"Make your point, boy," said Hrothgar.

"I have borne witness to acts of violence that no person should ever suffer under any circumstance. These are your people. They are our people. You say you are doing this for Midgard—but you are ruining lives."

Hrothgar stepped closer to Egil. Egil held his ground, but everything in his body was telling him to retreat and end this confrontation.

"You will support what I am doing, or you will . . ."

"I know why you felt the road was necessary. I don't disagree with you. I know the power imbalance between our realm and Asgard is great, and we all fear what the gods are capable of. And I . . ."

"You are tip toeing your way into disrespect son. I may be your father, but I am the Earl first."

"The creature is dead, and Asgardians have not threatened Midgard in ages. But you are. You and your guards and this damn road."

"Enough," shouted Solveig. "Egil, I think it is best you leave."

Egil observed Hrothgar place a hand on his once-soon-to-be wife and whisper something in her ear. She nodded and stepped back from Egil.

"Father, I cannot stand by while our people suffer. Your time of ruling is over."

"A bit presumptuous since I am still the Earl. I believe they are still just my people."

Egil, despite his shaky nerves, stepped forward. Solveig eyed him and then the Earl.

"Father, I am giving you an option to step down peacefully. Please take it."

"Son, when the nine realms are thrown into the chaos of Fimbulwinter, how will you lead? You are green and you have never known hardship. I know what happens on the road and at the mine and it bothers me not."

Egil clinched his fist.

"Father, you have lost sight of what your role is as the Earl," Egil said.

"My vision has never been clearer. The only thing humans have going for us is our intellect, but without direction that advantage does not serve us. And the only thing humans respond to is fear. Look around you. Look at this town. It wasn't kindness that got us here son. And I'll tell you this—no amount of cruelty enacted by any of my men will ever be worse than continuing to suffer at the threat of annihilation by creatures who see us as insects."

"So, our options are to live in fear of you or to live in fear of the gods?" Egil said.

"You think because you have ridden your horse along a road built on the backs of those too weak to protest my will that you are one of the people. I think what you need is to learn firsthand."

Just then Egil felt two men grab him by his arms.

"Wealhtheow thought like you. I know that's where you get it from. She refused to see Midgard for what it was. Hopefully, you are smarter than her. Whip him until he can't stand, and then lock him up."

"Sir, are you sure?" One of the guards said. "He is your son."

"Do what he said," said Solveig.

"Solveig," shouted Egil. "This is who you choose to be loyal to? A man who would have his own son whipped?"

"Get him out of here," Hrothgar said.

"He will betray you if he has not already," shouted Egil to Solveig. "Remember Destin. Remember your father."

Egil protested the men who held him, but he was not strong enough to break free.

"Father, you will regret this," he shouted as he was dragged out of the room.

Solveig stepped before Hrothgar after Egil was taken away.

"Do you regret your decision to stand with me?" Hrothgar said plainly.

She reached into her pelt and removed the glowing gem that housed the power stolen from Skadi.

"Within this orb exists the power of the World Tree. It worked and the road is nearly complete. We can move into the final part of our plan," said Solveig.

She handed the orb to Hrothgar.

"According to Hovard, Skadi had to consume the roots of Yggdrasil to gain its power. If you consume this orb, that same power will flow to you."

Hrothgar inspected the orb more closely before swallowing it. At first, nothing happened. Solveig inspected the Earl and there was only stillness. But then an arc of electricity danced along the ceiling of Heorot Hall, and the floor started to tremble. Dust in the rafters shook free.

Solveig stepped back as multiple arcs of electricity danced sporadically and the hall itself shook with increasing ferocity. She saw Hrothgar clench his fists and his frame fill out. A powerful wind tore through the hall, extinguishing the torches that lined the walls.

In the darkness, Solveig caught flashes of Hrothgar with each electrical arc and then there was nothing—only the darkness and stillness that was in stark contrast to the chaos from moments earlier. Solveig could hear breathing. She ran and opened the door of the hall to let in some light. The sight of Hrothgar shocked her.

He looked forty years younger and as strong as the most fearsome of warriors. It almost seemed like he glowed, but Solveig was not sure if her eyes were playing tricks.

The two made eye contact.

"So, this it," he said. "This is how *he* must feel at all times."

Egil resisted the entire way to the cell, but the guards that held him were too strong; his fighting was futile.

"It is not my desire to punish you this way, Egil, but the Earl has spoken," said one of the guards.

"He is right. I don't know my people's hardships. Not really. Do your worst. I can take it."

"Just know there is no shame in crying. Most men do."

Hovard spied the open door and the busy street beyond it. He walked out onto the street and looked left, then right, but did not see Skadi.

Down the street, he saw the silhouette of a broad-shouldered woman and took off in her direction. He quickly caught up to her, grabbed her by the right arm, spun her around, and took a sudden step back.

"You're not her," he said.

She quickly jerked her arm free and pushed him.

"Get away from me," she shouted.

"I'm sorry," he said.

Hovard looked around—again up the street and down the street. There were plenty of people who could have been Skadi but none he was sure were her.

"I had her. How did this happen?" he whispered. "She must pay for what she did to my son."

Skadi watched from the shadows as the woman Hovard thought was her pushed him away. She observed her uncle search for her with no success, and a sadness crept into her mind. She remembered a time when she was young and he had searched for while she hid, after stealing an extra loaf of bread. When he had found her, he scolded her but not because she had taken the bread, but because she had been caught so easily. The two had laughed and shared the bread together. The ground trembling beneath her feet caught her attention and her gaze shifted to the lightning bolts above Heorot Hall.

"What has he done?" she whispered.

NO FORGIVENESS

Hege moved ahead of Carr, staying low to the ground to not give away their position. She pried apart some brush and looked upon an encampment of guards.

"We must stick together. Do you understand?" Hege whispered to Carr and the small group of followers they recruited from the campsite earlier.

"We are with you, Hege," Carr whispered.

Hege scanned the encampment and eventually spotted what she was looking for, then looked back at Carr.

"Now is our time," she said.

Hege waited for a moment longer to ensure no one had noticed her, then moved through the brush and down a slope that was shrouded just enough in darkness. As before, the guards were drunk off mead but were still awake singing songs around the campfire. Beyond them was a collection of swords, axes, and bows. There were also multiple cottages locked from the exterior. The fire effectively lit up the surrounding area, leaving little room for sneaking around. But Hege spied a path that clung to the tree line. She looked at Carr and with her pointer finger gestured for the shadowed path. He nodded.

Hege stayed low and so did those who followed her. The group made its way around the campsite to the side nearest the weapons and the imprisoned workers. She gestured for them to stop.

"Stay here," she whispered.

She waited for a few people to acknowledge her before proceeding to creep toward the weapons.

"What are you doing?" Carr whispered a little too loudly for Hege's liking.

She gestured for him to stay where he was, then continued towards the weapons. Hege remained vigilant as she moved closer and closer and it was good she did, because one guard approached from her right, having just relieved himself in the forest. Thinking quickly, she scurried to the opposite side of the weapon stockpile and ducked as low as she could.

"Who are you?" said a voice behind her.

She was not vigilant enough. Hege turned around and standing over her was a guard she had not seen. His hand was on the hilt of his sword.

"It's you. The rebel."

He started to unsheathe his sword, but Carr tackled the man to the ground.

"Help," shouted the man.

Hege acting as quickly as she could, pulled the man's sword from its sheath. Carr jumped out of the way and Hege plunged the sword through the man's chest, lodging it into the ground beneath him.

She heard them before she saw them—the other guards rushing to aid their fellow man. Hege took a knife from the body of the dead man and handed it to Carr.

The first guard arrived and caught sight of his friend on the ground. His gaze then shifted to lock eyes with Hege. Hege pulled the sword free.

"This is the last time you interfere," said the guard.

She blocked his first and second sword strike. Behind her was Carr with his knife looking for a way to support her without getting in the way. In front of her, more guards were rushing over.

"What are you doing? Open the cottages," shouted Hege.

"Right," said Carr, turning around to face the people they'd brought with them. "You heard her. Let's free our people."

Hege cut down the man she was facing but as soon as he was down, two more took his place. Carr stepped up to help but with his knife, he was more of just a distraction.

"Grab a sword," shouted Hege.

Moments later, Hege had help, but more and more guards were rushing their way, and they would soon be overrun. But as soon as the odds were beginning to truly shift away from their favor, Hege heard the voices of men and women showing up on either side of her. She looked left and right and there were her fellow, former captives. They were unarmed but outnumbered the ten guards who remained.

"Give up. You can't kill us all," said Hege.

The guards all looked at one another and dropped their swords to the ground. A few more moments after that, the weapons were collected and distributed to some of the more able-bodied people who had been freed. And a few more moments after that the surviving guards were tied up in one of the cottages.

Standing over the guards, Hege said, "For everything you have done to us we should kill you."

"Your rebellion won't last. As soon as the Earl learns of this, he will make you pay."

"We should kill them," said Carr, entering the cottage. "They would not have mercy on us."

"I have all the reason in the nine realms to kill them and yet I am showing restraint. You should do the same," Hege said.

"These men will cause problems for us in the future."

"If we start acting like them, we are no different."

"I'm not concerned with being different. I'm concerned for us."

Hege looked down at the men they had captured.

"How many of you have families?" She asked.

"We all do," said one of the guards.

Hege turned to Carr.

"What kind of Midgard do you want to live in, Carr? One where every misdeed is met with retribution?"

"I want to be able to *live* in Midgard, Hege," Carr said.

"There is no weakness in showing mercy."

Hege and Carr looked at each other for a bit, and then he sighed.

"For the record. I want you to know if the Earl . . . no . . . when the Earl finds out, we will all be killed. Our only hope is that it is swift," said Carr before exiting the cottage.

"Not all of us are cruel like the man who took your children. Some of us warned him not to take such extreme measures," said one of the guards.

"But you did not stop him," said Hege.

She gripped the hilt of the sword attached to her waist so hard her knuckles turned white. She breathed in deep and let out a long sigh before turning and exiting the cottage.

"Carr, I want every person capable of wielding a sword, knife, bow or axe to have one. We will make camp here and decide what we shall do next. The next closest encampment is a day's ride. We'll need to be coordinated if we want to keep this liberation going."

"Hege, it would not be fair to you if I did not say that I think leaving those men alive is a mistake."

"They live," Hege said. "We are fighting for justice, not revenge."

"You are not the only one who has lost family while building this damn road."

"Let's not lose sight of our ideals."

"I've not claimed to have ideals. My wife is still missing, Hege."

"I know."

"Now is not the time to be the better people."

"When is the time?"

That night while most were asleep, Carr opened his eyes and saw the embers of the fire glowing. The night sky overhead was filled with stars and the full moon. He sat up and surveyed the camp. Men, women, and children were scattered about sleeping. Hege, too, was asleep near his feet. He was careful not to disturb her as he stood up.

Carr looked at the cottage where the guards were tied up. Two men with swords stood outside of it. His skin was covered in goosebumps and his brow a bit sweaty. But he got up and walked over despite his reluctance, wiping the sweat away from his forehead.

"Sorry Carr, but Hege said not to let anyone in," one of the guards said.

"I just need to speak with them," Carr said. "We are going to liberate more encampments. These men may know about their fellow guards and how prepared they are."

"She said no one. We all agreed."

"You are a young man but old enough to remember the time before these guards. What have you lost?"

"The same as most."

"Before us is a small chance to take back our lives, but Hrothgar's guards are in greater numbers in either direction. Do you not want to have an idea of what their strategy might be?"

The young man eyed Carr.

"I will be in and out. I promise. All I'm looking for is information."

"Be quick about it," said the young man stepping aside.

"Thank you," said Carr.

He entered the cottage and saw the guards tied up in a circle. Most were asleep. One was not.

"Come to finish us off?" the guard said.

Carr approached and knelt by the man.

"A year ago," he whispered. "My wife tried to escape. I encouraged her not to, but she was insistent. She was braver than me. She would go and set markers in the forest so others could follow her path. It is how we knew where to find this camp. But the markers stopped here. Where is she?"

"You're going to need to be clearer than that. Many have ended up here in search of freedom."

"You would be wise not to make light of the situation you are in."

"Why should I not? You mean to kill us."

"How you die can be painless. There is mercy there," Carr said.

The man hesitated for a moment, but only a moment. "We caught her sneaking around."

"Where is she now?"

"We do not know *where* she is."

"What do you mean you don't know *where* she is?"

"We do not mark the graves."

Carr did not respond.

"You said it yourself—you encouraged her not to flee."

Carr breathed in deeply.

"Escapees don't last long in these forests. If they aren't killed by wolves or trolls, then usually one of us finds them and . . ."

"You admit guilt so casually."

"I am tired. More of us are than you know. You might as well get it . . ."

The man couldn't finish his sentence. Carr jammed his knife into the man's neck, spewing blood over his right hand. The gurgling sound of the guard gasping for air filled the room. It was replaced with Carr letting out a long sigh.

Carr stood up and spit on the dying man.

"Hege is right about a lot of things, but not about this. Each of you must die tonight," he whispered.

Hege shifted in her sleep, slowly gaining consciousness. She looked back and saw Carr was no longer by her. Her eyes immediately turned towards the cottage with the captive guards.

"Did anyone go inside?" she said to the men standing out front.

"Uhm."

"Get out of the way," she said pushing the man aside.

Hege burst through the door and was taken aback by what she saw. Nine of the ten men they'd captured were dead with their throats slit. Carr was moving to the final.

"Stop," She shouted.

"It had to be done," he answered.

Hege scrambled across the room and tackled Carr to the ground before he could execute the final guard. The knife flew from his hand as he hit the floor.

"We have to be better," Hege said struggling to restrain Carr.

"Why?" he shouted. "They killed her."

Carr continued to resist under Hege's weight but eventually gave up.

"You have to trust me," Hege said. "We can change Midgard, but only if we know what we want to change it to."

Carr averted his gaze, tears streaming down his cheeks.

"Midgard can never change," he shouted back. "It needs to be burned down."

"We can change it, Carr. We. You. Me. Everyone out there," shouted Hege, pointing beyond the door of the cottage.

Hege looked at where she pointed.

"Oh no," he then said.

Hege looked in the direction he was facing. The tenth man was gone, and his ropes were severed. Hege jumped to her feet and ran out the door. The man who was to be guarding the front was on the ground and pulling himself to his feet.

"He surprised me," he said.

Hege scanned the tree line.

"I don't see him."

Carr caught up to her.

"Where is he?" he said.

"Wake up everyone and get them ready to relocate. I'm going after him. If I can't catch him though, then everyone here is in immediate danger. He'll bring reinforcements."

"This is my fault. I'll go."

"No, Carr. Listen to me this time. You stay here and help everyone get ready."

In Lejre, Hovard ran towards the front gate to speak with the guard on duty. He waved the man down from his perch.

"What is it?" said the guard.

"There is an escaped woman who must be recaptured. Do you recall seeing anyone suspicious pass by you recently? It is important she does not get too far."

"I am sorry sir, but I cannot say that I have. There are strange people who come and go from this town at all times, but none who have raised any concerns for us at the gate. Not lately at least."

Hovard looked beyond the man at Lejre's massive entrance gate.

"How many ways in and out of this town are there?"

"Just this way."

"And you are sure you see everyone?"

"We see everyone," said the guard pointing to several others in various perches. "The Earl likes to ensure no undesirables are let into the town. It's what keeps us from suffering the fates of smaller towns like Fensalir."

"Hmph."

"What does this woman look like? We will keep watch for her and apprehend her if she comes across our path."

"Her name is Skadi. She is tall. Almost as tall as me and has broad shoulders and thick arms. Her hair is dark brown. I should add that she is a skilled warrior. Do not underestimate her or it will be your death."

"And to whom should we contact if we find her?"

"Send a messenger to the guards at Heorot Hall for Hovard Hervor. That is I."

"We will stay on high alert for this woman. You have our word."

Hovard stood there for a moment, inspecting the gate then nodded and turned away.

Skadi ducked around a corner as Hovard neared. She was watching him interact with the guards, but he left them and moved beyond her. She turned her attention to the front gate of Lejre.

"This is why we never came here as a family. This town is just a fortress," she said rhetorically.

"You are not wrong, my friend," said an elderly voice behind Skadi.

She turned around and was face to face with a senior man, carrying a basket of bread and two flagons of mead. The clothes he wore did not fully cover his upper body and Skadi could see scars on his shoulders.

"I have seen you before," Skadi said. "Earlier when I first arrived."

"I was unsure if the Jötunn-Breaker was friend or foe journeying with the Earl's alchemist."

"I am no friend of the Earl if that is what you are wondering," Skadi said plainly.

"I realized that the way you watched that man at the gate. I would be careful around him. He showed up not too long ago and quickly earned the trust of the Earl by enforcing his will on some workers."

"What does that mean?" Skadi said.

"Come with me and I'll show you those who once lived in the cottages near the wall."

He handed Skadi the two flagons of mead. She debated refusing, knowing that she needed to find Mimir, but curiosity had gripped her. She wanted to see what Hovard had done to earn the Earl's ear. She took the flagons and started to follow the old man. They moved away from the busier part of Lejre—the town common and towards a quieter street with few passersby.

"I shelter them, and I bring food and drink to these poor souls when I can. Here it is just down these steps and through this door."

Skadi followed him below ground-level and through the door. They arrived in a dimly lit cellar with just a few torches burning on the wall. The men and women looked up at Skadi and the man as they entered.

She could not quite make out the faces of the people. The room was still far too dark and most quickly averted their gaze to keep from making eye contact. She looked to the old man as he proceeded to hand out the bread he carried with him.

"Fill their cups," he said to her. "Be mindful of your step. There are more down here than it may seem."

"Right. Sorry," she whispered. "I will."

Skadi approached the woman closest to her. She held up her cup but looked away. Despite her turning her head and the poor lighting, when Skadi got close enough, she could see what the woman was trying to hide. She was completely bald. Her scalp and half her face were covered in blackened scabs. She was missing one eye. And the wounds did not stop there—they were visible on her neck to her shoulder. Though a pelt covered the rest of her body, Skadi assumed the burns continued down her entire side.

At that moment Skadi thought back to the screams of those people in the inn from her childhood. The sounds they made as the fire consumed them haunted her still.

Skadi poured the mead into the woman's cup and moved to the next person. He was in no better shape with burns that covered most of his face and arms. Every person in the room was in a similar condition. When Skadi finished pouring their mead she sat down next to the youngest person in the room—a boy not much older than Bjorn. His injuries were the least of anyone's and there was a reason for that.

"His parents sacrificed themselves for him," whispered the old man appearing next to Skadi and the boy.

Skadi reached out to touch the boy's hand, but he recoiled.

"I'm sorry," she whispered.

"Come let's talk," said the old man to Skadi.

She nodded and got up. The two moved to a corner of the room furthest from the people.

"Where is the head they say you travel with?"

"Mimir has been taken," Skadi said. "If you are looking for my help, I no longer have the power of the World Tree. That was taken as well."

"By whom?"

"The Earl and his alchemist"

"That is unfortunate. The power you displayed against the jötunn is already legendary."

"I served my purpose."

"The people of this town need you as well."

"The one who did this is my uncle. He was violent, but I have never known him to be cruel like this."

"Our capacity for cruelty rivals that of the Aesir."

Skadi looked back at the room full of people who suffered at the hand of Hovard. She had seen this before. She had hoped to never see it again.

"I don't know how I could help. Your Earl and his alchemist are schemers, and they are powerful."

"Your uncle may have done this," said the man gesturing towards the room full of burned people. "But his actions were in direct response to the desires of Hrothgar. Skadi, we need help. We need your help."

Skadi hesitated to respond and looked once again at the people who were burned and living in this cellar, barely clinging to life. She was familiar with the look in their faces. She had seen it before. Not on those who had died years ago in the inn but on those of the parents who had lost children to the jötunn. It was a look of despair.

"I don't have the power anymore. I'm not going to be able to help you in the way you need."

"Let's go back upstairs."

Skadi followed the man to the main level of the cottage. In the kitchen, she took a seat at the table. As did the man.

"Your strength would be great, but it isn't what is needed."

"What is then?"

"You are a fighter. We need someone brave."

Skadi sighed and looked down at the table. There was still some mead left in the flagon and she took a swig.

"I'm here to find my friend. That's what I'm going to do."

She pushed away from the table and stood up.

"Wait."

"What?"

He hesitated.

"What?" she repeated.

"Skadi, I believe you can overthrow the Earl."

Skadi's brow was furrowed. Then she quietly snickered.

"Hovard is pursuing me, so we are bound to cross paths. I will do my best to kill him once and for all. But I cannot overthrow the Earl. I don't have the power of the World Tree because he stole it and even if that was not the case, overthrowing an Earl is not like killing a jötunn. How do you know the next person to take his place won't be worse?"

"Like it or not, you are an inspiration for people. Something must happen Skadi. Or we are doomed to suffer more of this," said the man pointing to the door that led to the cellar full of the burned. "Or more of the depravity that happens on the road and at the mine, we cannot go on as things are."

Hege returned to Carr thirty minutes after pursuing the escaped guard. The moon was high in the sky, dimly illuminating the encampment. She was breathing deeply as she arrived, having been running almost the entire time.

"I lost . . . his trail," she said between deep breaths.

"This is all my fault. I am sorry."

"We don't have time . . . for you to feel bad about the . . . stupid decision you made. We need to move these people now."

"What then?"

Hege took in a few deep breaths so she could catch her breath. She looked around at the folks they had liberated thus far.

"With time we could have built an organized resistance but now I'm afraid we'll just have to evade punishment."

"We could escape to one of the smaller towns like Fensalir. Maybe even Thrymheim."

"Either journey would take days if we avoid Hrothgar's road. If it was just us maybe that would be doable but not with all these children."

"This is my fault," said Carr. "Let me make it right."

"How?"

"The next camp over is just guards. I can sabotage it so they will not be able to pursue us."

"How?"

"I'll set fire to it. The guards there will be too flustered to go after our people and then you guide them along the main road until you reach the smaller path to Fensalir."

"There will be no way for you to return before they find you."

"I know."

"The plan was for us to get out of here together," said Hege.

"The plan was to liberate others."

Hege looked at her friend. She had never seen him so stoic.

"With a large enough fire, the smoke will be visible from here. That'll be the signal to take the road," said Carr.

Hege sighed and grabbed Carr's hand.

"Why could you not have just listened to me and let those men be?"

Carr gripped her hand tighter. She looked up at him.

"I was always stubborn. These people are in good hands with you," he said.

"I hope so."

Hege wrapped her hands around Carr, and he returned the embrace.

"I'm not going to stop you. It is the best option we have," she said looking at the children amongst the group. "I just wish we could have done this together Carr."

"I know."

Hege looked at her friend and embraced him a second time. The two held each other for a while before finally separating.

"Goodbye," he said.

NINE

FIRE TIPPED ARROWS

Carr moved through some brush and came upon the encampment he was seeking. He stayed low to keep from being found, and from his perch, he saw guards ambling around. Unlike the camp he called home for years, the only people here were men and women who served as enforcers for the Earl Hrothgar of Lejre. These were just the brutish guards who patrolled the road.

Carr stayed as low as he could behind some bushes and a few trees, staring down at the encampment. Men and women moved all around the site even this late at night. He knew why too. They were mobilizing. The guard that escaped must have reached them and warned them.

Carr looked right. There was a path down to the campsite—possibly the path of a reindeer or some other woodland creature. It wasn't a walking trail, but it was clear enough for him to move along without causing a disturbance and drawing attention to himself. He quickly, but cautiously, made his way down the path until he saw a guard start to look his way. He ducked to avoid being seen. Carr waited, then poked his head up just a bit to see if the guard had spotted him. The guard was gone. Carr waited a moment longer, looked for the guard, and saw him walking away. He was in the clear, but his hands were shaking.

He continued to move down the path until he was so close he could hear the footsteps of the guards. He remained hidden by the brush and just far enough away that if he needed to, he could run, but close enough that danger was imminent.

Through the leaves, he could see figures roaming around, grabbing swords, and connecting them to their waists. Some had bows and others had axes. If Carr had to guess, he would estimate there to be 50 or more guards readying themselves for battle.

He looked around, assessing the landscape, and thinking about what his next move would be. He saw some cottages to his left with fewer people near them. Continuing to stay low, he made his way over. Every few steps he would stop, look around, then continue. A few minutes later, he was near the cottages and searching for a way in.

Two men walked by, and he ducked. His heart nearly jumped out of his chest.

"Breathe, Carr. Breathe," he whispered.

He heard more footsteps.

"The fools think they can avoid their responsibilities to the Earl. They'll learn soon enough to regret that decision," one of the guards said.

"The Earl loves to make an example of rebels."

"A hanging perhaps?"

"I've heard him make reference to Ivar the Boneless."

"And here I thought he hated Vikings."

The two guards laughed and moved beyond Carr.

Carr's nerves were nearly fried. He could not express in words how he was feeling and considered what fear his wife had faced when she was caught.

"She still tried," Carr whispered. "So, pull yourself together."

Carr gave himself some breathing room before poking his head up again. The door to the cottage was only a few steps away, but he would have to be in the open for longer than he felt was safe or wise. Everything hinged on his being able to get this done.

To the right of the cottage was a quiver of arrows and beyond that a barrel of oil for torches. He looked around him, didn't see anyone, then just as he was about to emerge from the brush, he heard voices. Quickly he dropped back into hiding as four guards passed by him.

Carr's heart was beyond racing at this point. He felt like it would burst from his chest. He wiped the sweat from his brow, let the guards move away, looked around again, didn't see anyone, and stepped out. He was exposed. If anyone showed up at this point it was over—he would be a dead man. Guards were moving all over the campsite. Carr could hear them—footsteps and voices everywhere. But he did it—he grabbed the arrows, dipped them in the oil, and stole a bow leaning against the cottage.

Then he moved to the door of the cottage. Carr put his ear against it. He didn't hear anyone on the other side and opened the door.

He sighed with relief.

But the sound of a woman clearing her throat shook him.

Staring back at Carr was one of the most fearsome guards he had ever seen. She had broad shoulders and biceps the size of his calves. Her face was covered in war paint, and she wore a black bear pelt. He looked at her and she at him.

Without saying a word, she went for her sword. It, too, was massive. Too big for this tight space, Carr thought.

He dodged the first strike but just barely. He felt the air shift around him and knew that would not have just killed him but split him in half. He had never seen a woman or sword so large. He managed to evade a follow-up strike. It, too, was just as powerful. But this blow hit a wall and got lodged in it. Carr knew this space was too small for such a warrior and such a blade. He used this moment to his advantage and pulled one of the oil-dipped arrows from the bin.

With no room or time to fire the arrow, Carr lunged at the woman. She let go of the sword and caught him in the air and the two fell to the ground. Despite his momentum, the powerful guard quickly took control of the situation and pinned him. He struggled but she started to hit him. He defended as best he could, but block or not her blows had the intended effect. With the arrow still in hand he found the one vulnerable spot on her he could reach and stabbed it into her thigh. She flinched, but it barely slowed her down.

Carr tried to pull the arrow free, but she grabbed his hand and ripped the arrow out herself. Blood started pouring onto the floor as she lifted the arrow above his head.

"No stop," Carr shouted.

She attempted to put it through his face, but Carr blocked with his hand and the arrow went through his palm instead. Acting fast, Carr turned his hand around, snapping the arrow and slammed his palm against her face. The arrow went through her eye. Stunned, she fell back, and Carr proceeded to push her off him.

The guard was dazed and losing blood. Carr was convinced he was the victor, but she had yet to fall. Then, all sense of confidence left him when she smiled and dropped her hand from her bloody eye. The warpaint was replaced with crimson blood that flowed into her mouth and over her teeth, giving her grin the look of a troll. She lifted her hand and waved her finger.

Carr's body trembled and a chill crept up his spine, as she started to slowly advance towards him. Then, she charged. Carr jumped to his feet and yanked the arrow from his hand. It hurt like nothing he had ever experienced, but as she leapt for him, he moved quickly and jammed the arrow through her neck. She crashed into him, taking him back to the ground, but this time she was dead. He was truly confident this time since her dead weight made her nearly impossible to move.

He slowly got up. His injuries were significant. In the short bout, the guard had done a number on him. Carr made sure to inspect her to make sure she was dead. He used some of the guard's pelt to bandage his hand. His face was bruised and bloody, his vision was slightly blurry, but he had survived the encounter.

On the wall was a single torch. He took it down, grabbed the remaining arrows dipped in oil, and used the ladder within the cottage to reach a small hatch that led to the roof of the structure, making sure to maneuver around the giant blade lodged in the wall.

Carr peeked out a tiny bit and could see the camp in all directions. There were ten cottages total. Most of the guards were mobilized to the north of the camp, preparing to move along the road. Carr checked the number of arrows he had in the quiver.

He whispered. "Please guide my hand."

Carr lit the first arrow and pulled back on the bow. He let out all the air in his lungs and let the first arrow fly. It streaked across the night sky and impacted the building the furthest away. The blaze took hold immediately. Carr did not hesitate to shift his focus and let fly the remaining arrows with precise accuracy. When the last one hit the remaining cottage, Carr dropped the torch on the roof of the building he perched on before hopping to the ground. Each cottage blazed spectacularly and just as Carr had hoped, the guards who were preparing to strike down Hege's growing rebellion were scrambling to find out what happened.

He swiftly looked around him. Guards were rushing to put out the fires and it did not seem anyone noticed him yet. But the path he used to sneak into the encampment was crawling with guards. The remaining pathways were far too open to provide the cover he needed to escape.

Carr heard a man approaching and opted to hide within the cottage he just leapt from. Every movement hurt and he got inside a bit slower than he should have.

"What was that?"

"What?"

"I think I saw someone."

"Damn it," whispered Carr.

"I saw him go inside that cottage there."

"Surround the cottage. It is burning."

Carr looked up and saw the fire he started, thinking he would be long gone, breaching the ceiling. Embers were floating down around him.

"We should just let him die by the fire. He caused enough of a headache," said another guard.

Carr was dripping sweat. He removed his pelt and threw it to the ground. The injuries he sustained fighting the guard were throbbing and his mind was racing with thoughts of his past life and regrets of recent decisions.

"This is a distraction," shouted a guard.

"He means to keep us here."

Carr heard that last two comments and knew if he did not act, they would shift their attention away from him and away from the fires. He pulled the sword that was still wedged in the wall.

Carr took in one big deep breath and burst through the door, sword in hand. Twenty or so men and women stood around him and when they saw him with his sword ready to strike, some started to laugh.

"What do you hope to do with that all by yourself?" one guard said.

Carr did not respond. He just kept his eyes on all who was around him. This was not about survival. But this was something the guards knew as well.

"How many are there?"

Carr said nothing.

"You can tell us now or we can just count the bodies later. It does not matter."

Carr saw five guards approaching him. None were as intimidating as the woman from earlier, but it did not matter. The odds were so far from his favor that they could have been children with wooden blades.

"If you surrender maybe we'll let the children live. I am sure the Earl would find forgiveness in his heart for them and there is surely work for tiny people. The mine has tight spaces does it not?"

With a swift motion, Carr struck down the guard who spoke. The sudden act of violence surprised everyone, including himself. He looked at the man who was now dying on the ground with a gash across his chest and Carr gasped.

"Get him," shouted another guard.

Carr pivoted and took off in the opposite direction. He led a horde of guards on a chase through a fire-engulfed camp. He dropped the heavy sword to lighten his load. He had always been fast and now it was proving more helpful than ever. Carr to his own surprise put much distance between him and his pursuers. He then ducked around a cottage and heard footsteps run past him. He sucked in some air and tried to steady his heartbeat. With a bit of reservation, he looked to see if his pursuers were still after him. He did not see anyone.

"I might actually . . ."

A well-placed arrow caught him in his stomach. He looked down at the arrow protruding from his body and touched it. A second, then a third, connected with his shoulder and chest. Carr fell to his knees.

As the horde caught up to him, Carr looked skyward. He reached up, then his body fell over in the dirt. Fires were raging, and most of the guards were still organizing or trying to extinguish the flames. It was chaos all spurred on by one man.

Hege stood at attention watching in the direction that Carr made off in. Behind her were families prepared to move as soon as she gave the word. Each adult male and female was armed with a sword, axe, or bow, but Hege hoped none would have to use them.

"Carr, you can do this," she whispered.

As soon as the words escaped her mouth, she saw the smoke beginning to rise in the distance. It was black and grey and billowed towards the moon.

"Let's go."

Hege saw young a couple helping their daughter attach a sack to her back and an elderly woman struggling with her own sack. She hustled over to help her.

"Thank you," the woman said.

"Are you going to be ok?"

"I can handle myself."

Hege let a few people pass her as they headed towards the main road, then she walked with the elderly woman alongside the large group.

"Do *you* think we will be ok?" said the older woman.

"I hope so," Hege said.

TEN

THE BURNED

Skadi looked at the old man who was fastening the tattered pelt of one of the burned survivors. The room was cool. The man's hands were shaky, and he was struggling with a knot, so Skadi stepped in.

"What is going on in this town?" She asked as she tied the pelt. "What is the Earl and this alchemist up to?"

The man looked at the survivor, then at Skadi, and pointed upward.

Skadi made sure the pelt was properly situated, then followed the older man upstairs to the kitchen.

"What do you know?" Skadi said.

"My name is Stigr, and you are not wrong. There is certainly something sinister happening here."

"What?"

"I can only speak to what I have seen."

"And what might that be?" Her patience slipped just a little at the man's elusiveness.

"I suspect the Earl is on a path of war. Lejre was not always such a big town, and those massive walls are relatively new."

"With whom is he seeking war?"

"Who is a good question. At this point, I do not know who could challenge him. The Vikings are long gone and the Guards of Lejre are mostly well-trained, save for a few exceptions, of course."

Skadi shifted in place and looked at the man.

"If you do not know with whom it is he is seeking war, tell me why you think he is seeking war."

Stigr grabbed the teapot and poured himself a cup. He took a sip before speaking. "Many years ago, this town was nothing like it is now. These huge walls that surround it did not exist and it was not nearly as sprawling. It was more like your home of Fensalir, but even less so. The Earl had just come to power, but he was faced with a challenge. There was a monster in those days that would terrorize the people. Much like your jötunn, it would consume people. Men, women, children—everyone. I was a guard at Heorot Hall the first night it attacked."

Twenty Years Ago

Stigr clanged his mug full of mead against the mug of his friend who sat across from him. His face was red, and his spirits were high. The mead was doing what mead did best.

"Shall we sing?" Stigr shouted.

"Stigr, if you wish to sing then do so," said Hrothgar who sat next to his wife, Wealhtheow, at the end of the hall.

Stigr slammed his mead down and climbed onto the table.

"Get down, Stigr. You know your singing is terrible," said Bard.

"Bard, you should sing with me."

Bard laughed and took a swig from his mug.

Stigr looked around the room at the men and women merrymaking. He breathed in deep and began.

"WE SWUNG OUR SWORD THAT WAS EVER SO LONG AGO WHEN WE WALKED IN GAUTLAND TO THE MURDER OF THE DIG-WULF . . ."

The people who celebrated in the hall joined in.

"THEN WE RECEIVED . . ."

A shriek cut through Stigr's belting and the laughter of the audience. It was a shrill that pierced the veil of drunkenness brought on by too much mead. As quickly as Stigr climbed on the table, he got down from it and put his hand on the hilt of his sword.

The whole hall was quiet. Stigr looked at his fellow men and women with concern and curiosity.

"What was that?" Bard whispered.

"Shhhhh," said Stigr with his finger to his lips.

Then the primary door burst open. Wooden shrapnel flew across the room, piercing partygoers. Some were skewered against the opposite wall by pieces of wood the size of arms and legs. Stigr checked himself and found he was fortunate enough to have avoided serious injuries. His attention shifted to the open doorway and saw the silhouette of a massive, lanky creature with a misshapen head.

Whatever it was that stood in the doorway shrieked again. The sound was guttural and unlike anything Stigr had experienced in Midgard.

Stigr noticed a woman who was standing near the door when it burst open, was picking herself up. She was just out of the view of this creature standing in the door. But as she righted herself amongst the chaos, she turned to face it.

"Don't," whispered Stigr.

The woman screamed as soon as she saw the beast. The beast screamed back and with its long, tendril-like fingers grabbed her by the waist. She batted its hand, but it was a fruitless effort. This ogre was strong.

Stigr averted his gaze as she was lifted overhead of the creature. But even though he could not see it, the sounds she made as the monster consumed her would haunt him for the rest of his days.

When Stigr found the courage to look, the creature was gone and only parts of the woman's corpse remained. Right before him was Bard, who looked to still be checking if he, too, was injured.

Stigr turned around to face the Earl. Hrothgar was standing with a sword in one hand and a shield in another. His wife was seated just behind him, surveying the scene.

"Sir," said Stigr.

The Earl's attention shifted to him.

"What should we do?"

Hrothgar did not answer immediately. Stigr understood his hesitation to respond, since what could he say? But what Stigr did not understand was that on his life, he swore he saw the faintest smile pull at the corner of the Earl's lips.

Present

"The terror that happened that night would continue for years—12 actually, until the Earl seemed to have exhausted all of his resources. No man or woman in Midgard could stand against this monster, but one day a mysterious warrior showed up. I had long stopped guarding Heorot Hall. I wanted to study runes to become an alchemist. There was a man here named Destin who was very skilled and inspiring. I had an idea for a powder that exploded. I shared the idea with his daughter . . . sorry I digress . . . I saw this warrior arrive by sea and that night I heard music in Heorot Hall for the first time in years."

"Did the beast show?" Skadi asked.

"It did, but the next morning word was shared with the people of Lejre that the beast was dead, and I saw the warrior's ship in the harbor was gone."

Skadi looked at Stigr who was clearly recalling some past trauma he would have sooner never spoken of again. She placed a hand on his shoulder.

"I think about the woman often. Had I never started singing, she may not have . . ."

"You are no more at fault than the maker of the building where the death occurred."

"With the monster dead, things got better for a while. We weren't under the constant threat of the creature anymore. But rumors started to circulate amongst the people of Lejre that the Earl was talking about needing rare resources. Guards and former guards were recruited to be scouts. I was one of them. Another was my dear friend, Bard . . ."

Skadi noticed Stigr drift off in thought.

"Bard found an iron depository rich in Seidr magic."

"Bard Mine."

"You have heard of it?"

"I have."

"Bard gave his life trying to take the Ironwood from the Vargr. The real suffering began when the Earl called for the construction of his road connecting Lejre to the mine. We have lost more lives building that road than during the 12 years the monster attacked Lejre."

"We are the monsters," whispered Skadi.

"This is why we need your help. Your exploits in Fensalir are legendary and we are being crushed by this man."

Skadi fidgeted slightly when Stigr spoke. She looked at him, then at the door that hid where the victims of her uncle attempted to heal. She saw Stigr massage his forearm.

"You were burned too?" She asked.

Stigr rolled up his sleeve, revealing burns up and down his arm.

"I stood by while that woman was killed—I vowed I would never stand by again and yet when the man with fire came, I was too scared to intervene. I was burned and fled. I am trying to make amends for my cowardice, but I can only do so much and I'm no hero."

"Heroism isn't just about physical ability," said Skadi.

"But it is about taking action and standing up for those who cannot stand for themselves."

Skadi let out a deep sigh.

"So, you'll help us?"

Skadi looked back at the door to the victims of Hovard's flames.

"I will," she said. "I am not sure how, but I know I'll need Mimir's help."

Hovard pounded on the door of a cottage on Lejre's Market Street where homes were more ornate, and the people better dressed. When the door cracked slightly, he pushed his way past the man who opened it. Sitting by a fire was a woman with a baby. An iron skillet was positioned near the flames. She looked his way as he entered their home.

Hovard scanned the living space before addressing the man and woman. The interior was just as, if not more decorative, than the exterior. Gold pieces adorned the area around the fireplace and the smell of flowers permeated the room—but there was something a bit off.

"Who are you?" said the woman.

Hovard turned his attention towards her.

"I am seeking someone," he said. "Did a tall woman pass through here or down this road?"

The woman appeared to think for a moment but then slowly shook her head.

"I don't know who you are talking about," she said. "There are many tall women in this town. You would need to be more specific than that."

Hovard stared at the woman then shifted his attention to the man.

"Mind if I look around then?"

"I would mind," said the woman standing up.

Hovard turned his attention back to her.

"We don't know who you are, and this is Market Street. You cannot barge into our home and treat us like commoners."

Hovard took more offense to her statement than he expected himself to. He moved further into the home. The woman stepped between him and the baby. Then her husband met them and stood by her side.

"The easier you make this for me, the easier I make it for you," said Hovard.

"Why not search the workers' cottages near the wall?"

Hovard's mind flashed back to those people by the wall, and he winced.

"This is near where she last was," Hovard said, patience waning.

"Well, there is no one here," said the woman. "So, it is best you be on your way."

Hovard shifted his attention from the woman to the man and then to the baby. The smell of flowers was mixed with something he could not pinpoint right away, but soon realized it was something rotting.

"There is a putrid odor in this cottage. You are trying to mask it with your flowers, but the truth is coming through quite strong," Hovard said. "The cottages of those by the wall did not stink like this. Quite the opposite."

"We had meat spoil," said the woman, her nerves a bit shaken. "But we are not hiding anything."

Hovard stepped forward and the couple held their ground, but his massive frame and bear pelt loomed over them. His one hand started to warm.

"Are you hiding Skadi?" He said flatly.

"We do not know who that is and . . . we do not appreciate being harassed in our own home," said the woman.

Hovard's hand warmed some more. Any hotter and the flames would burst forth.

"You do have one thing in common with the cottage wall folks—they were resistant too. In the time you spent trying to impede me, I could have done my search and left."

"I think you should just go," said the husband putting a hand on Hovard's shoulder.

Hovard shifted his gaze towards the man's hand.

"Do not touch me," he said.

"Or what?" said the man, growing bolder despite Hovard's stature. "My wife already told you this is Market Street. You can't do this here."

Hovard grabbed the man's hand and burned it.

His eyes shot open at the sudden violence. His wife, too. She jumped to his aid, but Hovard swatted her away while keeping hold of her husband's hand.

"Stop," shouted the man. "Let me go."

The flames moved up the man's forearm. He screamed and his wife attempted again to come to his aid, but Hovard knocked her to the ground a second time. Finally, Hovard stopped the fire and let the man go. He grabbed his burned arm and fell back into the embrace of his wife.

"Step out of the way and let me search the home."

The man and woman showed one last bit of defiance but ultimately decided to move aside and allow Hovard to search the home unimpeded. He peeled back parts of the wall, rummaged through various rooms without concern for tidiness, and quickly tore the home apart in a way that conveyed more anger towards the owners than interest in Skadi's whereabouts. When he was done, the house was in a shambles.

"Be sure to do something about that spoiled meat," said Hovard as he made for the door.

"That's it," shouted the woman. "You nearly burn my husband's arm off and destroy our home then just leave."

"You have the resources to rebuild. Do it. I might have inconvenienced you but thank the Allfather I did not do more. The woman I am looking for is dangerous. It is important I am thorough."

"You are a brute," shouted the woman. "Look at what you have done to my husband."

Hovard looked over at the man. His arm was covered in significant burns.

"He is a hunter. How will he fire a bow now? How will he provide for us? We'll starve."

Hovard leaned in close to the woman while grabbing a gold ornament from the mantle. He held it in front of the woman's face.

"Trade these," he said flatly.

She looked up and snatched the gold from him and threw it away. It smashed against the wall a few feet away.

"Hmph," Hovard murmured and turned to exit.

"You'll be sorry," said the woman as she moved to hit Hovard with the iron skillet that was near the fire.

He caught the woman's hand and pushed her away from him but as he did so, accidentally lit her pelt aflame. She flew across the room and crashed against the wall furthest from him. She hit the ground with a thud and the flames spread over her entire pelt, engulfing her body in a blaze. The woman hollered as her body burned. She rolled around and the flames spread to the walls, furniture, and floors. Her husband leapt to her aid, but there was little he could do to extinguish the flames before they consumed her.

"You killed her," shouted the man. "You killed my wife."

He picked up the iron skillet.

"Think of your child before you do something foolish."

The man looked at his baby who was wailing.

"Be mindful of what you do next," Hovard said.

The man gripped the skillet handle tight but waivered and dropped it. The skillet bounced on the floor by his feet.

Hovard backed up, towards the door.

"Leave us," said the man. "Please."

"Gladly."

Hovard exited the home. Once in the street, he looked down at the line of homes he entered before this one where the folks were a bit less combative. The people were outside looking his way, having heard the screams. He could see there was talk amongst them but could not hear them. That did not matter—he knew what they were whispering.

"Get back inside?" he shouted, fires raging around him.

Most retreated but a few remained. Hovard sighed and disappeared around a corner.

A few hours later, Hovard found himself sitting in a mead hall downing his second mug. His motivation to pursue Skadi had stalled and he opted to drown his sorrows. As he put the mug to his lips, two guards approached him from the rear.

"What do you want?" he said.

"The Earl would like to speak with you."

Hovard finished the mead, put the mug down on the table, and looked back at the two guards.

"Fine," he said.

"Leave us," said the Earl to the guards who escorted Hrothgar into Heorot Hall.

The two men exited immediately, leaving Hrothgar alone with Hovard in the dimly lit hall.

Hrothgar stepped from behind his desk and as he approached, Hovard could see how young Skadi's power made him.

"You did it," Hovard said.

"I never doubted Solveig's abilities. Like her father before her, she is incredibly skilled."

"I can see that."

"But I have doubted your abilities. I hoped for the best, however, you have confirmed what I suspected would be the case and my people have had enough."

"You are referring to the woman who died earlier?"

"And the people whose homes you terrorized in search of one person."

"Need I remind you, how we met?" said Hovard. "Were those not your people too?"

"Those were laborers, who were supposed to be giving their bodies for the greater good. The people who you are drawing into your family squabble are some of Lejre's most upstanding. Discretion should be paramount, and you are doing everything but."

Hovard stood up straighter and stepped closer to Hrothgar.

"Your reputation as Earl is that of one who enjoys making examples of people. Am I not doing the same?"

Hrothgar smiled, glanced at the floor, then looked at Hovard.

"What does this town have that no other town in Midgard has?" Hrothgar asked.

"What?" Hovard responded plainly.

"Guards. Trained ones. People who everyday put the lives of others before their own to maintain peace in Lejre. How do you suppose we keep those guards fed and armored? The wealth generated on Market Street is a vital resource for the stability of this town. And you disturbed that peace."

"That family was difficult."

"They are all difficult, Hovard. Control is a balancing act. I'm not opposed to making examples of people. I have been eager to put someone to the blade in the town common, but there must always be a purpose for such actions."

"Is this why you have summoned me? To scold me? I have killed for lesser offenses," Hovard said.

"And yet here I am . . . still alive. Still scolding you."

Hovard grimaced and clenched his fist.

"You were a Viking," said Hrothgar.

"I still am."

"You're a broken old man," said Hrothgar. "I was, too, once upon a time."

Hovard chose to ignore the slight.

"In your day, I'm sure you were quite intimidating. Vikings in general were quite menacing. The berserkers who would raid and pillage settlements big and small. Oh, you were a fearsome lot."

"What is the point you seek to make with your blabbering?" Hovard said, patience waning and not inclined to endure the patronizing speech.

"But times changed, and your numbers dwindled. Most Viking clans disbanded. Or in your case, abandoned their leader altogether."

"Make your point," said Hovard. "Or I am leaving."

He began to turn away from the Earl, but Hrothgar tapped his foot, and the hall shook.

"Try turning your back on me again."

Hovard slowly turned his attention back to Hrothgar.

"You have mistakenly believed I care about this issue with your niece. I do not. I gave you a gift in return for what you brought me, and you have wasted it. Something you should not have done, because in the past

I would have simply killed you for stepping foot within Lejre. Vikings, or *former Vikings*," said Hrothgar gesturing at Hovard. "Are not welcome in this town. And yet I let you roam free to pursue this revenge quest of yours."

"It is more than that. It is a blood debt."

"Another dead Viking is not a concern of mine."

Hovard felt his stomach churn and the heat in his hand grow. Hrothgar looked down at Hovard's hand.

"You wish to strike me down? You would not be the first today."

Hovard reigned in his emotions and let the heat dissipate.

"I used to offer a huge reward for any fool brave enough to attempt to slay the creature that plagued this town. Vikings would come from all over Midgard to try, and none prevailed. This went on for twelve years until I sent a raven to a man in the Geatland. I thought your savagery would benefit me, but you all failed. So, you see I do not care about your dead son. What I do care about, however, is that the upstanding people of Lejre will not be terrorized by a relic of an age that ended years ago. Do you understand me?"

Hovard did not respond. He did not shift his footing or break his eye contact with Hrothgar. But in his mind, he was strangling him.

"I'll accept your silence as a yes. I have already sent a raven to the Geatland for help tracking down Skadi. This man is a skilled warrior— more than capable of dealing with your niece and with far less destruction to my town and my people. He will be here within a day. I want you to wait for him at the docks."

Hovard hesitated. It had been so long since he was given orders.

"Do you understand?" Hrothgar said.

He waited a little longer then nodded subtly and moved for the door.

"Hovard, you're angry, but do not let that anger blind your judgment."

ELEVEN

A NETWORK OF TUNNELS

"The people of Lejre always knew when the ogre was coming because its wail was steeped in agonizing dread. When it reared its ugly head, we used a network of tunnels we created to travel and seek safety. I will take you to the nearest entrance," said Stigr.

"Lead the way," Skadi said.

"A few guards patrol these tunnels, but no one uses them anymore. If you do run into trouble, however, the tighter spaces will help keep you from being ambushed."

Skadi followed Stigr out of the cottage, and the cool air of Midgard prickled her skin where it was not covered by her pelt. In her years traveling Midgard, these days were the coldest and she was afraid to admit to herself what that meant. Skadi let the gloomy thought fade from her mind as she and Stigr maneuvered through the town, sticking to the shadows as best they could, taking care to watch for roaming guards and Hovard. Not before long they arrived at the entrance of a cellar.

"This it?" Skadi asked.

Stigr nodded.

"The network is simple but do be careful."

Skadi moved to grab the handle of the door but stopped and looked back at Stigr.

"Dark times do not last forever. The sun always rises," Skadi said.

"That is why you are here."

Stigr grabbed a torch off a nearby wall and handed it to Skadi.

"Those people are lucky to have you watching out for them," she said.
"And now they have you too."

Skadi extended her hand.

Stigr grabbed her forearm, she took hold of his, and the two shook.
Skadi then proceeded to enter the tunnel. The torch was bright enough
to light up the surrounding area, but it was very dark underground, and
it fiercely competed with the torch. She moved cautiously, slowly putting
distance between herself and the way through which she entered. She
looked back only briefly when she heard Stigr close the cellar door.

Though it was cold above ground, beneath it, the temperature felt
nearly unbearable. Skadi was missing the power Yggdrasil afforded her.
With it, the cold had no effect on her, but without it, she felt every
degree below freezing.

With one hand on her sword, and the other holding the torch just
above eye-level, she inched her way through the cramped quarters. As she
walked, she thought about Bjorn, Fensalir, Eirdóttir, and the two missing
council members. She recalled the fight with the jötunn and the journey
to consume the roots of Yggdrasil. Her thoughts then shifted to that of
Loki. For a while she walked in peace. But that did not last.

Skadi's thoughts were interrupted by the sound of footsteps in the
direction of an approaching intersection. She looked left and right. There
was nowhere for her to hide, and the footsteps were getting closer. Skadi
debated throwing the torch to the ground and extinguishing the flame
but then she would be left in the dark. Instead, she listened intently to
the footsteps with the hope of deciphering the number of people.

"Two . . . maybe?" she whispered.

"Do you see that light?" said one of the approaching persons.

"Someone else is down here," said another.

"Two," she confirmed for herself.

Skadi quickened her pace towards the intersection, meaning to catch
the approaching guards by surprise and use the tighter space to her
advantage. She was confident in her abilities as a warrior, World Tree, or
no World Tree, there had been plenty of battles in her past that would
give her an edge.

She hit the intersection and standing before her was a guard taller than her who looked comically big in such a small space. Behind him were two other guards, smaller in stature but each quite formidable.

Skadi unsheathed her sword.

"Who are you?" shouted the guard out front.

Skadi did not waste a word answering his inquiry. She merely let go of the tension in her muscles and readied to strike. It was one of the other guards who answered for her.

"She is the one the Earl is looking for. I was just at the front gate and overheard her description."

"Apprehend her then."

The guards unsheathed their swords and lunged for Skadi. She deflected all their initial attacks. The tight space made maneuvering difficult, but she was an experienced warrior, and the guards were hired swords. But their strikes were powerful enough; each blow reverberated up her arm. She was quickly remembering the toll combat took on the body. Strike, deflect, strike, deflect, strike, deflect . . . Skadi did her best to contend with the three warriors, but they were gaining ground on her.

Skadi looked behind her and saw the tunnel narrowed. She pondered what her next move was. It had been months since she had felt the pressure of a battle. Skadi hesitated, but then pivoted and ran.

"This is all the Jötunn-Breaker can do," laughed the large guard. "Get her."

Skadi continued running and as she did, glanced back. When the narrowing tunnel forced the three guards into a single file, she stopped, spun around, and threw the torch at the largest guard in front. Reflexively he tried to catch the torch and Skadi used the distraction to pierce his chest with Ridill. The force with which she stabbed him, pushed him into the guards behind him and they all fell to the ground.

Skadi pulled her sword free as the two remaining guards scrambled to get to their feet. The guard immediately behind the large one, swung at Skadi but she parried and cut his neck. Blood spewed onto the tunnel wall. The final guard, having witnessed his two comrades meet their end quite violently picked up the torch and waved it at Skadi.

"Get back," he shouted. "Get back."

Skadi did not give any ground and swiped at the torch. The remaining guard took a step backward, then another and another. Skadi was now the one gaining ground. But as she neared, and with the torch close to the man's face, she saw that he was just a boy, not much older than Bjorn. Skadi paused then glanced at the two men lying dead at her feet. She sighed, stopped inching forward, and lessened her combative stance.

"I will let you live," said Skadi.

"It's a trick," said the guard. "You will kill me as soon as I turn around."

"It's not a trick," said Skadi. "I am showing you mercy. Just promise not to do anything stupid."

The man with the torch in hand hesitated to do anything and Skadi could see his grip around the torch was shaking.

"I don't know what to do."

"Take my offer," Skadi countered.

"I have to kill you, or you'll kill me," shouted the guard.

He jabbed the torch in Skadi's direction, but she deflected it and knocked the man to the ground. He screamed and put his hands up to block what he suspected would be a killing blow . . . a killing blow that never came.

"I could have ended you multiple times by now."

He scrambled backward a bit then tried reaching for the sword he'd dropped. Skadi stepped on it and slid it away. He turned over and tried grabbing the torch, but Skadi hit him in the back of the head with the hilt of Ridill.

"Idiot," she whispered.

Skadi looked around the tunnel for a way to hide the bodies and lock up the one unconscious guard. It took a moment, but eventually, she found a room, cordoned off by a wooden door. She tried to open it but was locked so she opted to kick it open—inside was a store closet with ropes, chains, and other miscellaneous items. Skadi dragged the bodies and the one unconscious guard into the room. She tied up the living guard and gagged him with torn-off pieces of his pelt.

She gave the guard one last look before closing the door behind her and continuing her journey through the tunnels underneath Lejre.

Two Days Ago

"Alfhild, Gosta, what did I tell you about leaving my sight?" said Hege.

"Sorry, Mother," said Alfhild. "We thought we saw a deer and wanted to pet it."

"You cannot run off like that. It's dangerous. What if a guard catches you where you are not supposed to be?"

"Mother, we know why it is dangerous. The guards tell us you won't work," said Gosta.

"They're talking to you?" Hege said.

Alfhild and Gosta looked at one another.

Hege knelt to be at their level. She put a hand on each of their cheeks.

"What have they said to you?"

"Not a lot," said Alfhild.

"You can tell me. I won't be mad."

"They say that you will be the death of us," answered Gosta.

Hege made a fist. She looked up at the sky for a moment then back at her two children.

"We don't believe them though mother," said Alfhild. "They're just trying to scare us."

"They're scaring me," whispered Hege.

"Mother, we are brave. Don't worry."

"Do you two understand what I am doing?"

The two kids looked at one another curiously.

"The Earl of Lejre has taken advantage of people who cannot fight back. He has destroyed families in service of this road and that cannot persist."

"But mother, why do you have to be the one?" said Alfhild.

Hege hesitated.

"Because it has to be someone," she answered.

"Why can't the people just run away to Fensalir? Have you heard of the Jötunn-Breaker, Mother?

"No."

"She killed the monster in that town. We can go there and leave the Earl and his road behind," said Alfhild.

"And what of our friends like Uncle Carr? What would happen to him if we left?"

"What will happen to us if we stay?" asked Gosta.

Present

Hege walked with the elderly woman and a few children who did not seem to have adult caretakers along the main road that connected Bard Mine to Lejre. Behind them, the smoke was still rising from the campsite Carr sabotaged. Hege looked back and thought about her friend, acknowledging the sacrifice she knew he had to make for them to pass unscathed.

"Where to now?" asked the older woman.

"We are going to Fensalir. Up ahead is the junction of this main road and the path that leads to the small town."

"Is that town not just as dangerous? There are rumors of a jötunn."

"I have heard the same," said one of the children.

"It has been freed of the jötunn's grip," assured Hege. "Tales of the Jötunn-Breaker reached my children and they . . ."

"They what?" said the old woman.

Hege wiped a tear from her eyes.

"They told me it would be safe there if we went."

"I'm sorry," said the elderly woman somberly.

Hege nodded one time then broke eye contact with the woman. Moments later she felt a hand wrap around her own. Hege closed her eyes as tears streamed down her cheeks.

"My worst nightmare has come true," Hege whispered.

"Don't cry," said one of the children near her.

Hege wiped the tears from her face and smiled at the small boys and girls that walked alongside her.

"I lost a son many moons ago. My husband succumbed to grief and took his own life not long after. I learned to live with their deaths, and my own mother supported me until her passing. Do you have someone to lean on?"

"I thought I did."

"We are all grateful for what you have done for us. I can't do much, but I can listen. My name is Bergljot."

Hege gripped the woman's hand tighter. The group reached the intersection and turned onto the path that led to Fensalir. It was a tighter and less traversed route. The brush was overgrown and the path barely visible, but it was a known passageway. The group narrowed into a line as they started along the path. Concerned that a threat was more likely to come from the rear than the front, Hege hung back as those she escorted passed her so she could bring up the rear. Bergljot stayed by her side.

As soon as they were all on the smaller, narrower road, Hege looked back one last time at the smoke which was starting to thin out and mouthed the words "thank you".

Hege and the Bergljot walked in silence along the path to Fensalir. The smoke from the sabotaged campsite was no longer visible. The group had gone too far, and it had faded too much. For Hege, the quiet of Midgard was mildly unsettling. She did not like how it let her mind wander. She thought about her children. She thought about her home before her parents relocated her to the mainland. Deep down, she wished they had just stayed—she would never have been conscripted into the Earl's ambitions and her children would never have been killed.

"But they would have never been born," she whispered.

"What was that?" Bergljot said.

"Nothing."

A few hours passed with no disturbance. The darkness of the Midgardian night sky was held at bay by the full moon which cast light onto their path. Hege stayed with Bergljot but kept an eye on everyone who was with her, especially the few young children without parents.

"How long is the journey to Fensalir?" asked Bergljot.

"It has been some time since I was there, but I believe it is a few days on horseback so even longer by foot."

"You have been to Fensalir before?"

"My mother and father were nomads. Like Vikings but without the pillaging," Hege laughed. "They first traveled to the mainland many seasons ago and we moved from town to town, never spending more than a few years anywhere. We lived in Fensalir before the dark times."

"I heard of the troubles Fensalir faced. Few have not I trust. It is as if the Allfather has turned his back on us."

"Or perhaps turned his attention to us," Hege said.

"You don't trust the gods?" Bergljot asked.

"It is said that humans and the Aesir are the most alike of any creatures of the nine realms. Not in strength or magic but in personality. If they are anything like us . . ."

"That is a terrifying prospect. I always thought of Thor as a protector but if he were . . ."

Hege put her pointer finger to her lips interrupting Bergljot.

"What?"

"Quiet," whispered Hege.

Hege knelt and placed her ear to the ground.

"What?" whispered Bergljot.

"Oh no," she whispered.

"What is happening?"

"Riders on horseback. We must hide now."

Hege ran up to the middle of the group.

"Hrothgar's men are on their way. Get off the path. Use your pelts to clear your footprints and hide."

"What if they stop?" said one man.

"I'll distract them," Hege said before turning her attention to the children. "If anything happens, do you all know what you are supposed to do?"

One child shook his head.

"You are to listen to Bergljot here. If anything bad happens to me, she is in charge."

The children nodded in understanding.

"Now everyone hide," Hege commanded.

All the people with her immediately scattered. The few families that were whole stuck together and individuals paired up. Within minutes the path was cleared, and everyone was dispersed amongst the trees and wildlife around the path. Hege grabbed Bergljot and the two found refuge behind a massive bush.

Hege kept as low as she could while keeping an eye on the trail. From her position she could see far back quite a way and could hear and feel the trembling of the guards on horseback.

"Hopefully they'll pass us," Bergljot whispered.

Hege looked at the Bergljot and did not say a word. She turned around and saw the first guard on horseback charging down the narrow path. He was followed by another and another and another, each more fearsome than the last. The road shook violently under their horses' hooves.

As soon as the first was within earshot, Hege heard what she feared she would hear.

"Let us stop here," said the first guard. "The tracks end here."

It was then Hege's brow began to drip with sweat. How could she be so stupid she thought—it did not matter if they erased their tracks to escape into the woods, the path they had been walking for hours was covered in them.

Hege continued to watch the guards pour into the area and fill the space she and the others had occupied only moments ago. She looked around and did not see any of them which she hoped meant they had decent hiding spots, but there were so many guards that she knew deep down it was only a matter of time until they were discovered.

"Dismount," said the lead guard. "I want you to fan out into the trees and find them. They could not have gotten far."

Hege heard this and knew it was now or never. She wiped the sweat beads from her forehead and was about to stand up when she felt the tug on her pelt.

"Don't," said Bergljot.

"I must."

Hege grabbed Bergljot's hand and moved it away.

"It'll be ok," she whispered.

Hege maneuvered away from Bergljot and stood up.

"You found me," she shouted.

Hege stepped onto the path in front of the dismounted guards. They looked at her and she at them. There was an eerie stillness in the air.

"Where are the others?"

"It's just me who remains. The others are gone."

"Your friend did quite a bit of damage for being alone, but he only managed to slow us down."

"Is he dead?" Hege asked.

The guard held up the head of Carr and tossed at Hege's feet. She jumped back as it rolled to a stop, eyes looking up at her.

"It is days to Fensalir even on horseback. You didn't think you would make it there, did you?"

"I thought *I* would try," Hege said.

"We know there are more. The narrow path to Fensalir might mask your numbers but we know it was not just one set of footprints that led to here. Tell them to show themselves and spare my guards more exhaustion. Maybe we'll let some of you off with a warning if you give up now."

"I swear it is only I. The few who fled with me abandoned me. One was actually taken by a remaining Vargr from the Ironwood"

"The Vargr are all gone."

"The Witch breathed new life into their kind."

"Enough tricks," said the guard. "There is no Witch, and there are no more Vargr. But there are workers whose punishments grow more and more severe as you stall."

Hege remained stoic and looked deep into the eyes of the guard before her.

"I am alone," she said.

"I commend you for trying. But look at your feet."

Hege looked down at Carr's head.

"If my guards must continue looking for these runaways it is going to be a lot worse for everyone. Do you understand?"

Hege started to shift slightly, fear rising. She glanced around her. There were too many guards to count—more than the number of escapees.

"We are done waiting. Men move into the trees and find them," said the guard.

Hege's heart was racing, and beads of sweat had reformed on her forehead. She was not panicking yet, but she was about to. She did not know if everyone had an opportunity to get far enough away or if they even had gotten away. Some—all may have just hidden not far off the main road. In fact, she was almost sure that was what they did. But she did not immediately hear screaming. Her concerns started to subside.

She glanced from side to side as soon as the guard ahead of her broke eye contact with her. The other guards were slowly making their way into the trees. Maybe they did escape, she thought.

Her hope was premature. Just as she thought it was going to be ok, she heard the first man and woman yelling. A couple that had not moved from their hiding spot when Hege stepped up. She looked their way as four guards wrestled them out of the forest. She recognized them—they had a young girl.

"I thought it was just you out here," said the lead guard to Hege.

Hege watched the four guards drag the couple to the pathway. She hoped to intervene but knew it was a futile effort.

"Let them go please," she said instead. "You have me. I am the instigator."

The guard ignored Hege's plea and said "For everyone who is out there hiding. I want you to see what happens to these two and reconsider whether you want to follow this woman to your doom," said the guard.

"Stop," said Hege. "Do not do this."

"I should be drunk off mead and asleep right now. But I have a duty to perform as a Guard of Lejre, and as a result, I have been putting out fires and trekking through the backwoods of Midgard, even Heimdall dare not observe all so I can find you and these runaways."

Two guards grabbed Hege and pulled her hands behind her back so she could not fight them. She was then forced to face the couple. She did her best to resist, but the strength that remained in her body betrayed her will.

Another set of guards grabbed ropes from sacks on their horses and proceeded to toss them over a large branch of a nearby tree.

"Stop this madness," said Hege, seeing the fear on the faces of the couple. "Your point is made."

"Remember this is your fault," said the guard.

The ends of the ropes were tied into nooses and placed around the necks of the couple. The man and woman were profusely crying and pleading for their lives, but the guards handling them were cold and distant.

"Please don't," said Hege, defiance leaving her.

"Pull," shouted the guard.

The ropes went taut, and the couple was lifted into the air by their necks. Their legs flailed as they fought for air and freedom. A guard laughed.

Hege lunged forward to intervene but was met with the tip of a blade to her abdomen.

"I wouldn't," said the guard. "You can only observe."

The couple struggling began to slow as life left their bodies, each jerk hastening their demise.

"Enough. Let them go," pleaded Hege. "Can't you see? Everyone else has fled clearly. They would have said something by . . ."

"Mother! Father!" shouted a small child from the forest.

"You were saying?" The guard said.

Hege looked the way of the child as she came running from the forest. Her face was red and covered in tears.

"Mother," she shouted again. "Father!"

Bergljot jumped and grabbed the girl, but in doing so revealed her location to the guards. Knowing they were caught, others started revealing themselves as well. Hege assumed it was that they wished for mercy, but she knew mercy would not be granted and because of that, her heart sank deeper than she thought possible.

"You have been led astray by this woman," said the guard. "Step onto the path. We are going to escort you back to your camps. If you comply peacefully, you will all be spared."

"Why are you lying to them? You're going to kill them," said Hege.

The guard glanced at her and winked.

"They're going to kill you. Don't listen to him," shouted Hege. "Run as fast as you can. Try to escape."

The next thing Hege saw was the hilt of a sword coming straight for her face. When she awoke, she was surrounded by darkness. She reached out ahead of her and was met with a wooden barrier. She pushed against the barrier, but it did not budge, and she soon realized how stale the air was. She took a few deep breaths and there was a strange taste to the air. It was then she knew where she was.

TWELVE

REUNION

Hovard made his way to the pier where he was to meet Hrothgar's mystery man. He took a seat at the end of the dock and looked out at the bay. The sun was set, and the full moon that replaced it reflected in the water.

A boat docked at the pier and a few men jumped off to secure the longship. Hovard watched them work and reflected on his own crew. He remembered being at sea with Skadi when she was a child and their adventures on land by horseback. He remembered his own son and the joy those early years brought him.

Hovard heard one of the crewmen mention getting mead from the hall near the pier. He turned his gaze towards the hall and decided that's what he would do to pass the time. The self-loathing on the pier was not like him. Self-loathing with alcohol was more appropriate.

The mead hall was bustling. Men and women of all ages were serving and drinking mead. Hovard took a seat in the quietest section he could to avoid the stares of the townsfolk he may or may not have terrorized while looking for Skadi.

A barmaid approached him. Hovard put up a single finger indicating he wanted a drink for one. The barmaid nodded and scurried off to collect his mead.

"Hovard Hervor," said an unfamiliar voice. "I thought that was you who entered."

He turned around and standing over him was a skinny, elderly man with a scar across his reddened face. The man was swaying ever so slightly, giving away his drunken state.

"Speak your name," Hovard said. "I do not know you."

"Is your memory so short? I know we have not seen one another in some time, but I thought you would remember the man who made you who you are today."

The barmaid delivered Hovard's mead.

"Do you need anything . . ."

Hovard waved off the barmaid before he could complete his sentence. As the barmaid left, the old man with the scar took a seat next to Hovard.

"Leave me be," Hovard said. "I do not have the patience for anyone's games right now."

He proceeded to lift the mead to his lips.

"The strong do what they will and the weak suffer what they must. Who taught you that lesson?"

Hovard put the mead down and turned to face the man.

"It can't be. I thought you were dead. Is that really you, Fell?"

"How is the old berserker?" Fell asked.

Hovard struggled for a moment to find the right words to answer. He landed on, "I am . . . fine."

"Who is it you seek to convince—yourself or me?" Fell muttered. "You don't look fine. That is all. One might say you look terrible."

Hovard half-smiled and laughed just a tiny bit.

"That's a bold claim coming from you," Hovard said.

"It is true. I have aged."

"It does not appear the years have been kind to you," said Hovard.

"It's only the gods and elves who do not feel the impact of time. We mortals do not last forever."

Hovard nodded and took a swig of his mead.

"What happened to you?" Hovard asked. "I thought you were going to die by the sword—a good warrior's death as I remember you saying."

"If only . . ."

Hovard observed the frail spirit next to him—a shell of what he once was.

"After you and Skadi left, I found a new clan. And honestly even though part of me missed you as a right hand, it was refreshing not having to hear your insincere moral superiority all the time," said Fell.

"I wanted us to be better."

"Is that so?" Judgment spread across Fell's face clear as day.

"Wanted," said Hovard. "I didn't say we were."

There was a moment of silence between the two men. The only sound was the fervor of the hall.

"I heard what you did to those workers and the people on Market Street," Fell said.

"Word travels fast around this town."

"It does when the people of Market Street are harmed. If you think I was bad, just consider the guards these people empower," Fell said.

"What happened on Market Street and with the laborers by the wall was . . ."

"It was not an accident. You are like me—more so than you want to admit. Power over others is intoxicating."

Hovard did not answer.

"After you two left, those of us who remained in the clan heard about the treasure to be had by slaying the monster here. They said it was unstoppable, but whoever slayed it would be wealthy beyond their wildest dreams," said Fell.

"That treasure and that monster ended the Vikings."

Fell laughed.

"I wondered if the Age was over."

"Why did you stay here?" asked Hovard.

"See this scar. Remember the innkeeper? She did this after my men were killed by the monster. I didn't know she had it in her, but I guess she still had the fight in her that I lost."

"I'm surprised she did not kill you."

"You see it is a scar across my face, correct? She tried but in the struggle that ensued, she ran."

"And you let her go?"

Fell pulled back his pelt revealing his mangled right leg. "The monster broke it in two, and it healed poorly."

"Looks like it hurt."

Fell took a swig of his mead.

"It did. And the cold still makes it throb."

"It's always cold here," whispered Hovard.

"Terrible situation I have found myself in then, haven't I?"

Hovard took a huge swig of his mead and looked Fell in the eyes.

"I will never apologize for taking Skadi away from you. Her parents entrusted her to me, and she had to be protected."

"I know. I used to say all the time that the strong do what they will and the weak suffer what they must. The only thing I never considered was that one day I would be the weak," Fell said.

Fell finished his mead.

"I should go," said Fell. "I have been here all day, and you don't want to hear an old man drone on about how things are now."

"Do you regret how you lived your life?" Hovard asked as Fell stood up. "Would you have made different decisions if you knew this is where you would be?"

Fell took a moment to respond.

Then he said, "I could do a thousand good deeds a day for the rest of my life, and it wouldn't make up for all the pain I caused. I see every single person I hurt or killed when I close my eyes. My life was not just a waste; it was worse than that."

"When I was younger, I hated you."

"I know you did."

"I thought I would do things differently one day. But in time I fear I became just like you. My son grew up to be a bastard. This I know to be true but because Skadi killed him, now I want nothing more than her head. And I know I should move on, but I can't."

Fell placed a hand on Hovard's shoulder and said, "I never had a drive as motivating as revenge. I enjoyed the thrill of the hunt. But forgiveness is strength. I've tried to forgive myself, but every time I try, I just end up here drunk and alone. You don't want to end up like this. Live or die for something important."

With those final words, Fell left Hovard. Hovard sat at the table with his mead and watched the old man hobble out of the hall. And as if the hustle and bustle of the hall had stopped for his conversation with Fell, he became aware of the sound of others again once the old man was gone.

He looked around the room at the people of Lejre. Many of them appeared happy, but Hovard could sense beneath the exterior something toxic that pervaded them—an angst that he could not quite put a finger on. He downed his mead and raised his hand for another.

Hours went by and finally Hovard decided to head back to the end of the pier to wait for Hrothgar's warrior. The sun was just starting to rise, and the light glimmered on the Midgardian Sea. But Hovard's attention was drawn to the small mass of people gathered at the end of the pier. He made his way over and moved two of the folks near the rear of the gathering.

"What is going on?" he said.

The group parted.

"We pulled him from the water moments ago," said a man. "It would seem he drowned himself."

Lying dead at the end of the pier soaked from head to toe was Fell. His face was blue, and feet were bound in chains.

"I saw him just beneath the surface. It took two of us to pull him up," said the man.

Hovard looked down at Fell, who once struck fear in his heart and made him so angry all he could see was red, but now, strangely, to his surprise, he pitied him. Or was it fear that he would suffer the same fate? He could not tell.

Skadi moved through the tunnels with even greater caution, having encountered some of Hrothgar's guards only moments ago. She passed by doors with thoughtfulness and intersections with mild trepidation, but in time, she made her way to the base of the incline which she knew would take her to Heorot Hall. She put her ear to the door and did not hear anyone on the other side, so she opened it.

The torches, though sparing throughout the rest of the tunnel were nonexistent beyond the door. The only light was that from the torch she carried with her.

She stepped on something that snapped under her foot. She turned the torch so she could see what it was, and her eyes widened.

She picked it up and said, "Pieces of a Bifrost key."

She looked around the space she was in. In the corner, just before the incline began was a rusted hammer and a few other pieces that also appeared to be part of a Bifrost key.

Skadi placed the pieces of the key within her pelt and started the climb towards Heorot Hall. And as she did, she could hear the voice of another guard.

"You see that light? Someone is there."

"Damn," whispered Skadi before extinguishing the flame.

"In there, by Eitri's workshop."

"Eitri?" whispered Skadi. "The dwarf?"

Skadi turned and started running up the incline to put as much distance between her and the approaching guards. She stopped running only when she felt she put sufficient space between her and them. Looking down from up high, she could see two small lights flickering—the guards who were inspecting what they thought they saw. She watched the lights move about the space for a bit and eventually leave, choosing not to follow the incline she was on. Skadi let out a small sigh of relief and then continued in the darkness.

Not before long she reached another door. Again, she listened for voices on the other side or any sights of life and having heard nothing, entered. But unlike before, this room was well-lit. There were burning torches throughout and two doors—one to her left and one to her right.

She heard footsteps approaching from the right door, so she quickly scurried to the left. Skadi scanned the room—no one was there so she put her ear to the door.

"What about Hovard?"

Skadi recognized the voice as belonging to Solveig.

"I sent him to wait at the pier for his arrival. I can't have him running through my town burning up my citizens on his crusade."

She recognized the other voice as belonging to Hrothgar.

"Has the bond worked?" Solveig said.

Skadi felt the room she was in shake when Hrothgar stomped his foot.

"It has," said Hrothgar.

"With the road near completion. We can start the next steps soon. I am going to finish clearing out Eitri's old forge, then make sure he is ready with the first armor, sword, and shield."

Skadi heard the door to the tunnel she had arrived through open and close.

So Eitri is here? Skadi wondered, what are the next steps if Hrothgar already has the power of the World Tree?

She listened intently and sensed no one was on the other side of the door.

On the other side of Midgard, Hege was starting to panic. Her palms were clammy, and her entire body was drenched in sweat. Her breathing increased and her hands shook.

"Help," she shouted. "Somebody help me."

When she quickly realized her pleas were going unheard, she stopped yelling.

"Calm down, Hege," she whispered. "Calm. Down."

She slowed her breathing to measured, deliberate breaths, and reached out to touch the top of her encasement. It was made of wood. She pushed against it, but nothing happened.

She took another slow, deliberate breath and removed her pelt as best she could while confined to the tight space. She placed some of the clothing over her face and wrapped another piece of it around her right fist.

With as much might as she could muster, she punched the ceiling of her confinement. It did not budge. She punched it again and again nothing happened.

"What am I doing?" she shouted.

Hege made a fist again and hit the roof of her prison. Though she had wrapped her pelt around her hand for protection, her knuckles started bleeding.

"There is only one way out of here," she whispered and hit the ceiling again.

Finally, a crack formed where she had repeatedly made an impact. Hege kept on punching and the crack grew. Dirt eventually fell through, which Hege made sure to push to either side of her within her prison.

Finally, so much of the wooden encasement was broken that Hege was able to start digging her way out. She made sure to keep her face protected so she did not suffocate from the falling dirt. Inch by inch, she exited the encasement and pulled herself through the soil to freedom. When the weight of the dirt lessened, she knew she was almost free.

The light of the full moon shone down on Hege as she emerged from her would-be grave. With her body half underground and half above, she removed the pelt from her face and took the deepest breath she had ever taken in her entire life. The night air never tasted sweeter. She pulled herself up and out of the soil and collapsed on the ground, continuing to take deep breaths.

Hege looked at the hole she emerged from then up at the full moon. She was atop a hill, surrounded by trees. Just beyond the trees was a cottage with smoke rising from it. Hege willed herself to her feet and moved towards the cottage, being careful to keep to whatever shadows she could find.

She peered through the window of the cottage and saw a man asleep. A fire was dwindling in the corner. She recognized him as the guard who ordered the hanging of the couple and the recapture of her people. She also laid eyes on a dirty shovel in the corner.

Hege crept around to the entrance of the cottage and slowly pushed the door open. The sleeping guard did not budge. She moved towards the shovel. The man moved and Hege stopped. She waited, frozen, hoping he would not wake. When she was confident, he was still asleep, she continued.

She took the shovel into her hand and stood over the guard. As if aware of her presence, his eyes started to open. The look on his face went from surprise to shock as Hege brought the shovel down on his abdomen, piercing flesh. She repeated to strike him until she was sure he was dead, and then she threw the shovel to the side.

Hege was breathing deeply and gave herself a moment to calm herself before moving on. She grabbed the guard's sword and exited the cottage.

Further beyond the tree line was a cliff. She stopped at the ledge and saw the sun peaking over the horizon. The light illuminated the clearing below and, in the center, Hege saw her people digging a massive hole.

As the sun crested over the horizon, Hovard looked beyond Fell, whose corpse laid on the ground, and saw the silhouette of a menacing drakkar longship approaching the pier.

Hovard stepped beyond Fell and said, "He is here."

THIRTEEN

HOVARD'S BARGAIN

"Wake up," said Mimir. "Can you hear me? Wake up."

Egil did not respond to the calls from the cell adjacent to his. He stirred a little, but nothing indicated that he heard Mimir's pleads.

"Hello," shouted Mimir. "Wake. Up."

Mimir saw the young man start to move more and more.

"Are you ok? You look badly hurt."

"Where . . . am I?"

"They brought you in hours ago. You were moaning and groaning, but completely unconscious."

"Everything hurts," Egil responded.

"I would imagine it does. Your back is . . . well rather raw."

"My father did this to me."

Mimir said nothing as Egil sat up.

"Your father is the Earl?"

"I am Egil Hrothgarson."

"I am Mimir."

"I know who you are."

"Am I so popular?"

"A talking head. I can't imagine there are too many of you around Midgard."

"I grew so accustomed to being alone atop that mountain, that I sometimes forget being amongst the people, I must be quite the sight."

"And you travel with the Jötunn-Breaker."

"Where is Skadi?"

Egil did not respond.

"Is she alive?"

"If Hovard was successful then no."

"Hovard is here?"

"You know him?"

"What is his involvement in all of this?"

"Aren't you supposed to be the wisest man alive?"

"Wise does not mean all-knowing."

"Why bother locking you up? What could a head do?"

"Isolation is punishment with or without limbs, my friend."

"I didn't mean for it to come out that way."

"Tell me what Hovard is doing here."

Egil sat up despite the pain and looked directly at Mimir.

"Not long ago, Hovard showed up in Lejre seeking an audience with my father . . ."

A Few Months Ago

"Earl, a man at the gate with one hand is demanding an audience with you," said a guard. "He has some sort of mastery of fire, but he cannot get beyond our walls. What should we do?"

Egil watched his father shift his attention from the scroll he was reading to the guard before him.

"Mastery over fire?"

"He can project fire from his body, sir. It is unlike anything I have ever seen before."

"Where did he come from?"

"He claims to be a Viking sir, but he is alone."

Egil saw his father glance his way briefly before turning his attention back to the guard.

"What would like you me to do, sir?"

"He wants an audience with me?"

"Yes."

"Vikings are long gone, but I am still not fond of their ilk. Give him a test and if he proves useful, he can meet with me."

"What sort of test, sir?"

Egil watched his father consider the dilemma before him, wondering what he would say.

"My friends on Market Street tell me some of their workers who live along the edge of the wall have been especially rebellious as of late. See if this *Viking* can whip them into shape. If he can do that then I will grant him an audience with me."

"Father," said Egil, standing up in protest.

"See that it is done quickly."

"Father," shouted Egil.

Egil watched Hrothgar wave off the guard then ran over to his father's desk.

"What, son?" Hrothgar said.

"You don't know who this man is, and you are just going to unleash him on our people?"

"I am growing tired of your cowardice, boy. If you are to be the Earl, one day you will need to grow a backbone."

"Your road is nearly completed. Why are you still working our people so hard?"

"Everyone has a role to play. Including yourself. But you seem less inclined to want to do what you need to which worries me. Go with the guard. See what this man can do and report back."

"But Father . . ."

"Go."

"Yes sir."

Egil exited Heorot Hall and ran after the guard, who had not made it very far. The two walked in silence towards the gate of Lejre.

Just as was stated, the man with one hand was waiting at the gate.

"What is your name?" Egil said.

"Where is the Earl?"

Egil paused for a moment before repeating himself.

"What is your name?" Egil said.

The man looked at him with a coldness Egil had never seen. It was as if there was nothing behind the man's eyes but blackness.

Egil hesitated but started to ask a third time.

But the man said, "Hovard."

"Hovard, what is the reason for the audience you seek with my father?"

"Begrudgingly I must admit he has resources that can aid me."

"Aid you with what?"

"I seek justice."

"You may be seeking an audience with the wrong man if justice is what you seek."

"Is this not Lejre, the largest and most powerful town in all of Midgard?"

"It is."

"And is Hrothgar not the Earl?"

"He is."

"Then he can aid me with my quest," said Hovard.

"Hovard, my father is not one to do anything for free."

"I would not expect the would-be king of Midgard to do anything if there was nothing he could personally gain. I have something to offer him in exchange for those resources."

"What might that be?" asked Egil.

"I would rather speak with him."

It was then the guard stepped in and said, "The Earl has stated he would entertain you if you did something for him."

Egil stared at the guard.

"What does he want?" Hovard asked.

"He wants you to quell a rebellious group who refuse to work."

Egil looked at Hovard, then at the guard, and then back at Hovard.

"You do not have to do this," said Egil. "Find another way to seek your justice."

To Egil, it seemed as though the one-handed man contemplated this proposal. But this was only for a moment.

"Show me where they are," said Hovard plainly.

"No," said Egil. "You don't have to do this."

"You would defy your father?" the guard said.

Egil hesitated.

"Either I can be granted an audience with the Earl or not, but what I will not do is spend any more time speaking with either of you."

"We are going," the guard said.

Egil said nothing as the guard turned to Hovard.

The guard turned to Egil. "You may come with us if you like," he said.

Egil looked at the guard then at Hovard. Knowing he would not sway the guard to disobey the Earl, Egil opted to follow the two men as they walked from the gate. The group stopped at a hill that overlooked a small encampment of people along the wall that surrounded Lejre.

"The fine people on Market Street supply the Guards of Lejre, like me, with the supplies we need to survive and do our jobs. But they can only do that if their workers work. The Earl wants you to remind the workers that they have a responsibility to Lejre just like the rest of us. You do that and the Earl will meet with you," said the guard.

"No," said Egil unsheathing his sword and maneuvering between Hovard and the people below. "This is too extreme. What is it you wish to tell the Earl? Tell me instead and I will convey it to him."

Hovard looked to the guard as if he was considering Egil's proposal or making sure it was ok with the guard—Egil could not tell either way. But then Hovard raised his hand and in his palm, fire started to form.

"Move or be moved."

"Don't," said Egil. "Those people are innocent."

"No one is innocent," said Hovard.

"Get out of his way," said the guard. "Getting yourself killed won't change anything."

"I would die for my people."

"Then you should live for them," said Hovard.

The guard positioned himself next to Egil and placed a hand on his shoulder.

"There is nothing you can do."

Egil looked at the guard then down at the people below.

"Prove it. Kill me."

The guard quickly looked from him to Hovard. Egil stood his ground with his sword stretched out ahead of him. Hovard reached out and touched the tip of the sword. His hand glowed and shortly after so did the sword. Egil felt the heat making its way up the blade and into his hand. The blade turned shades of yellow and orange. The hilt was becoming unbearable in Egil's hands, but he would not break his grip. Even though his will persisted, the blade did not, and the tip started to melt.

"Damn it," shouted Egil as the sword flashed into flames, and he was forced to abandon it.

"Step aside, boy," Hovard said. "I would rather not kill the son of the man I am trying to meet."

"You're going to kill those people," Egil said.

"I will try not to."

Egil gave Hovard and the guard one final look before hanging his head in defeat and stepping aside.

"This is a test," said the guard to Hovard. "Succeed, and the Earl will see you."

Egil watched in quiet horror as Hovard strode down to the unsuspecting people below. He hoped for the best—that the people would comply, but his fears were quickly realized when the flames erupted, and the screams carried through the air.

It was not long until Hovard returned.

"The Earl will see you," said the guard.

Egil kept to the rear as he, Hovard, and the guard returned to Heorot Hall. The entire journey back, his mind raced with the images of those who were burned by Hovard's fire. It wasn't until they reached the hall that his attention shifted to the present.

"This is where I leave you," said the guard before departing.

The doors opened and Egil entered first.

"Your being here means you must have proven your worth," said Hrothgar.

Egil gestured for Hovard to approach his father.

"The people along the wall fought bravely for their freedom, but those who remain able-bodied will return to work," said Hovard.

"I take no pleasure in seeing others suffer, but it is a necessary evil," said Hrothgar

"That is a lie," Egil whispered.

"What say you, son?" Hrothgar said.

"I said that is a lie," Egil responded.

"Anymore defiance from you, child, and you will sorely regret it," said Hrothgar, before turning to Hovard. "Now speak, Viking. Why are you here?"

"There is a woman named Skadi who has ingested the roots of Ygg-drasil and absorbed its power. She killed the jötunn of Fensalir and now travels with Mimir, the bodiless man who once advised Odin. It is known you have a skilled alchemist in your service."

"I do," Hrothgar said.

"If she could steal Skadi's power from her, would that not be of inter-est to you?"

"What is in it for me if my alchemist can do this?" Hrothgar asked.

"You can take Skadi's power for yourself. All I ask is that you let me kill her."

Present

"Solveig crafted a means for stealing Skadi's power using gems within Bifrost keys."

"Your father has access to Bifrost keys—plural?"

"My father is one of the wealthiest men in the realm."

"I have never heard of a single human acquiring such resources and power," Mimir said.

"My grandfather and grandmother owned a gold mine off the main-land. When they passed, their wealth went to my father, and it has only grown since. In a realm where so many are poor, someone like my father can seem like a god."

"But he isn't one."

"If Hovard was successful, then he has killed Skadi, and my father has her power."

"Having seen Skadi in action, I would not count her out just yet. That woman is resilient."

"I hope you are right, because my father's ambitions do not stop with him acquiring her strength."

Skadi pried open the door to the room where she heard Hrothgar and Solveig speak. The two were gone, but a crack in the ground showed where Hrothgar slammed his foot.

To Skadi's right was the entrance to the tunnel from which she had emerged and, directly across from her was a door to which she assumed led aboveground.

She walked across the room to the opposite door and pressed her ear against it. Nothing. Skadi opened it and felt the cool breeze of winter air brush against her skin. She poked her head through the doorway and saw stairs and did not sense a presence at the top of them.

Skadi emerged from the staircase into the room she was first taken captive in. It was empty. Early morning light shined through the windows along the wall to her right. She walked over to the desk where Hrothgar was sitting earlier but did not find anything placed upon it that would give her a hint to Mimir's whereabouts. She did, however, find a scroll that had two words written on it, "Remember Nyköping."

She continued to inspect the desk and the area around it. While nothing more seemed to provide clues to Mimir's location, she started to find signs of the great struggle that once occurred in the hall—deep scratches in the walls and splintered wood that had been poorly repaired.

"What are you doing?"

Skadi looked up and saw three guards standing just below her in the middle of the hall.

"Go inform the Earl," said the guard out front.

Another started to head for the door, but before he could exit, Skadi hurled her sword, Ridill, across the room and forced the door shut, wedging it place.

"Now you are without a weapon," said the head guard.

Skadi leapt over the desk and brought her right elbow down on the head of the guard who spoke. He immediately lost his composure and hit the ground with a thud. The remaining two drew their swords and attacked as a pair. But Skadi dodged when necessary and countered whenever she could and even managed to strip one guard of his sword, which turned the fight in her favor rather quickly.

But she was attempting to spare the lives of these guards. So, the fight dragged. The guard without a sword broke off from the altercation to try pulling Ridill from the door. That was a mistake on his part. Skadi made him a priority and broke away as well. She slammed into his back, knocking him unconscious against the large wooden door. He fell to the ground in a slump, and Skadi quickly turned her attention to the one guard remaining.

116

He looked at her with fear in his eyes. He dropped his sword and raised his hands.

"I give up."

"Where is Mimir?"

"Who?"

"The bodiless man I arrived here with."

"I don't know. Please, I don't want any trouble."

"It is too late for that. Where is Mimir?"

"I cannot say," said the man, panic creeping into his voice.

"I am trying not to kill, but you are between me and my friend."

The guard hesitated.

"Do you wish to die for someone who would not do the same for you?"

He hesitated a moment longer then gestured over his shoulder at the desk.

"Under the desk is a hatch. It is the only door that is strictly off limits."

Skadi moved past the guard towards the desk. When she hit the ledge, she glanced back at the floor beneath the desk.

"There is nothing," she said.

"I promise I have seen the hatch open before."

Skadi inspected the floor more closely and saw where the edges of a hatch had moved but did not see a handle.

"Runic magic perhaps," said the guard.

Remembering the runic symbol to open the tomb in Nidavellir, Skadi traced two parallel lines in the middle of the hatch. Then from the top of those two lines, she traced a V, then an inverted V. She finished by tracing an X through the left line and the right line. As soon as she completed the runic outline, the desk shifted to the side as if pushed by an invisible force, and the hatch opened.

Skadi looked back at the remaining guard and said, "You're coming with me. I want to learn as much about this place as possible."

Moments later, Skadi and the guard, having finished hiding the other two guards in a storage room, made for the open hatch.

"Have you ever been through this way," asked Skadi as she gestured for the guard to go ahead of her.

"I have not. This passage is for only the Earl and some guards he seems to trust a bit more than others."

"Tell me about this place," said Skadi as she grabbed the top rung of the ladder leading underground.

"What do you want to know?"

"Tell me about the guards. I have never seen this sort of organization anywhere in mainland Midgard."

"It is something new that the Earl created. He wanted to emulate the armies of Asgard and Vanaheim here on Midgard. We learned all about his grand design while training."

"You are trained?"

"At first, we are sent to the Geatland and then we are required to maintain a certain level of skill here in Lejre. It would seem, based on how you made such quick work of the others, that we do not train hard enough, but for most we are competent."

"How loyal are the guards to the Earl?"

"Some are more loyal to the seat than to him, but we all recognize what this man is doing. The Earl is doing more for Midgard than any other human has ever done before. Trolls took my parents. The Earl had the wall constructed that surrounds Lejre, and now most children do not even know what a troll is."

"I see."

"Life has improved under his reign. That I can assure you of."

"I saw two children murdered on my way to this town."

The guard stepped off the ladder, having reached the ground floor. He took a step back as Skadi moved off the ladder as well.

"The guards working on the road have a tough job. Sometimes the workers like to rebel and making sure they do not requires punishment."

"And that is punishment?" Skadi asked.

The guard did not say anything; he just looked away from Skadi at a torch flickering in the distance.

"You've heard of the Nyköping massacre have you not?"

"Everyone has heard the story of the human settlement lost during the Great War," answered the guard.

"Roaming Aesir gods tortured and killed for sport. No man, woman, or child was spared. You guards are like those Aesir."

"Before you go passing judgement, Jötunn-Breaker, know that your reputation is known, not simply your recent heroics. You think slaying one monster is enough to absolve you of your misdeeds?"

Skadi gripped the hilt of her sword tightly, but an image of Bjorn popped into her head, and she let it go.

"Keep walking," said Skadi. "We have plenty of ground to cover."

FOURTEEN

DO NOT BURN PINE SO DEEP IN MIDGARD

Hege's hands were raw, having saved herself from being buried alive, and her body ached all over. But despite every ounce of her body telling her to rest, she proceeded to climb over the ledge leading down to the people she was attempting to guide to freedom.

The guards had them surrounded and were forcing the more able-bodied to dig a massive hole. Hege knew exactly what they were digging—a grave. Surely, they knew too.

She found her footing while holding onto a root and dropped a few feet onto a clear path. She ducked behind a brush to keep from being spotted, before poking her head up briefly to see the people below. No one was looking her way, and the grave was getting bigger.

What can I do? she thought.

Hege looked left and did not see anything that caught her eye, other than the ravens used to communicate with Lejre and the other campsites. The birds were relatively still despite all that was happening around them. Hege looked right where she saw barrels of oil used to light torches. Beyond that she observed the tree line.

Hege moved cautiously but quickly down the path towards the base of the hill. She was well-covered by the brush along the side, and she could hear the conversations between the guards and the folks digging.

"Keep going," one guard said.

"You brought this upon yourself," said another.

Hege pulled the brush apart that hid her so she could get a closer look at what was happening. The people she had been guiding were busy digging. They all looked broken and defeated.

"Will that be enough?" said a guard.

"I think we are deep enough," said another.

This made Hege perk up. Was she out of time?

"Just a little deeper," said a third guard. "There are a lot of them."

"It would be a shame if they came back as draugr."

A collective laugh broke out amongst the guards.

Hege watched until the guards nearest her all faced away from her, then she moved from her hiding place. As fast as she could she moved to the cottage between the guards forcing those to dig and the barrels of oil she spied from her perch on the path. When her back was to the cottage, she heard whimpering on the other side. Hege turned around and stood on the tip of her toes to peer through the window. She saw the children of those digging.

She tapped on the window gently.

"It's going to be ok," she whispered.

Some of the children looked her way and wiped their tears.

"Hang on just a bit longer."

Hege moved to the edge of the cottage and peeked around the corner. There was no one between her and the containers of oil. She looked around one last time and then ran to the barrels. Hege knocked one on its side, uncorked it, and pushed the barrel so it rolled away from the others into the tree line that surrounded the encampment. She ran after it as the oil started to pool at the base of a pine tree and proceeded to dip some branches in the oil and toss them about. After she felt she had sufficiently covered the surrounding area with oil-soaked branches, she moved on and let the remainder of the oil spill out of the barrel.

Hege ran back to the cottage where she found the children held captive. She got up on the tip of her toes again and looked through the window.

"Pssshhh," she whispered.

One of the children looked her way.

"Come here."

The child got to her feet and walked over to the window.

"See the torch on the wall?"

The child nodded.

"Will you hand it to me?"

"It's too high," said the child.

Hege considered trying to enter through the front of the cottage but knew she would be caught.

"You'll have to work together. It'll be ok. Can the child next to you lift you up?"

The girl nudged the boy to her left.

"Can you lift her?" whispered Hege.

Hege heard footsteps approaching.

"I must drain the sea snake. Give me a moment," shouted the approaching guard.

"Please hurry," Hege said to the child.

The boy got to his feet and grabbed hold of the girl.

"Quickly now," said Hege.

The young boy lifted with all his might to get the girl off the ground. The girl extended her hand towards the torch, but it was still just out of reach.

"When I finish, it's time," said the approaching guard.

"Come on just a little bit more," said Hege.

The boy lifted, the girl reached out, Hege listened intently for the guard getting closer.

"You're almost there," said Hege.

The girl's hand was just about to grasp the torch. The anticipation was palpable. She was so close now.

"What are you doing?" shouted the guard.

Hege dropped from the tip of her toes and unsheathed her sword immediately.

"Guards, she escaped somehow."

As soon as he shouted, ten more guards showed up alongside him. Hege scanned all of them. She knew how to fight, but this was not winnable.

"Burying you alive was a stupid idea anyway." said one of the guards. "Bodies are best put in the ground already dead."

At that moment, all the guards present started to charge Hege. She readied herself for the end but then the torch she was trying to get from the two children dropped in front of her.

"Good luck," the little girl said.

Hege quickly picked it up.

"What are you going to do with that?" one of the guards said.

Without answering, Hege pivoted and started running towards the oil barrels. But as she neared an arrow caught her in the shoulder causing her to drop the torch and fall to the ground herself. She continued to crawl towards the torch and the oil barrels but as she did so, the guards caught up to her.

"Your foolish escapade has caused us way too much headache," said one guard as he kicked her in the abdomen. "For all you have put us through tonight, we are going to do the children first."

Hege heard the guard's words and found the strength in herself to propel her failing body to the torch, which she then tossed to the barrels of oil. The flames caught immediately and traced along the path created by the uncorked barrel that was pushed into the tree line.

"Your friend already tried this and if I'm being truthful, more effectively. The goal is to burn the cottages, not the trees," said one of the guards.

Hege turned over on her back, looking up at the guards.

"These trees are pine," she said.

"This we all know."

At that very moment, a powerful roar cried out from just beyond the tree line.

"We are where trolls still roam. Burning pine drives them mad."

From the tree line emerged four massive creatures. Hege scrambled to her feet as the guards were dumbstruck by the powerful beasts. Quickly she ran away from them to the other side of the cottage.

"Trolls," she shouted.

The guards who were still overseeing the people digging turned their attention to Hege. The people digging also stopped and looked her way.

"Everyone run," she shouted before ripping open the cottage door where the children were being held captive. "Come on, let's go."

The young people flowed out of the cottage and kept close to Hege as she did her best to direct her people away from the encampment. The trolls meanwhile were slaughtering the guards who had cornered Hege. The whole scene was chaos and, in that chaos, Hege made her escape with her people, while the guards mostly met their doom at the hands of the wild beasts of Midgard.

When she felt there was sufficient distance between them and the battle between the guards and the trolls, she stopped and took stock of who made it. Surprisingly all the original group was with her.

"Is everyone ok?" she said.

Most did not answer, they simply grumbled.

One person asked, "What happened?"

"The trolls should be enough to preoccupy Hrothgar's men, but we need to make it to Fensalir. Can everyone walk?"

"I think we are ok," said another.

"Keep an eye on each other and if anyone starts to struggle, carry them. It's a long way to Fensalir and we must go now."

The young girl who provided Hege the torch tugged on Hege's pelt.

She looked down at her and said, "What is it?"

"My mother and father were . . ."

Hege remembered the couple who was killed.

Hege wanted to pick the girl up but winced at the pain in her shoulder from the arrow. Instead, she reached out and took the girl's hand.

"You're going to be ok, little one."

Bergljot appeared next to Hege. "I thought you . . . we were all dead."

"They should have buried me deeper."

"You're a brave woman."

"If word of what just happened makes it back to Hrothgar, it may get a lot worse."

"It surely will."

"We'll have to be ready."

As the trolls barreled through guard after guard, tearing limbs from bodies and crushing skulls under feet, one guard ran to the cage where the ravens were kept for sending messages. He scribbled out a quick message, attached it to the raven, and let it fly. The bird left his hand just as a troll crushed him.

FIFTEEN

IMPRISONED SON

Skadi and the guard, who she had forced to answer questions about Lejre, traversed the dimly lit paths underneath Heorot Hall in silence. Skadi hung back behind the guard but kept a small gap she could close, if necessary, in a moment's notice. The two moved from room to room looking for Mimir.

"Where is he?" whispered Skadi in frustration.

"This is a fool's errand," said the guard. "Even if you do find him, what then?"

Skadi ignored the question.

"The Earl is trying to make a better Midgard for all of us. Why do you want to get in the way of that?"

"Hello," shouted an unknown voice.

Skadi shifted her attention away from the guard and towards the voice. The voice was coming from the door on the right at the end of the hall. The guard with Skadi turned around.

"You have to stop," he said.

"Move."

"You would undo all we have worked for here."

"You saw what I did to your fellow guards."

"I responded with cowardice, but this has gone on too long," the guard said.

The guard lunged for Skadi. She sidestepped and guided the momentum of the man to the ground. He tumbled but caught his footing and pulled a knife from his boot. Skadi responded by unsheathing Ridill.

"Don't throw your life away."

"I throw away nothing. If this is how I die, then I die with honor."

The man leapt at Skadi with the knife directed out front. She smacked his hand away with the flat side of her blade.

"Enough," she said. "Have you all lost your wits?"

Skadi tackled the guard to the ground. He struggled under her weight, but his strength was no match for hers.

"You'll die for this," he shouted.

Skadi brought the hilt of Ridill down on his forehead and he was immediately unconscious.

Skadi got to her feet and threw the man over her shoulder before making her way to the door through which she heard the voice.

"What's happening out there?" said the voice.

Skadi opened the door at the end of the hall and found a series of cells, only one of which was occupied.

"Who are you?" Skadi said as she placed the unconscious guard in the adjacent open cell. She closed and locked the cell and then stood in front of the other prisoner.

"My name is Egil," he said.

"Skadi."

"The Jötunn-Breaker."

"You know of me as well?"

"Your story is one of hope for many across Midgard. Please will you help me be free?"

"Why are you imprisoned?"

Egil hesitated.

"If you seek freedom, it would be wise to speak honestly," Skadi said.

"I am the Earl's son. My father and I have been increasingly agreeing less."

"Tell me more."

"I do not like what he has done to our people. The road and the mine have caused too much harm. He disagrees."

"He imprisoned you over a disagreement?"

"I would also wish to see his other plan be halted."

"And that is?"

"The creation of his weapons."

Hrothgar opened his eyes as the morning sunlight washed over him. He sat up in his bed, dropped his feet to the floor, and moved to the window that overlooked all Lejre.

He took in the view of the town common and the people who were moving about the town. He thought back to when he first arrived in Lejre decades ago.

"We have come so far, haven't we?" he whispered.

He looked off beyond the town common at the pier and saw a drakkar longship in the harbor.

The caw of a raven sitting on his window's perch shifted his attention. Tied to the foot of the raven was a small scroll. Hrothgar grabbed the scroll and read it. His face soured as he concluded the note. He moved to the door of his bed chamber.

"Guard. Fetch me Solveig. Now."

The guard ran off. Moments later he returned with Solveig. Hrothgar handed her the scroll.

"Make sense of this," he said.

He watched as Solveig scanned the scroll then hold it to her side.

"Trolls attacked an outpost near Bard Mine?" she said.

"I thought we did something about trolls?"

"We did. Rune writers inscribed runes near choke points and encampments. No trolls should have crossed those barriers . . . unless . . ."

"Unless what?"

"This marking indicates it came from the encampment nearest Bard Mine which is approaching the Ironwood. The trees out there are mostly pine and burning pine drives trolls mad."

"My guards would know better than to burn pine if trolls were looming. Which means they did not do this."

"Who would be foolish enough to attack one of your encampments?" said Solveig.

"We can only keep a tight grip for so long before people start pushing back."

"Let me go," Solveig said.

"No, I am going to handle this myself. Keep an eye on Eitri."

"What about Skadi?"

"An old friend just arrived to assist Hovard with tracking her down. I saw his ship in the harbor. I am going to bring whoever started this act of defiance back to show the people of this town what happens when they turn their back on me."

Solveig nodded and turned to do as she was instructed.

"One more thing that I want you to do while I am away," said Hrothgar.

"Yes?"

"Begin questioning Mimir. He, more than anyone, knows the most about the gods. He served Odin during the Great War."

"It will be done."

Solveig left Hrothgar's chambers.

Hrothgar adorned his pelt, attached his sword to his waist, and made for the front of Heorot Hall.

"Your horse, sir," said a guard bringing forward a powerful steed.

Hrothgar put up a hand and waved the man off. He flexed the muscles in his legs and felt a surge in power throughout his entire body, unlike anything he had ever felt before. The shockwave from Hrothgar's departure caused the horse to rear and kick the guard to the ground.

Skadi looked at Egil curiously.

"The walls contain a tiny portion of the iron ore from Bard Mine," said Egil.

"I would have assumed more."

"The walls are mostly made of wood and mud. They've been enhanced with runes by rune writers, but for the most part, they're simple. Just big."

"Then the ore is being mined for what?"

"I should show you."

"Tell me."

"You're going to want to see what is happening here. I could tell you, but it just won't have the same impact."

"Try."

"I suspect I know where Mimir is—I can take you to him as well."

Skadi did not respond.

"Free me. I am speaking the truth about my father and Mimir's whereabouts."

Skadi again did not reply. But she did walk closer to the cell and look at Egil.

"You were whipped?" she said noticing the blood on the back of his pelt.

"This was my father's doing."

Skadi inspected the hinges of the cell and grabbed two of the bars.

"One of the first things you learn as a Viking is how to escape a cell like this. They're surprisingly ill-constructed. You simply lift and pull," she said.

Egil pulled himself to his feet but stumbled because of the pain.

"Be mindful of your injuries," Skadi said.

Egil grabbed hold of a separate set of bars.

"With all your strength. Lift and pull," said Skadi.

At the same time, the two strained their muscles and lifted the cell door. Egil pulled while Skadi pushed, and the door came free from the hinges. Skadi kept a grasp on it, so it did not fall on Egil, and he quickly repositioned himself out of the way.

"Show me where Mimir is."

Hovard watched in silence as the drakkar longship docked at the pier. The people behind him were busy cleaning up the body of Fell, but he mostly ignored them since the anticipation of this warrior intrigued him.

He stood with his one hand and nub behind his back. A broad-shouldered man with long flowing hair stepped up onto the rail of the longship. He watched the man leap from the rail and land on the pier in front of him.

"I take it you are who Hrothgar sent for?" Hovard said.

"I received his raven at night and boarded a ship immediately. He tells me the Jötunn-Breaker is causing a problem in his town."

"You have heard of her, too?" Hovard said.

"The tale of Skadi the Jötunn-Breaker spread like a plague, my friend. It even reached the Geatland. I'm excited to meet her. It is not a common occurrence that a human kills a jötunn. But first, I do want to pay a visit to my old friend. Take me to Heorot Hall."

"Take you to Heorot Hall? You know the way."

"Are you not here to greet me?"

"I'm here to . . ."

"Hrothgar has a way of commanding even the mighty to follow him," said the mystery man.

"Follow me," Hovard said.

He turned to lead the newcomer to Heorot Hall and just as he did a loud boom emanated from the direction of the hall.

"What was that?" said this mystery man.

"I recognize that power," whispered Hovard under his breath.

"What was it?"

"I'm afraid your friend just left," Hovard said. "Hrothgar has acquired the power of the World Tree for himself."

"Help," shouted a guard fast approaching Hovard.

"What is it?" Hovard said.

"Skadi . . . she is in the tunnels."

"How do you know this?" asked Hovard.

"I was just there. She killed the guards I was with, but she spared me for some reason. Her mistake. I just got free."

"The tunnels lead to Heorot Hall," Hovard said.

"Then it seems that is still our destination," said the mystery man.

SIXTEEN

THE GEAT

Solveig stood at a window overlooking the entrance of Heorot Hall. She watched Hrothgar depart faster than the fastest of horses.

"That is what the World Tree is capable of . . . incredible," she whispered.

As soon as he was out of view, she left the window and headed for the door at the end of the hall. She descended the stairwell and found herself in the central room of the hall where Hrothgar's desk was located. She moved it aside and opened the door beneath it, using the runic lock she had inscribed in it.

She descended another stairwell and moved through the hallway towards the series of cells in the room at the far end of the hallway. Solveig opened the door and found Egil asleep and Mimir staring at her.

"Let me go," Mimir said.

"How is he?" Solveig said gesturing towards Egil. "I'm assuming you talked."

"He is worried. And rightfully so. He told me what you and Hrothgar are planning. Your plan is incredibly foolish."

"What is foolish is allowing ourselves to continue to live at the mercy of vain gods."

"Vain. Sure. But the gods are dangerous and cruel too. Those are the adjectives I would be more worried about."

"Don't fret, Mimir. We know what we are doing."

"Do you? Weapons made from magic ore are not going to be your salvation. They'll be your doom."

"Spare me your concerns. I came to collect you because I want to talk about the Aesir. Long ago you served as Odin's advisor. You, more than anyone, must have an intimate knowledge of the Allfather and his kin, namely Thor."

"I once served the God of Hanged Men. And for my troubles, he left me to live alone without a body for hundreds of years."

"If someone did that to me I would pretty angry."

"I'm Mimir, the wisest man alive. You are not going to be able to mind game me into helping you."

"No mind games, just commenting on what I see as an unfortunate outcome for someone who has so much to offer the nine realms," Solveig said.

"You should leave me be and give up this noxious dream. You are only going to get everyone you love and care about killed."

"What do you know of it?" Solveig asked.

"I know that despite your betrayal Egil still loves you. I know that it causes him much grief that you support his father in this endeavor."

"I did not force him to go against us."

"I think he would argue otherwise. He thinks you are seeking the approval of Hrothgar since your father passed when you were young."

"My father was killed."

"By whom?" asked Mimir.

"Enough questions of me. I came here to fetch you so that you, Eitri, and I can speak at length regarding the Aesir. And the Vanir too. If there is to be a new pantheon, we should be knowledgeable of the current ones."

"A new pantheon?"

Solveig moved to open the cell that housed Mimir. She picked him up and turned him over.

"I don't really know what I expected, but there is no hole. You are a bizarre creature," she said, tucking Mimir under her arm.

"You can stop this. It was your alchemy that transferred Skadi's strength to Hrothgar. You can undo it."

"I would need to have the desire."

"A blind man can see Hrothgar is a tyrant. I should I know, I used to serve one."

"And that is what we will discuss."

Skadi helped Egil move through the halls and ascend the stairs to the main room of Heorot. She retraced her steps towards the tunnel she had traversed to gain access to the hall.

"The place where Eitri works, he shares with Solveig. I remember before she chose her allegiance, we would spend time together there, and I would watch her work. She had invented a powder that explodes."

"Exploding powder?" Skadi asked.

"In a perfect Midgard, she could use her intelligence for good. But instead, she has let my father manipulate her into trying to harness something wicked."

"The council in Fensalir sought to harness something they did not fully understand or appreciate, and it costs most of them their lives," said Skadi. "What makes your father so confident he can do better?"

"We know all about what happened in Fensalir. We had a similar problem years ago. But whereas your monster manipulated your council members, my father manipulated our monster. He saw that it was nigh unbeatable and decided to let it do his bidding, destroying Vikings until he no longer needed it."

Skadi said nothing.

"My father sees moments of distress and turns them into opportunities. When this town was at its lowest, he saw a way to make it work to achieve his goals."

"You speak as though you respect him," Skadi said.

"I do. I just disagree with him. My mother disagreed with him also, and he cast her aside. My father demands loyalty . . . especially from family, and he likes to make a show of those who are disloyal."

"Family can be . . . difficult."

Egil smiled.

"That, my friend, is very much an understatement."

"While on my journey to Lejre, I came across a mother mourning her children who were hanged by guards. Later, I saw what my uncle did to those simply seeking freedom from oppression. If Hrothgar wishes to make weapons, I will help you stop him."

Moments later, Skadi and Egil, having retraced Skadi's steps, came upon a wooden door, and seeping out from the other side was the smell of coal smoke.

"When I was here before I found only the remains of broken Bifrost keys."

"You did not enter Eitri's forge?"

"No."

"It is beyond this door. Eitri should be there, and Mimir, but also . . ."

"Solveig," whispered Skadi.

"My father might have the vision, but she is the key."

"Can she be reasoned with?" said Skadi.

"Her parents died when she was young. Her mother, of natural causes, but she believes it was the Aesir who took her father. She sees what my father is doing as a means for making Midgard a safer place and the atrocities just a means to an end."

"She is lost, then," Skadi said.

"Solveig has a dream of Midgard atop the World Tree."

"It took traveling around Midgard and consuming the roots of Ygg-drasil to acquire power she stole in moments. With that kind of skill, she could be a powerful ally."

"Which also makes her a powerful foe," said Egil. "She is talented in an art known only to a few, but her need for validation and her quest for revenge means she will be unlikely to aid us."

"Then perhaps I have sworn off killing prematurely."

Skadi moved to open the door.

"Wait."

"What?" she said looking back at him.

"Never mind."

She pressed on the door, and it creaked open. There was no one on the other side, so she and Egil moved deeper within. They walked for a while before stopping. The smell of coal smoke was strong.

"Mimir," said Skadi announcing their presence.

There was no response.

"Eitri," Egil said.

Again, there was no response.

Skadi looked back at Egil.

Nothing.

"Where is everyone?" Skadi asked.

She continued; the smell of coal smoke grew stronger and stronger.

"Deeper within, perhaps? Eitri's forge goes further underground than the rest of Heorot Hall," said Egil.

They entered a room—Eitri's living quarters they supposed. In the corner was a stove and atop a tea kettle. Skadi put the back of her hand near the kettle. It was warm to the touch. Egil appeared next to her.

"Someone was here, and they have not been gone long," she said. "We should . . ."

"Skadi Hervor and Egil Hrothgarson," said an unknown voice.

Skadi pivoted and saw a man she did not recognize standing in the entrance. He had long flowing hair and shoulders so broad he filled the doorway. He looked older than her by at least ten years, but his body was that of someone far younger.

"Do I know you?" she asked.

Egil turned his attention to the man and moved closer to Skadi.

"A few moons ago, a sailor returned from the mainland with a story. He said that in the town of Fensalir, for years there had been a jötunn that fed on the children and grew more powerful by the day. But one day, a woman showed up with a boy, who embarked on a journey, and when she returned, wielded so much power she was able to kill the jötunn. When I heard this story, I was immediately intrigued, because I once performed a similar duty for Lejre. But I had no help of the World Tree, Skadi. I killed that monster with my bare hands because I needed no aid to be its equal in strength. When I received notice the Jötunn-Breaker was here, I decided I would see who the World Tree granted its gifts."

Skadi stepped in front of Egil.

"Who is this guy?" he whispered.

"Stay behind me."

"I understand the power has been taken from you so you may use your sword if you like. It will not matter either way," said the mystery man.

Skadi unsheathed Ridill and prepared herself for battle.

With no sword in hand and hardly any armor save for a bear hide pelt, the man lunged for Skadi. She responded by jabbing forward with her sword, but the man caught the blade between his two hands and ripped the weapon from her grasp. This caught her by surprise. He tossed it aside, and the blade clanged against the stony floor. Skadi followed the sword with her eyes, but the quick distraction proved to have major implications, because she caught two feet to her chest and abdomen. The impact sent her flying across the room and just like the sword, she went tumbling across the floor, crashing violently into the wall to her rear.

"Get up," Egil shouted, shaking Skadi. "Get up."

Her eyelids flickered as she rocked her head back and forth. She was dazed and her breathing was ragged. It was as though she had been standing behind a horse. She could not remember ever being hit so hard.

Egil stepped between Skadi and this mystery man.

"I do not think your father would be pleased if I crippled his son. This is between her and I," said the man.

Skadi got to her feet, put a hand on Egil's shoulder and gently pushed him away from her.

"Find Mimir."

"I can't do this alone," he said.

"I would listen to her," said the man. "Hrothgar will understand a broken limb or two if I told him you got in my way."

Egil hesitated and then stepped backward.

The man once again leapt after Skadi. She deflected the initial few punches and even landed a counter of her own, but once the first of his punches connected with her jaw, the rest went unblocked. She only received a reprieve from the onslaught when he let up.

Skadi's left eye was bloodshot. Blood and saliva dripped from her mouth. Her arms and legs were scraped up and bruised.

"I did expect a little more fight from you," said the man. "The World Tree had to see something in you worthwhile."

Skadi took a deep breath and wiped the blood from her lips. She raised her fists.

"At least you have spirit," said the man.

Skadi went on the offensive, throwing punch after punch, but hitting only air. Whoever this man was, he was fast despite his size. When it was clear to Skadi that he was tired of evading, she raised her fists to defend her face, but he went low and clipped her legs from underneath her. She landed with a thud and then rolled, just barely avoiding the bottom of his foot connecting with her face.

"Run Egil," shouted Skadi.

"But . . ."

"I'll be alright. Get out of here."

Skadi observed Egil hesitate before running to the second door within the room that led to a tunnel deeper underground. He looked back at Skadi, and she nodded. He disappeared through the door.

"You'll have no witness to your demise," said the man. "Sad, even for me."

Skadi's legs wobbled as she picked herself up again. She spit the blood in her mouth onto the floor.

"I do not fear death, and I do not fear you. Tell me who you are. I would want to know the name of my would-be killer should I need to seek vengeance from beyond the grave."

"That sounds like a Jötunn-Breaker. I am the destroyer of giants, slayer of sea-monsters and killer of Grendel. I am the son of Ecgtheow and king of the Geats. I am Beowulf."

As his last word escaped his lips, he went on the offensive again. The next few moments for Skadi were a blur. Every hit went undefended. She could no longer fight back. It was not for lack of will. Every instinct in her told her to strike and to defend, but while her mind was willing, her body was unresponsive. She was beaten and after a few moments found herself once again lying on the ground.

Skadi sensed Beowulf kneeling by her side. He lifted her head off the ground, and she looked at his face.

"Even without the gift of Yggdrasil, you have fared better than any other human who has stood against me. Not even the fearsome ogre, Grendel, survived my wrath. You are strong, but only a few can be mighty."

He dropped her head.

"She is all yours," said Beowulf.

Skadi looked past Beowulf at the doorway. Standing in it was Hovard. His good hand was glowing. Next to him stood the guard she spared.

But just as she was coming to terms with the end, the room exploded and became shrouded in greyish cloud. Skadi felt herself being dragged from the room and passed out in the chaos.

She awoke in semi-darkness. A burning torch provided some light far in the distance, but it wasn't much. She shifted her weight to her elbows and sat up.

"Where . . . am I?"

"You're awake," said Egil.

"What happened?"

"I saved you."

"Where is Hovard? And Beowulf?"

"I don't know," Egil said.

"Where are we now?"

"This is the room Solveig used to experiment in when we were younger. It's where I got the exploding powder."

"They'll find a way to get here."

"No, they will not. It is only accessible with this rune and Solveig has not ventured here for some time," said Egil holding up a small stone with a carving on it.

"Beowulf," whispered Skadi. "Have you heard of him? He knows your father."

"I know of him. He showed up many years ago at the behest of my father to slay Grendel. He comes from the Geatland, a large island north of the mainland. As far as I know, he is just a man, but he fights like he is more than that."

"He said he is king of the Geats. Does your father command other rulers?"

"I don't know," Egil answered.

Skadi looked off in the distance, thinking.

"Hovard and this Beowulf are a powerful pair. I'm not sure this fight is winnable without the World Tree," said Skadi.

Skadi attempted to shift her weight so that she could stand. She struggled and then fell to the ground.

"Give it a moment. He knocked you around quite a bit."

Skadi looked at Egil.

"I almost forgot what it was like to be in danger. Even before the World Tree, I rarely faced another I could not handle."

"My father sends the guards to the Geatland for training. This must be who they train under."

Skadi spit up more blood.

"His movements are so fast, and he hits with more force than a horse."

"I sense admiration in the way you speak."

"It is not every day you meet someone who has so artfully mastered the craft of combat."

"But so have you. You are the Jötunn-Breaker of Fensalir. A warrior. A hero."

"A weapon maybe. Not a hero."

"You are here, now, helping me fight for a town that you owe nothing. What is that if not heroic?"

Skadi smiled and despite the pain put a hand on Egil's shoulder. Skadi's eyes adjusted to the dimly lit room. The torchlight bounced off a few benches, atop which there was round, glass containers.

"We need to keep moving," Skadi said once again attempting to stand.

"This is Solveig's experimentation room. She once created a solution that heals most wounds. I'll find it and then we can continue."

Skadi watched Egil light a second torch and proceed to move around the room in search of the healing solution. While he searched, she thought about Bjorn and Fensalir. Then her mind shifted to Eirdóttir and her whereabouts.

"You say Solveig is doing this because of the Aesir. What do you know about the gods? Specifically, Loki?"

"Not a lot I'm afraid. Why do you ask?"

"The Aesir God arrived in Fensalir not so long ago."

Egil stopped searching for a moment.

"You met him?" he said sternly.

"Not I, but I trust who told me."

"My father's mine is built in the Ironwood, where some believe the witch Angrboda still resides, mourning her children."

"Who?"

"She is the wife of Loki . . . or at least that is what people believe," said Egil as he began searching again for the potion.

Skadi contemplated what Egil said.

"His father was the jötunn I killed," Skadi said plainly.

Egil stopped rummaging again and looked at Skadi.

"What?" Egil said, less sternly this time and more fearful sounding.

"Mimir figured it out. It is part of why we came here. I don't know when or even if he will want revenge, but it is a concern I cannot shake."

"I do know one thing—Loki is known as the trickster, which means he is a plotter. He may not act right away, but he will. When the time comes, I'll do everything in my power to help you. Facing a god should not be done alone. Found it," said Egil lifting a small vile. "This should fix you up."

Skadi took the tiny container from Egil.

"I just drink it?" she asked.

Egil nodded.

Skadi observed the contents of the container, then in one swig downed it all. At first, she felt nothing, but after only moments the pain in her face and body quickly disappeared. A few moments after that, the wounds she sustained during her bout with Beowulf began to heal.

"How do you feel?" Egil said.

Skadi set the vile aside and stood up with no problem.

"This is the power of a Valkyrie. Solveig can make this and yet chooses to follow the Earl."

"She sees my father as her own," Egil said.

"If the time comes, are you prepared to stop her?" Skadi asked.

"When you say stop . . . do you mean . . ."

Skadi let her question linger.

"We grew up together. We were to be wed. We love each other . . . loved each other. I do not know now."

SEVENTEEN

SEARCHING FOR THE TRUTH

"Take this," said Egil, handing Skadi the rune he used to access Solveig's workshop. "If something happens, the instructions for how to make more of the solution are here."

"It works like a Bifrost key?"

"She used a Bifrost key as inspiration. This workshop has no doors. This rune allows you to transport instantly in and out of this room from wherever you are."

"She understands Bifrost keys."

"She spent a lot of time studying them. The gem inside a Bifrost key stores the power of Yggdrasil. Solveig correctly believed it could be a means for further harnessing godly power such as what you wielded."

Skadi placed the rune stone in her pelt.

"That Hrothgar now wields," added Skadi.

"She won me over with this," said Egil pointing at his head. "She was . . . is so intelligent. Do you know what a skogvættir is?"

"A forest spirit," answered Skadi. "I am fortunate to have never encountered one."

"They require anyone who comes across their path to answer a series of riddles, and just one wrong answer will mean your death. When Solveig and I were children, no older than ten each, we came across a skogvættir in a forest near Lejre. Solveig answered each riddle so quickly the spirit honored her."

"I cannot say I would be able to do the same," said Skadi.

"Me neither. I was useless. She told me that she and her father used riddles to keep their minds sharp for alchemy."

"Which Aesir does she believe killed her father?"

"The Thunder God himself."

"What reason would Thor have for killing her father?"

"What reason would he need? The gods simply do. They need not a reason, Skadi. You know this."

"And yet I sense you question Solveig's belief."

Egil shrugged.

"There is something more to all of this. I know this to be true. I just cannot believe she would follow my father as smart as she is."

"Even the smartest and strongest amongst us seek comfort," said Skadi.

"Perhaps you speak the truth. No matter . . . when we transport out, we will be in the room where we left. It is not a true Bifrost key. It can only go here and back to where you came from. We'll be taking a risk that Beowulf and your uncle are still there."

"For how long was I out?"

"Some time but not very long actually. I was actually surprised to find you still breathing."

"There is a chance they're still there."

"What do you want to do?" asked Egil.

"Time is not on our side," said Skadi. "Your father's road seems near completion if it is not finished already."

"When Solveig came to collect Mimir, I overheard her mention my father's absence."

"Beowulf may have been strong, but the power he displayed pales in comparison to what the World Tree has given Hrothgar."

Skadi extended her hand, and Egil took it. Then just as she would a real Bifrost key, she triggered the rune and, in a flash, they disappeared from the workshop. They reappeared in the room where moments ago Skadi had failed to best Beowulf in combat. To her's and Egil's relief, neither Beowulf nor Hovard were present.

Egil let out a deep sigh.

"My knuckles had whitened."

Skadi looked at Egil and admitted, "Concern had consumed me as well."

"This room descends deeper underground to Eitri's living quarters. If they were not here, then it is possible he, Solveig, and Mimir may all be there."

"I will follow your lead."

The hallway was dimly lit and filled with the smell of coal smoke. As they walked, Skadi checked her arms and legs. She was fully healed.

"Everything ok?" said Egil.

"That was not the first time I experienced being healed like that," she said. "There was a Valkyrie named Eir."

"You have met a Valkyrie?"

"Two. Her daughter is who is missing."

"Eirdóttir?"

Skadi nodded.

"Her mother gave her life for my son and me. It was my uncle's doing. The power you have seen him display was a gift from the jötunn."

"Your uncle is disturbed."

"I killed his son, Magnús," Skadi said plainly.

"Did he deserve it?"

"He was a violent man. Eager to start a fight and careless with people's lives."

"I see."

"Magnús could have been an honorable warrior, but my uncle spoiled him in our youth."

"Oddly, that is something I am sure my father would blame my mother of."

"She is gone now?" Skadi asked.

"She cared little for how my father handled Grendel and was convinced he could have done something sooner. She started speaking out."

"And he killed her?" asked Skadi.

"He never loved her, and I have not turned out to be the child he wanted. Solveig, however, . . ."

Skadi continued behind Egil until they reached a door.

"We're here," said Egil.

Skadi rested a hand on the hilt of her sword to be ready.

"Open it," she whispered.

He pushed on the door, expecting there to be people, only to reveal an empty room. Only glowing coals in the hearth inhabited the room.

"They should be here," said Egil.

Skadi walked over to the hearth, and hanging by it was a pair of tongs. She put the back of her hand near the end of the tongs.

"Warm," she whispered.

"They have to be around here somewhere?" Egil said.

"What about over there?" said Skadi pointing at a closed door.

Egil, standing closer to it, opened it.

"There's a bed in here. And a desk."

Skadi joined Egil in the room. Egil went to the bed and peered under it. Skadi opened the first desk drawer.

"Anything?" she asked.

"No. Did you find anything?"

Skadi opened the second desk drawer. In it was a scroll with runic symbols on it.

"I may have" she said taking the scroll into her hands.

Egil appeared by her side.

"I am not familiar with this language," she said.

He looked at it.

"This is written in the runic alphabet of Nidavellir. I do not know how to read it either."

"Who does?"

"Solveig."

"Anyone else?"

Egil paused and thought for a moment. Then Skadi saw him come to a realization.

"Actually, yes," he said. "He is a rune writer in Thrymheim."

Skadi's expression shifted to a mild frown.

"We do not have time to go to Thrymheim."

"We will send a raven. He can translate it and send it back. It should not take more than a few hours."

"And you trust him?"

"He is one of the best rune writers in Midgard and he is a friend. His name is Roar."

"Ok then," Skadi said, looking around the room further.

She looked up and painted on the ceiling was an elaborate mural of the World Tree.

"Odd painting," Skadi whispered.

Egil looked up.

"Asgard is out of place," said Skadi, pointing to the middle of the tree. "Normally Midgard is here which means . . ."

She shifted her focus to the top of the tree.

"Midgard at the top," she whispered.

"I almost forgot about this."

"You knew this was here?" Skadi asked.

"This was once Solveig's room. She painted that before Eitri moved in."

"It perplexes me that a dwarf would follow a human. I have met dwarves, and they are . . . passionate about their own realm and their own kind."

"We can ask him later. Let us send this raven to Roar."

Moments later, Skadi and Egil moved to his chamber within Heorot Hall. Egil removed a raven from its cage and attach the scroll to its leg.

"Now we wait," he said.

Hovard covered his face and quickly backed out of the room as the explosive powder filled the space with chaotic energy. Beowulf joined him.

"Neat trick," Beowulf said.

"How did you do that?" said Hovard.

"That was the boy."

"Not the powder. The way you fought. Even without Yggdrasil, Skadi is still one of the fiercest warriors I have ever known, and you bested her as if she was still green."

"Most combatants, Skadi included, seek to overpower their opponent. They want to dominate them and bend them to their will. But unless the odds are overwhelmingly in their favor, that tactic will not work against someone like me."

"What makes you different?" Hovard said.

"I, my friend, do not seek to overpower and dominate. I redirect, channel, and use my opponent's strength against them. Using your mind, skill, and strategy will allow you to defeat almost any adversary. Whether it be Grendel or the Jötunn-Breaker. I choose to flow like water."

Hovard observed the man who bested his niece as he peered back in the room.

"Like water you say?"

"Water is resilient and flexible. It flows peacefully but it can crash with the fiercest of strength. You, my friend, are the opposite of that. Fire has little direction and consumes all."

Hovard stared at Beowulf for a moment, contemplating what he said. Before he had a moment to comment, Beowulf spoke up.

"Any thoughts on where they may have gone?" Beowulf asked.

"I think I know where they'll be heading. Follow me."

A VALKYRIE IN LEJRE?

As Hrothgar moved along his road, to others, he appeared as a blur. He moved at a speed nearly unfathomable by any creature other than the gods. Behind him, a trail of dirt and debris followed as each footstep left its mark. And yet, despite his pace, he was completely aware of his surroundings. It was a paradox he had yet to make sense of. He could smell everything more intensely. He could hear everything more clearly. In every capacity, his senses were improved beyond what any human should be able to comprehend.

It did not take long for him to arrive at the remains of the encampment, destroyed by trolls. He slowed his run and strolled onto the site. As he walked, he took account of the area. It was burned to the ground. The fire had spread from the trees to the cottages. Mostly just smoldering embers remained.

"There were over one hundred guards here," Hrothgar whispered to himself.

He heard a man scream in the distance and the roar of a massive troll. Swiftly, he was standing between the man and a troll with its arms stretched overhead prepared to strike. Hrothgar caught the troll's arms on the downswing. And with ease lifted the creature into the air and threw it deep into the forest.

"Behind you," shouted the man.

Hrothgar turned just as the second troll grabbed him by his waist. The creature's hand was so big it engulfed half of his body. To Hrothgar, the embrace felt like a strong hug, not life-threatening as it was intended. The troll lifted him off the ground and near its face. It roared, and Hrothgar flinched only at the smell of the troll's breath.

Hrothgar clapped his hands together on either side of the troll's head and the beast dropped Hrothgar as it slumped to the ground. He wiped the blood off his face and turned back to the guard.

"How?" whispered the man.

"Is there anyone else?"

"Just I."

Hrothgar looked around the campsite. Fires were burning. Others were smoldering. Not a single cottage stood intact. The remains of dead guards were everywhere—some were so thoroughly smashed by the trolls that only red paste remained.

"From the beginning—tell me exactly what happened."

"Last night, we became aware of a rebellion. We were quick to act and tracked down the those who were causing the disruption. There were not many, but enough that a mass grave was necessary. While they dug, the one who we suspected started the rebellion, Hege, managed to light some pine trees on fire, which attracted the trolls."

"How did she manage to get the better of you all? Are you not trained?"

"We had buried her already."

"Alive?"

"She had given us trouble in the past. The men wanted to make an example of her."

"Next time see it through to completion, you fool."

"We failed you, sir."

"What happened after?"

"The trolls arrived, and in the chaos that followed, most of the rebels escaped while the guards contended with the furious creatures. All gave their lives."

"Where were the rebels heading when you caught them initially?"

"Fensalir. Under the Jötunn-Breaker's protection, it would be the safest place in Midgard for them."

Hrothgar smirked.

"The Jötunn-Breaker is no more. Return to Lejre and prepare the execution stage in the town common. I will show you how to properly make an example of this Hege."

The caw of a raven made Skadi perk up. The bird touched down on the perch outside of the window. Tied to its foot was a scroll. Egil collected it and removed the scroll.

"What does it say?" Skadi asked.

"I knew my faith was well placed in Roar. The runes refer to a special project for my father."

"We already know about the weapons."

"Something other than the weapons."

"What?"

"It does not say."

"Then was this a waste of time?" Skadi said.

Egil looked up from the scroll at Skadi.

"I thought the weapons were it. The mine, the road, Eitri, and Solveig—those were all for the weapons."

"Is there anything else to the scroll?" Skadi said.

"There is a second forge. It is . . . in the center of town."

"In the common?"

"The door of the Valkyrie will lead the way."

"Do you think your friend translated this wrong?"

"Not at all. Roar is one of the mainland's most skilled rune writers. He wrote the runes that protect the walls of Lejre and Thrymheim. Neither town has had its walls breached," Egil said.

"Then could a Valkyrie live here? It is a massive town."

"It's possible, I'm sure. Why they would live here I do not know, but clearly stranger things have happened."

"Let's find her," Skadi said, before heading to exit the room. "Wherever this second forge is, we will likely find Mimir."

She looked back when she realized Egil was not following.

"What?" she said.

"I am worried about what this could mean. I thought the weapons were the extent of his machinations, but if Eitri knows of something

149

more then so does Solveig, and that means she has been keeping this from me."

"Your relationship is hardly the issue here," Skadi said coldly. "Best not to dwell on it. Those closest to us can be the ones who hurt us the most. Let's find Mimir and get this whole mess sorted out."

"You're right," said Egil, looking down at the ground.

Skadi looked at Egil and sighed.

"I did not mean to be so . . ."

"Let's go."

He then slipped past Skadi and out the door. She followed him for a moment with just her eyes before continuing behind him.

The sun was inching higher and higher into the sky, but it was still early enough that the cottages and storehouses cast long shadows. Skadi and Egil left Heorot Hall and stuck to the shadows of the adjacent buildings to evade detection by any nearby guards. They descended from the hilltop without issue and reached the beginning of Lejre proper, where the citizens of the town ambled around, opening shops and taking care of morning chores.

"My father uses guards who dress as regular people to keep an eye on the happenings. Even I may not be able to spot them. I'm certain if we knew exactly where the Valkyrie was, we could talk to her without detection, but if we spend too much time searching then we'll be caught."

"Your father does not trust people very much."

"An Earl can trust no one. Especially one as ambitious as my father."

Skadi took in her surroundings while considering what Egil said.

"I have an idea."

Moments later, Skadi and Egil reached outside of Stigr Gudmund's cottage. Stigr opened a slot in the door.

"Skadi," he said and opened the door immediately.

"Stigr this is . . ."

"Egil, the son of the Earl. Yes, I know. Come in."

Skadi gestured for Egil to enter first. She followed and closed the door behind her.

"Have a seat," said Stigr, grabbing two chairs from against the wall.

Skadi sat first, followed by Egil.

"You went looking for one friend and seem to have found another."

"I hope it is ok I brought him here."

"He has always been a friend of the people," Stigr said.

Skadi shifted in her seat.

"We need your help," she said. "There is a conspiracy unfolding in Lejre, and we fear for what it means for this town and Midgard."

"What sort of conspiracy?" Stigr asked.

"Stigr, we have a request of you," Skadi answered.

The older gentleman seemed to hesitate for a moment before answering. "I asked for your aid, Skadi, and you gave it freely. It is only right that I do the same."

"What we are asking is potentially dangerous," added Egil.

"And we do not ask lightly," said Skadi.

"What do you need?"

Skadi reached out to Egil for the scroll. He placed it in her hand and Skadi proceeded to hand it to Stigr.

"What is this?" Stigr said.

"Those are notes taken by Eitri."

"The dwarf?" Stigr said before scanning the scroll. "There is a forge in the center of town?"

"We need you to find the entrance," Skadi said.

"My father uses guards dressed as commoners to patrol Lejre. They will spot us. I am his son, and she is the Jötunn-Breaker, but you can go undetected," Egil added.

"What is the door of the Valkyrie? Is that what you need me to find?"

"Yes," Skadi said.

"A Valkyrie lives in Lejre?"

"We do not know," Egil said.

"The people here will need someone to watch over them while I'm gone."

"We will," said Skadi.

"Finish preparing the food for them and tend to their injuries."

"We have it under control," Skadi said.

"I'll be back with whatever I find."

Skadi stood up when Stigr stood and extended her hand. He took it and the two shook.

"Be careful," she said.

"Thank you," added Egil. "My father's actions are inexcusable, and he will pay."

"Son, if there is one thing I have learned in my time in this realm, it is that we all have a role to play."

With that said, Stigr departed the cottage.

Stigr looked back at his cottage one time before entering the hustle and bustle of the early morning in Lejre. He blended into the crowd of folks opening their shops and preparing to sell their wares.

The sun was cresting over the massive walls that surrounded the town. Stigr hated the shadow they cast and longed for the time when they did not exist. It had been so long since they were finished that he almost forgot the time before them.

The center of town was not far, so he walked casually as to keep from drawing attention to himself. He knew the Earl disguised some of his guards as commoners. When he was younger, you knew who the guards were and who they were not; things were simpler, and Stigr yearned for those simpler times.

The road Stigr walked along opened into a very large common, surrounded by cottages, shops, and storehouses. Smoke from burning hearths pumped into the sky and the smell of baked goods permeated the air. One could not be blamed for finding the common a pleasant place to be. But it was also the largest communal space in all of Lejre.

Stigr looked at all the doors and said, "This may take some time."

Skadi led Egil underground. The people Hovard maimed were still huddled in groups around the cellar. Some hadn't moved an inch since she was last there, hours ago.

"These are the people your uncle burned?" whispered Egil.

"The healing potion Solveig created; would it work on them?" whispered Skadi.

"She did not create nearly enough."

"What would it take to create more?"

Egil seemed to think for a second, then said, "Energy from the World Tree."

"We know where we can find the energy," said Skadi.

"Stigr said for us to finish the food. Perhaps we focus on that for now," said Egil.

Skadi watched him return to the kitchen on the first floor of the cottage, before she looked back at a woman whose face was nearly gone and a man whose midsection was wrapped in bandages.

"You don't deserve this," she whispered before following Egil to the kitchen.

"Here," said Egil, handing Skadi a basket of bread.

She took the basket and placed it under her arm. She turned back towards the cellar but paused.

"When I was a child, I witnessed a man take the lives of an inn full of people. He burned them alive, and I had to watch because he thought it would make me strong."

"That is terrible," said Egil.

"For a long time, I thought it did make me strong, but really it just made me numb to other's suffering . . . until I had my son. My uncle was not a kind man, but he was never a truly cruel one either. He has changed."

"Power and anger are a dangerous pairing."

"I do not blame him for his anger, but this is unforgivable."

"If we can know how power and emotion impact our decisions, we might make Midgard a better place."

Skadi laughed.

"What is funny?"

"Mimir is always saying he is the smartest man alive, and yet in less than two days I have been better counseled by my son and now you."

Egil laughed.

"I had a lot of time to read growing up as the son of the Earl."

She then returned to the cellar with the basket of bread and proceeded to hand out the loaves to the people scattered in the cellar. Egil followed with pieces of cod and cups of water.

Stigr moved from door to door around the town common, attempting to look as unsuspicious as possible while still inspecting each cottage door for the name of the owner. He was three quarters of the way around the common when a cottage sign caught his eye. The sign showed a woman with wings pointing.

The image was of a Valkyrie pointing in a direction left of Stigr's current location. He looked and saw a cellar door. As he neared, he smelled the faintest hint of coal smoke, and he knew that was it.

Skadi lifted a cup of water to a woman's mouth to help her drink. She struggled, but Skadi ensured she finished it. Her attention shifted to the door of the cottage when she heard it open and close.

"I found it," said Stigr.

Skadi placed the cup down and ascended the stairs of the cellar. Egil was already in the kitchen with Stigr.

"You found the door?" Skadi said.

"It's on the eastern-most side of the common. It was not a Valkyrie at all. It was a sign. There is a storehouse with a sign of a Valkyrie pointing in the direction of a cellar door and a faint smell of coal smoke rising from the cellar door. I think that is where you will find your hidden forge."

"That's it. Thank you," said Egil.

"Thank you," Skadi said. "Let's go, Egil. We had best be on our way."

"I should go with you. I can help. I once guarded Heorot Hall. I can still fight."

"Stay here," Skadi insisted. "The people of Lejre do not need your body, just your kindness."

Stigr nodded and stuck out his hand. Skadi embraced it and then so did Egil.

"Farewell," Stigr said.

NINETEEN

THE DWARF

Skadi laid eyes on the storehouse with the sign of the pointing Valkyrie and the cellar that it pointed to. She tapped Egil on the shoulder and gestured towards it. They each looked around to make sure no one was paying attention to them and quickly slipped through the cellar door. Just like the forge under Heorot Hall, the smell of coal smoke was strong.

Skadi cautiously walked in silence with Egil close behind. The smell grew stronger the deeper they went. She had a hand on the hilt of her sword and so did Egil. Not before long, Skadi could sense the presence of others. She heard the faint, distant sound of voices.

"That's Solveig," Egil whispered.

"If we move quickly, we can stop her."

"You mean to kill her?"

"I tried to keep from killing and it led Beowulf right to us. There is a permanence in death that is advantageous in situations like this," said Skadi.

"I'm no fool. I know what we face."

"Right now, we have the element of surprise. We need to take advantage of it," Skadi said.

"The element of surprise may not be enough."

"Then what?"

"We talk to her," Egil said.

A subtle look of confusion spread across Skadi's face.

"It's the only way. I promise you this is not me trying to save her life. She is more powerful than us. We will lose surprise or no surprise."

Skadi breathed in deeply and let out a long sigh.

"I'm not comfortable with this approach."

"If I'm unsuccessful and she tries to attack, then let's pray you are quick enough with that sword."

Stigr took a kettle of tea off the flame and set it aside before pouring his cup. Just beyond the kettle, behind the tabletop, was a door. He got up, walked over to the door, and grabbed the handle.

"I shouldn't," he whispered.

He hesitated but opened the door, and before him was a broad sword and an armored pelt.

Skadi let Egil lead as they approached the innermost door of the underground forge. Three distinct voices could be heard on the other side. Skadi recognized two; Mimir was one and Solveig was the other, but she had not heard the third before.

She watched Egil place his hand against the door. He looked back at her, and she nodded.

"Solveig," he announced as the door opened.

Skadi rushed to stand beside Egil.

"My love," said Solveig shifting her attention towards Egil.

"Skadi," Mimir shouted.

"Skaði is here?" shouted an unfamiliar voice. "I am before the jötunn goddess of winter? I wish someone would have told me she was in Lejre. I would have shaved. I am sorry, goddess, for what the Aesir did to your father, Þjazi. He did not deserve that."

"No Eitri, this is *Skadi,* not Skaði. She is a human," corrected Solveig. "But her presence here is just as surprising."

"Solveig, Eitri . . . we are here to persuade you to abandon this mission my father has set you on. It will only result in ruin for us all."

"It's no use," Mimir said. "I've been trying to convince them that their plan is foolish this entire time."

"Mimir, as I have said numerous times, I would expect the *wisest* man alive to be able to see the larger picture." Solveig said.

"Mimir, have they hurt you?" asked Skadi.

"Only my ego."

Skadi readied her hand near her sword. Whatever happened she knew would happen quickly.

"Egil, why are you fighting the inevitable? Do you still fail to see the Midgard your father is trying to create? That *we* are trying to create," Solveig pleaded.

Skadi watched Egil to see what he would say and do.

"Solveig . . . my love," Egil said. "Remember your father. Remember Destin. Would he want this for you? For you to align yourself with a madman? Your father was a man of knowledge and wisdom. He wanted peace."

We cannot have peace while the Aesir rule," Solveig said.

"Is that you talking or the Earl?" Egil asked.

Solveig did not respond.

Skadi saw Egil shift his attention to Eitri.

"Eitri."

"Yes, human?"

"I know the story of how Loki challenged you and your brother."

Skadi paid closer attention. She was curious to know what Egil was about to say.

"I know when Loki challenged you and your brother, Brokkr, that you could not craft anything as fine or as useful as the objects created by the Sons of Ivaldi, you proved the trickster wrong. You crafted the golden boar, Gullinbursti, faster than any horse, Draupnir, the golden ring of Odin himself, and Mjölnir, Thor's mighty hammer which he used to slay jötnar. Something only one other person in this room has done. I say all this not to flatter you but to remind you that you did all of that because you and your brother chose to of your own volition. Why now would you take the direction of a single human when you are capable of so much?" said Egil.

"I am not stupid. You did say that to flatter me."

Skadi thought the same thing.

"And I have not forgotten all that my brother and I have achieved," said Eitri. "What you do not understand is that your father's goals will be a benefit to my realm of Nidavellir as well. The gods are not just a terror for humans. Thor has done more with that hammer than slay jötnar. Brokkr is dead. Making that hammer was our biggest mistake."

Skadi put a hand on Egil's shoulder. He looked at her and she stepped forward.

"Let me say something," she whispered.

Egil nodded.

"Eitri," Skadi said, directing her attention his way. "Consider how many have lost their brothers while building the road to Bard Mine and many more will lose their brothers when Hrothgar uses the weapons you are building for him."

Eitri did not respond.

"Do not listen to her. Hrothgar knows loss. That is what unites us. We have all lost our families to Aesir. But times are changing. The nine realms will soon know what humans . . ." said Solveig before turning to Eitri. "And dwarves can do."

Skadi glanced at Egil. He met her gaze.

"Solveig. Eitri. You are making a mistake," pleaded Egil.

"I'm afraid the two making a mistake are you," said Beowulf as he entered the room behind Skadi and Egil.

Skadi pivoted and shifted her attention to the man who not long ago bested her quite handily. Her skin grew clammy and sweat formed on her brow. She did not pick up on it immediately, but she realized that she was nervous.

"Please be careful in here," said Eitri. "My work is not yet complete. If you are to fight, please take it outside."

"What's so delicate about forging weapons?" Egil said. "What is this secret plot?"

"Time for you to leave," Solveig said.

"We found a scroll that made reference to it. Tell us what is going on!"

"If only you chose your people," said Solveig. "Then perhaps you would live to see it."

"I am choosing my people," shouted Egil. "It's you who has abandoned us. I lost my mother, and I would do anything to fill that hole in my heart, but I would not do so at the expense of others. Your father would not want this!"

Skadi placed a hand on Egil's shoulder.

"Some do not see the error of their ways until it is forced upon them," she whispered. "We do it my way now."

Egil glanced back at her. Then he looked away and nodded.

Skadi pulled from her pelt a bag of the exploding black powder and threw it at Solveig while simultaneously unsheathing Ridill. But to her surprise, Solveig did not move and simply raised her hand with a rune stone in it. A light flashed and the bag dropped to the ground with a thud. Sand spilled out onto the floor.

"That won't work," shouted Mimir. "You have to flee."

"Get them," said Solveig.

Skadi tackled Egil to the ground just as Beowulf leapt across the room. Skadi jumped to her feet, but as she gained her footing, Beowulf slammed his entire bodyweight into her and sent her flying threw through the door. It splintered upon impact, and she rolled to a stop down the corridor. Skadi shook off her injuries and looked up. She saw Beowulf charging after her, and behind him, Egil was still on the ground slowly gathering himself.

"Egil, move," shouted Skadi.

Beyond Beowulf, who was fast approaching, Egil was regaining his footing, but not fast enough.

"Get out of here. I will be fine," shouted Egil.

She turned to face the opposite direction. The corridor was empty, and she had enough of a head start that if she started running, she could probably escape. But . . .

She turned back around and said, "Egil, I won't abandon you."

"Skadi please . . . this is bigger than you and me."

Beowulf was almost upon her. She jumped to her feet and hesitated. Egil was beyond her reach. She clenched her fists.

"Damn it," she shouted before pivoting and fleeing down the corridor.

Beowulf pursued her, but as soon as Skadi burst through the exterior cellar door, she evaded him by merging into the crowd of people in the town common.

"Egil," Solveig said, standing over him.

He looked up at her.

"Get on with it," he said. "Kill me or lock me up. I won't fight you."

"I wish you could have seen the truth. Imagine how powerful we would be together. Your father will not be the Earl forever."

"Solveig, I just wanted us to be together."

"And we will be."

She reached out and touched Egil's forehead with the rune stone. It glowed red and immediately he felt his stomach turn and his body start to shift.

"What are you . . ."

"I won't lock you up or kill you, and you'll never leave my side again."

"I feel . . ."

Egil couldn't finish his sentence. His words became muffled, and the final word escaped his mouth as a bark. Egil watched Solveig grow bigger but quickly realized she wasn't getting bigger; he was getting smaller. He saw his hands turn to paws. He looked at his feet, they, too, were paws. Egil attempted to yell but all that came out was a terrified howl.

"I did not want this, but you forced my hand," whispered Solveig.

Skadi kept her head low as she mixed with the crowd of Lejrians going about their morning routines. With haste, she headed for the front gate. But as the gate came into view a familiar face did as well. Her uncle was standing by the gate and around him were a dozen of the Guards of Lejre. It appeared to her that he was in command.

Skadi put her head down and backed away.

"Now what?"

Stigr saw Skadi burst out from underground and attempt to disappear into the crowd. He followed her with his eyes for a while before shifting his gaze back to the cellar door where he saw a broad shoulder, long haired man chase after her.

He put a hand on the hilt of his sword and said, "Be brave Stigr. Be brave."

TWENTY

NYKÖPING

Solveig turned her attention towards Mimir. Whatever patience she once had was gone. A scowl formed where a slight smile once was. "If you are the wisest man alive then you know that you and your friends have lost. Hrothgar has the power of the World Tree. Beowulf will soon have Skadi, and you know what I am capable of. All that remains is for you to tell us what you know of the gods."

Mimir's eyes glanced at the dog that once was Egil, sitting in the corner with terror spread across its face.

"What do you hope to achieve?" He asked.

"Freedom, Mimir. Until the gods are dethroned, all the realms are shackled."

Mimir's gaze on the dog didn't break.

"Look at me," said Solveig.

He shifted his focus reluctantly.

"We know enough about you Mimir—you were there during the Great War. You advised the Allfather. You have lived amongst the Aesir and are familiar with the Vanir. This we know to be true."

"You, Hrothgar, and Eitri are fools. You can't possibly hope to achieve equal footing with the Aesir," said Mimir. "The gods are more powerful than you could ever imagine. Odin and his brothers Vili and Vé killed Ymir and fashioned Midgard from his flesh. And the tales of Thor . . . Do you know the true story of Nyköping?"

"I do."

"Do you really? Because I was there 200 years ago . . ."

200 Years Ago

Standing on a hilltop overlooking the town of Nyköping was a broad-shouldered man with arms the size of tree trunks and hair as red as fire. He held a hammer with a stunted handle in his right hand.

"What can the humans truly hope to achieve? Let them be. Even with all the weapons in the nine realms, they could never stand against the Aesir. You can ignore this," said Mimir, who was situated in a holster that was attached to Thor's side.

"There is but one power in all the realms," Thor grumbled in his deep, bellowing voice.

"Don't do this," begged Mimir.

"They have made their choice."

The god lifted the hammer to the sky, a bolt of lightning touched down around him, and the hammer pulled him into the air.

After hours of mayhem, Thor stood in the wreckage of the last cottage. Behind him was a burning town. A smoke plume was sky-high.

"This was the forge," he muttered. "But I see no blacksmith."

"Thor let us leave this place," pleaded Mimir. "The humans are no threat to the Aesir."

Thor looked around and spied the cellar door. But as he started to move towards the door, the sound of footsteps caught his attention. He looked beyond the cellar and saw a man emerge from the ground just a few feet beyond the cellar door.

"Spare him," Mimir said.

Thor smirked before launching into the air. Lightning swirled around him as he landed in front of the man.

"We made a mistake, but we did not mean any harm," the man said.

"Weapons have but one purpose."

"We only wanted to defend ourselves."

"You should have prayed instead."

"Please show us mercy," the man pleaded.

"I will let you attempt to strike me so that you might die in battle. That is as much mercy as I will grant you."

The man hesitated.

"Decide quickly. I mean to see the lady Sif shortly."

The man pulled a knife from his person and ran towards Thor.

"Wise decision."

Thor raised his hammer above his head.

"Thor don't," Mimir said.

A bolt of lightning struck down and when it was gone, only ashes remained where the man stood moments before.

"Mortals must remember their place, Mimir. You would be wise to take note as well."

Present

"It was one of the first massacres of the Great War. The only survivors were those who were not there that day," said Mimir. "Merchants and travelers who had taken to the road and sea while Thor devastated their homes. Thor was sent to send a message and he delivered it with merciless effect."

Solveig paused for a moment after Mimir finished speaking.

"Something on your mind?" Mimir asked.

"Your story is missing details," Solveig said.

A puzzled look took Mimir's face.

"I can assure you that I am telling you a complete story."

"The only survivors were not just those who were not there. There was one who survived the attack who was there."

"Who?" Mimir asked.

200 Years Ago

"Eirik, we need to hide," whispered Herlief as he rushed through the door of their cottage in a panic.

"What's happening out there?" said Eirik.

"We must go underground now," said Herlief, quickly moving past Eirik towards the cellar door.

Eirik did not chase after right away. Herlief stopped and looked back.

"What are you waiting for?"

Eirik pried open the front door and peeked outside. The screams of a woman and the loud boom of thunder passed through the cottage. It sent a shiver down his spine.

"Shouldn't we help?" Eirik said.

"It's too late for that. He's coming here."

"Who is?"

Herlief took Eirik's hand and pulled him into the cellar.

"Close the door," Herlief whispered. "Quickly."

Eirik and Herlief descended deeper and deeper underground until they reached the room where they stored axes and swords they had not yet finished. There had been no time to grab a torch, so the entire space was pitch black.

"We can't stay down here," whispered Eirik.

"Quiet."

There was a loud crash overhead, and the storeroom shook. Eirik grabbed Herlief and they embraced one another in the darkness.

"He's looking for us. We made the weapons."

"Who is?" whispered Eirik.

"Thor," said Herlief just before a loud boom reverberated through the storeroom. The entire cottage above was wiped out. It shook the foundation of the room they hid in and knocked hanging swords to the ground. They clanged around the two men.

"Stay here."

Eirik felt Herlief slip from his embrace. He reached out for him but in the darkness could not see where he went.

"What are you doing? Where are you?" Eirik whispered loudly.

But there was no response. Eirik could sense that in the darkness he was alone.

Present

"His name was Eirik. He survived Thor's assault. His love sacrificed himself by distracting Thor. Eirik told his descendants of what happened, and the tale passed through his family for generations."

"Are you . . ."

"I am his descendant."

A puzzled expression spread across Mimir's face.

"That would mean you know the truth about why Nyköping was destroyed."

"I do. And so does Hrothgar and Eitri."

"Then why would you . . ."

"Repeat history?"

"Not just repeat history but follow the same path towards annihilation. Nyköping was destroyed because the humans forged weapons against the gods."

Solveig smiled.

"Do not fret, Mimir. We have thought this through."

"The wise do not court death."

"We are doing no such thing. My ancestor was no dwarf. The quality has far improved. Plus, we have the advantage of hindsight. We also have one other item tucked away in our quiver that you'll see in time. But for now, you have a job. We want to know everything about the Aesir—their hierarchy, how they govern themselves what they eat, where they get resources. Personally, I would like to know where I can get some of those golden apples." Solveig said. "Is it really true or just legend that Odin hanged himself for nine days and nine nights so the Norns would fate-craft for him?"

"How am I going to do this?" whispered Skadi as she walked through a backstreet of Lejre.

The sound of the bustling town common was faint in the distance, but still audible enough to mask the footsteps of the man approaching. She only caught wind of him when he spoke up.

"You should have fled," said Beowulf. "Worthy of Yggdrasil perhaps not, but you are no coward."

Skadi pivoted and drew her sword. Beowulf lunged for her. She swung for him, but with only his hand he parried the sword, got in close, and forced Skadi to abandon her attack. She leaped backward to avoid an otherwise fatal blow.

The violent interaction happened so fast, that Skadi barely had a moment to comprehend his movements and he did not let up. She was forced to accept that Beowulf was too fast for her to strike him down with a sword, so she opted for the knife she kept on her waist, thinking it would give her more flexibility in attack. She sheathed Ridill, drew the knife, and struck, but he expertly blocked. Skadi struck again, he blocked again, and this time knocked the blade from her hand.

Beowulf headbutted Skadi, causing her to stumble through the door of a nearby cottage. She crashed into a table and the room full of people started yelling and scrambled for the exit. Skadi pulled herself to her feet as Beowulf entered and jumped to the side once he sprang for her. He split the table in half, just missing her.

"You're a king. Why do the bidding of an Earl?" said Skadi.

"I do no one's bidding," Beowulf said then he gestured for Skadi to attack.

Skadi clenched her fists and went on the offensive. She swung for him. He deflected, just as he had done multiple times at this point. Then Skadi did something unexpected, even for her. She dropped low and grabbed Beowulf's waist. She put all of her weight into his body, lifted him over her head, and slammed him into the ground, knocking the air from his lungs.

Beowulf stared up at the ceiling of the cottage stunned for a moment. Then, he started to laugh.

"That is it," he said. "That is what I expected of the Jötunn-Breaker."

Skadi stood over him for a moment catching her own breath.

"Beowulf, go back to the Geatland. You have no stake in this fight."

"What reason do you have for being here?"

Beowulf pulled himself to his feet. Skadi stood back and put her fists up. She shifted her posture defensively.

"You saved this town from Grendel. I know you and Hrothgar are *friends,* but he is killing this town. Why stand against me when he is the problem? Why fight for him when you're a king?"

Beowulf righted himself and brushed the dirt from his pelt.

"I will admit it gives me concern Hrothgar would take the power of Yggdrasil for himself. Power is to be earned. But I will deal with that later. You are supposed to be a warrior—a legendary one. But I must say you have proven to be disappointing."

Beowulf dropped to the ground and kicked Skadi's feet out from under her. She tried to catch herself as she fell, but with another swift kick from Beowulf, her hands flung out ahead of her and she hit the ground with a thud.

"We will meet again in Valhalla."

Skadi was completely dazed. She felt Beowulf grab her by the hair to lift her head, but she could not bring herself to fight back. She thought about Bjorn in what she was sure to be her final moments. But just as she thought the end was nigh, something or someone knocked her free from Beowulf's grip.

Skadi looked left and saw Stigr with his sword drawn, standing opposite Beowulf. His elderly body looked especially frail compared to the overwhelming stature of Beowulf. But there he was standing tall, protecting her.

"Stigr, what are you doing?"

"I thought you might need some help."

"You better get going," said Beowulf to Stigr. "I wish not to fight those who pose no threat. But if you stand in my way, I will take you down. This warning, I give you only once."

"Stigr," shouted Skadi, finally on her feet. "Go."

But he didn't budge. In fact, it appeared to Skadi that he became more resolved to do battle.

She shifted her attention to Beowulf who, while not ignoring Stigr, did not seem threatened by him either.

Skadi said. "Pay him no mind."

Beowulf glanced back at her and started to do as she had instructed. He shifted his attention away from Stigr and towards her.

"Skadi, let's take him together."

"Stigr, stay out of this," shouted Skadi.

Skadi put her fists in front of her chest and dropped one foot back. Beowulf grinned. He turned his back to Stigr and focused solely on Skadi.

"Show me you are not a disappointment. Show me you were deserving of the gift Yggdrasil granted you," he said. "You have this opportunity to prove yourself."

Beowulf charged towards her gracefully but with tremendous power. She met him blow for blow, recognizing finally how he opted to fight. She did her best to redirect his attacks, the way he did hers. But the advantage was still his. For every two strikes she parried, he landed a third. Every hit she attempted, he blocked. It was no use; within moments she was once again facing defeat.

Beowulf let out a deep sigh.

"You are strong. One day even, you may be able to best me but that is not this day. You'll make a great einherjar. See you in . . ."

He trailed off and blood splashed onto Skadi's face. She wiped it away quickly and saw Stigr had attempted to strike Beowulf while his back was to him. But Beowulf caught the sword in his left hand. He held it for a moment, letting his blood flow over his fingers and down the sword.

"You should have fled," Beowulf said calmly before snapping the blade.

Stigr stumbled forward due to the sudden jerk of the sword breaking. Skadi saw the look in Beowulf's eye as he observed the sword fragment still in his grasp. She lunged for him and attempted to grab his wrist as he moved to put the blade through Stigr's heart. But Beowulf, as Skadi knew all too well, was faster than her.

Time seemed to stand still for a moment as Skadi saw the life escape Stigr. She looked at him and mouthed the words "I'm sorry." She noticed Stigr pull the drawstring on a pouch attached to his waist and grey powder spilled out. Skadi quickly leapt over a table, turning it over as she did to protect herself from the explosion.

The blast rocked the very foundation of the cottage. Beams fell from the ceiling and stone crumbled. When the dust started to settle, Skadi stood up from behind the table. Stigr's remains were before her, ragged and charred, but Beowulf was gone.

Skadi poked her head out the door and looked in both directions for Beowulf. He was nowhere to be found. She turned back to the remains of Stigr.

"Your sacrifice will not be in vain," she whispered.

Skadi knelt and picked up Stigr's body and carried him outside. Beowulf was still nowhere to be found.

"What happened?" asked a passerby.

"This man gave his life for others. Would you see to it he is honored appropriately?"

The passerby who had come to investigate the explosion looked at the man in Skadi's arms.

"A pyre will need to be built," he said. "I will fetch others and we will see to it."

"Thank you," Skadi said.

As soon as the man left to find those who would help put Stigr's body to rest, she sat him down, then turned her attention to Heorot Hall.

TWENTY-ONE

DESTIN, FATHER OF SOLVEIG

20 Years Ago

Smoke filled the space, making it nearly impossible to breathe and the heat was almost unbearable. But Destin did not let those two things deter him. He wrapped his arms around his daughter, shielding her from the fire that raged around them. Though the smoke clouded his vision and burned his eyes, he could see clear enough that their only path out was blocked.

"Father, I'm scared," the girl shouted.

Destin pulled her tighter and kept both low to the ground, so the smoke did not fill their lungs. He regretted building a cottage so big. Had he exercised a bit more restraint, they would not have as great a distance to traverse to escape the fire and the beam blocking the door would not have been so hefty.

"It'll be ok," he assured his daughter. "We will get out of here."

But as soon as he said those words, flames leapt from the wall to her pelt. Destin quickly patted it but as soon as it was extinguished, more flames caught his own pelt. He patted that too, but the fire was encroaching faster and faster, and the smoke was thickening all around them.

"Father," shouted Solveig.

A banging on the front door shifted his attention away from his daughter.

"Destin. Solveig. Are you in there?" Shouted Hrothgar.

"We are, but the door is blocked, and I do not have my rune stones."

"I will fetch something to bust down the door."

The flames grew closer.

"Father," said the girl.

"It will be ok."

The fire continued to encroach and again took hold of the girl's pelt. Destin swatted at them, but they were spreading faster than before.

Then the banging returned, and the sharp end of an ax burst through the door. It quickly cut through the wooden beam blocking the door and Hrothgar crashed through, forehead drenched in sweat.

"Quickly now," he shouted.

Destin picked up his daughter and ran out into the cold Midgardian night. The shift in temperature was immediate and shocking. He fell to his knees as soon as he was clear of the flames; coughing up the smoke he had inhaled.

"Are you ok?" Hrothgar said resting a hand on Destin's shoulder.

"I'm fine. Daughter are you . . ." Destin said.

"I'm ok, Father," she said between coughing fits.

"How did this happen?" Hrothgar said.

Destin let go of his child so she could stand on her own then proceeded to stand up himself. He looked skyward.

"There was . . ."

"What?"

"A bolt of lightning," he said.

Hrothgar looked up.

"No storm clouds."

"It was him," said the child.

"We do not know that for sure," responded Destin.

"Father, you said it was a bolt of lightning."

"What reason would Thor have for striking us?" Destin said.

Hrothgar grabbed Destin's shoulder.

"He needs no reason, my friend. You remember."

"That was an accident."

"Does it matter?"

Destin looked past Hrothgar at his burning cottage and the smoke rising into the night sky. The home he built with his daughter and late wife was crumbling.

"Now will you help me?" Hrothgar said.

The sound of a beam cracking carried through the night air and the roof caved inward.

"I still don't know what you want me to do?"

"When you are ready, let us speak in private," Hrothgar said.

"I appreciate the help, but with her mother just passing and now our home in ashes I don't think I can give you what you need."

"Take tonight to get your affairs in order. But we must do something. This was their doing, and you know it," Hrothgar said.

Destin glanced at his daughter.

"Let us stay in Heorot Hall tonight and we shall talk in the morning."

"I would have had invited you stay either way. You are always welcome there."

Destin turned to his daughter. He knelt in front of her, and she looked up at him. He wiped soot from her face.

"I'm ok, Father," she whispered.

"Solveig, it is ok if you are not," he said.

She reached out and embraced him. He was struck by her empathy and hugged her back. Tears formed in his eyes.

"We are staying with Uncle Hrothgar tonight," he said.

Destin hardly slept that night. He stayed up remembering his wife and their life with Solveig in the cottage that just burned down. Solveig, he noticed, slept oddly sound despite all that had happened.

When Hrothgar knocked on the door, she was still asleep. Destin slipped out of the room without disturbing her.

"This idea of yours seems unnecessarily dangerous."

Hrothgar laughed.

"I am no fool, Destin. It is not as if I have not given this a lot of thought."

"Have you?"

"For years it is all I have thought about."

"I can't help you kill yourself. It'll mean all our doom, and Solveig is my priority."

"I would never ask you to do something that would endanger her."

Destin eyed his oldest friend for a moment. He remembered their youth and that fateful day at sea. "What is it you wish to speak about then?"

"I have traveled Midgard extensively in the past few years. Very few people I've met have impressed me as much as my oldest, living friend."

"I appreciate the flattery, but please get to the point."

"When we were kids, you began to study alchemy. And you study still."

"It requires a lot of time and patience to master."

"Most alchemists are glorified rune writers, but you are a truly skilled practitioner."

"Hrothgar, please get to the point."

"Sentient transmutation. Explain that to me again."

Destin shifted his feet uneasily. "Why do you want to know about this all of sudden?"

"I am curious."

"It is not a practice that should be taken lightly. It's powerful alchemy."

"How does it work?"

Destin paused before answering. He continued to eye his friend, looking for something. He couldn't quite tell what he was looking for, but he was uneasy with his friend's question. Nevertheless, he had no reason not explain the art to him.

"Alchemy is a relatively simple in terms of practice. We use a combination of advanced runic carvings and seidr magic to transform one material into another, otherwise known as transmutation. Wood can become stone. Iron can become gold."

"But what about sentient transmutation?"

"Sentient transmutation refers to a living, thinking creature turned into something else, usually another living creature. A dog can become a pig, or a rat can become a raven."

"What about something bigger?"

"How much bigger?"

"A small human. A dwarf. Can that be . . . transmuted?"

"Sentient transmutation is already taboo," said Destin.

"But it is something that can be done?"

"Why do you want to know?"

"Let's take a walk."

Destin looked back at the door to the room where Solveig was still asleep.

"We won't be gone long."

Hrothgar started to walk, and Destin reluctantly followed.

"I returned yesterday from my latest journey. It would seem I got back right in time too."

"Thank you for that. We owe you our lives."

"You don't owe me anything. I just want you to keep an open mind when I show you what I must show you."

"And what is that?"

"You'll see soon enough. We're almost there."

Hrothgar pushed open a door and led Destin down a dimly lit hallway before opening another door. Through the door, Destin saw the bars of a cell and the feet of a man chained up.

"Who is that?" Destin said stepping past Hrothgar.

The man looked up to see who had entered. But Destin saw that he had a sack over his head.

"What have you done?" Destin said.

Hrothgar let the door shut and walked over to the cell.

"Keep an open mind."

"It is open, but it looks as if you have taken someone prisoner. Who is this person?"

Destin turned to face the person in the cell. Second to the sack over the captive's head, he noticed the man was short in stature with stunted arms.

"Is this a dwarf?" Destin asked.

"Help me," said the man weakly.

"Destin, you were there that day that Vikings killed my father. The same day Thor and Jörmungandr battled and killed my mother. It was a rogue lightning strike from Thor's hammer that killed her. It was a lightning strike from that same hammer that destroyed your home last night. Thor wields the hammer, but do you know who made it?"

"Everyone knows . . . Eitri and his brother, Brokkr."

174

Hrothgar unlocked the cell and entered. He ripped the sack off the man's head, revealing the face of a bearded dwarf. He wore an eyepatch.

"Tell him your name," said Hrothgar coldly.

"Hrothgar, this is too much. What is going on?" asked Destin.

"Tell him . . . who you are," Hrothgar repeated himself.

"Brokkr. Brother of Eitri. Please help me."

Destin turned to Hrothgar with fear, shock, and disappointment.

"What are you doing?" said Destin. "You can't keep this man locked up like this."

"He and his brother made Mjolnir."

"And it is Thor who wields it."

"Destin," said Hrothgar getting close to him. "This dwarf knew what he was doing when he forged that weapon."

"Why have you locked him up?"

"That's where you come in my friend."

A few days later

Destin wiped the sweat from his brow, having finished hammering a nail through a support beam in the cottage he was building.

"Solveig, would you hand me the flagon?" said Destin.

Moments later the flagon appeared by his side.

"Thank you," he said without looking up.

"You're welcome," Hrothgar said.

Destin turned around and stood up.

"What are you doing here?"

"Why bother with a hammer and nail? Can't you just transmute it?"

"Doing things slowly makes it more meaningful."

"Have you thought about what I said?"

"Hrothgar, I am sorry you lost your mother and father. Truly I am. But alchemy is not to be used in this manner. This is not what I committed years of my life to. I'm mad that Thor's actions cause such destruction, but I will not be an accomplice in your quest for vengeance."

"Is it a quest for vengeance when the outcome you seek to achieve is noble?"

"Solveig," said Destin shifting his attention beyond Hrothgar to his daughter. "We're done for now. Let's go prepare for dinner."

"Ok, Father," she said.

Destin attempted to move past Hrothgar but was stopped by a hand on his chest.

"Let me go," he said.

"I am giving you a chance to be on the right side of history."

"I am doing the same for you, my old friend."

With that, Destin followed his daughter, leaving Hrothgar alone.

TWENTY-TWO

CAUGHT

Bergljot's feet ached, her legs burned, and her back was unbearably sore. But she would not put down the child, who only hours ago lost her parents. The young girl was asleep and Bergljot had no intention of disturbing her semblance of peace.

The path to Fensalir was hardly clear and the overgrown brush made it difficult to navigate, but as the sun inched its way into the sky, Bergljot and the children who followed her were able to move at a quicker pace. She could sense that morale was waning, even as freedom seemed within their grasp.

Bergljot looked down and saw their faces were dirty and sorrowful. She considered saying something to lift the spirts of all but feared disturbing the girl's sleep. Besides, what was there to say?

Just as she was about to decide, something caught her attention. It was the loud crack of a tree snapping at its base. She of course was not the only one who noticed—all did. The group looked around to face whatever it was that felled the tree far off in the distance.

Hege's heart felt like it would beat through her chest. She knew his face immediately, having seen him before making his rounds on horseback to ensure his road was being constructed according to his timeline. Though he looked younger, there was no mistaking him. She also knew the type of punishment he preferred. He was one that liked to make public examples of people. What she did not know was how he had become so powerful that his mere arrival felled a tree and kicked up a fearsome dust storm that blew over her and her entire group.

"Come forth now, she who leads this rebellion," said Hrothgar.

There was whispering throughout the group. Hege's heart continued to race and to her shame, her feet felt heavy like iron.

"Show thyself or suffer the deaths of all these people."

The fear that gripped her let go.

"It's me," shouted Hege, stepping forward. "I am the one who spurred this on."

She walked forward through the crowd towards Hrothgar. But as she progressed, one man grabbed her arm. She tried to pull away, but he looked at her and shook his head. Another man stepped in front of her. One by one, the people she was leading started to block her from confronting Hrothgar.

"He will have to go through me."

"And me," said another.

"Me too."

"Don't throw away your lives for me," insisted Hege.

"We are not scared."

"You should heed her advice," said Hrothgar. "There is much to be fearful of."

"I will be ok," whispered Hege.

"We're not going to let him have you," a woman said.

Hrothgar laughed.

"My patience has run out."

"There is not one of us who cares," shouted one of the people who stood between Hrothgar and Hege. "We will no longer work your mine or build your road. Those days are over."

"That I am certain of."

Hege felt a lump in her throat as blood and skull fragments sprayed over her face, painting her in a crimson red. The body of the man nearest her quickly dropped to the ground. Standing only inches away was Hrothgar with his hands clasped together, covered in the man's blood.

In a moment of shock, Hege didn't move. Hrothgar looked at her with his piercing eyes, then she stumbled and fell backwards. It had happened so fast; she could not register it. Hege turned her attention to the headless body of the man who had stopped her. Blood spilled out from his neck and pooled at her feet. She scrambled backwards.

The carnage did not stop with one. Hege could barely follow him with her eyes as Hrothgar tore through the group of people she was leading to Fensalir. One by one he eviscerated them. It was as if the ground parted and swallowed them up entirely. One man he threw into the air, not to be seen again. Another he wrapped around a large tree. No one was spared—all were all slain without mercy. When it was over, Hege and Hrothgar were alone amongst the dead.

"What have . . . what have you done?" she said, her whole body shaking.

"Perhaps their lives were miserable, but at least they were theirs to live. It was you who led them to their doom."

Hege was shaking from head to toe. She turned her head slowly to take in the massacre that happened as a blur before her eyes. The soil was soaked with blood. Bodies were broken and mutilated.

"Their deaths were quick. Yours will not be."

In an instant, Hrothgar was standing right before Hege. She tried to step back but he grabbed her by the arm.

"You will be made an example of for the people of Lejre."

With a thunderous boom, Hege and Hrothgar were gone.

Bergljot heard the boom as she neared the clearing left behind by Hrothgar's slaughter. She saw the red on the ground and knew immediately what she was looking at.

"Stop," she said to the children with her.

She woke the girl she carried on her back and placed her on the ground.

"Stay here," Bergljot said.

She ran ahead of the group and nearly fell over when she saw the massacre left behind. Bergljot put her hand to her mouth and gasped.

"How could . . ."

She scanned the bodies one by one in search of Hege.

"Who . . . what could have done this?"

"What happened?" said the young girl Bergljot had been carrying.
Bergljot ran back to her and grabbed the child.

"You should not see this," she said.

"Is everyone dead?"

Bergljot looked back, knowing she had not found Hege's body.

"Children, keep an eye on where you are stepping. We must go off the path for a while."

Bergljot grabbed the girl's hand and guided the children into the trees so that they could avoid the massacre.

"What happened?" one child shouted.

"Just keep following me," said Bergljot.

Not before long they had reached the other side of the clearing and were continuing to Fensalir along the path they had set for themselves. Bergljot made sure to account for all the children she had with her and when she was confident none had strayed, she let out a deep sigh.

"Hege, I will make sure these children get to Fensalir," she whispered. "I swear on my life I will."

Skadi spied the entrance she once used to enter Heorot Hall, but it was protected by two guards. One was a massive creature, even by Skadi's standard and the other was a slim woman.

Skadi hung back and observed the two guards for a moment, debating in her head how to approach. Was it better to barge through or should she be slyer? She gripped her sword and considered the scenario. To the left of the entrance was a stable. Skadi could hear the neighing of horses.

When neither of the guards were looking the way of the stable, Skadi slipped inside. There were three horses—each seemed to be well maintained and cared for. Perhaps they were the prized possession of a wealthy Lejrian. Skadi opened the gates, keeping each horse and maneuvered the creatures towards the front of the stable. She poked her head through the door and saw the guards were still there, then unhatched the main gate. She moved back to the way she entered the stable on the other side and poked her head out from that end. The guards were idling about. She picked up a midsize stone and held it for a moment before throwing it at the horses with all her might. It hit one of the horses on the buttocks and the beast reared its legs and bursts through the main gate. The other two horses followed suit.

Skadi watched as the two guards panicked and ran after the horses, then quickly slipped into the tunnel. As she was making her way, thinking she had gone unseen, she heard the voice of a woman call out to her. She looked back and saw the slim woman. But then the woman disappeared. Skadi did not like what that implied. But she chose not to focus on the strange behavior of the woman and headed towards the original forge she and Egil discovered earlier in the morning. Within moments, she was once again in the room that belonged to Eitri the Dwarf. Nothing had changed since she was last there. The room remained vacant.

She made for the desk where she and Egil found the scrolls with clues to the secret forge.

"If they could steal my power then there must be a way to steal it back," she thought.

Skadi opened drawer after drawer but found nothing. There were no other scrolls or clues of any kind as far as she could tell. Skadi closed the last drawer and stood up straight. She looked around the room. There was a cot against the wall. She took a seat.

"Thor killed Brokkr, so Eitri chose to work for Hrothgar? Why would Thor kill one of the greatest blacksmiths in all the realms? That doesn't make sense even for a bastard god. And even if it were true, why would Eitri commit his skills to a human? Why not another dwarf? Why serve Midgard when his own realm could use his talents?"

Skadi looked up at the ceiling. There was the mural of the realms. At the top was Midgard where normally Asgard would be located. Next to the out-of-place Midgard was Nidavellir where Vanaheim would normally be.

Skadi stood up to get a closer look. All the realms were out of place and those that were normally near the roots of the World Tree, like Svartalfheim, were shifted higher to the top, and noticeably, Asgard was missing entirely.

"Eight realms," whispered Skadi.

TWENTY-THREE

OLD MEN

20 Years Ago

Destin finished writing down his thoughts, tucked the scroll in a chest, and put the chest in the corner. He proceeded to open the hatch in the floor and climb down into the room he shared with his daughter. The smell of stew permeated the space.

Later, as he and Solveig finished eating, he turned to his daughter.

"I want to talk to you about something," he said.

"What, Father?"

He hesitated. "How are you?"

A look of confusion spread across her face.

"Ok," she answered.

"A lot has happened as of late. Sometimes people feel sad when those things happen."

"Mother is still with us. She watches out for us from the halls of Valhalla."

"And we are better off for having her watch out for us," said Destin.

"Father, are you ok?"

Destin was shocked at how mature his daughter seemed. He sat back in his chair and wrestled with the question.

"I want to be," he answered truthfully.

"You do not need to worry about me, Father. I am ok. I swear it."

Destin thought for a moment about what his daughter said.

"I fear it is no longer safe here."

"But we live in Heorot Hall," she said.

"Precisely my concern."

He could see that Solveig was confused, and he was not sure how much detail he should share with his daughter.

Destin paused for a moment before continuing.

"Did your mother ever tell you of her dreams of seeing the rest of Midgard? The lands beyond the mainland."

Solveig nodded.

"I want to do that with you."

Destin saw his daughter shift her gaze away from him when he said that.

"But . . ."

"What, Solveig?"

She delayed her response.

"Tell me, daughter."

"Father, I want to stay here."

He observed his daughter. She looked more and more like her mother with each passing day.

"I do not trust Hrothgar," he said plainly. "I think he is dangerous, and I want you to be safe."

She looked at him curiously.

"I love Uncle Hrothgar."

Destin stood up and moved from his side of the table to be closer to his daughter.

"I love him, too."

"Then how can you not trust him?"

"It is complicated."

"What about Egil? Do you feel the same about him?"

"Egil takes after his mother."

"Father, I do not want to leave. What about the cottage you are rebuilding . . . we can't just . . ."

"It is just one building."

"Father, Uncle Hrothgar is good to us. He can be fun to play with. I do not want to go."

Destin pinched the bridge of his nose. Solveig got up from the table.

"I know you miss Mother, and our home burning was scary, but please, Father I want to stay. Egil is my friend, and this was Mother's home. I am not ready to leave yet."

"But . . ."

He looked at his daughter with her pleading eyes. Destin took in a deep breath and let out a long sigh.

"Where would we even go?" she asked. "What lands are beyond the mainland?"

"We would figure it out. The Geatland. Northumbria. Anywhere. I once heard tales of a land with a monkey king and a dragon prince. I don't even know what a monkey is, but would that not be fascinating to see?"

"Father, let's stay. If you don't trust Uncle Hrothgar confront him about it. Let us not run."

Destin sighed again.

"If we are not to flee then I think it is time you learn alchemy. I need to know you will be safe."

Solveig smiled and removed a rune stone from her pelt. She placed it on the table in front of Destin.

He took the stone into his hand and inspected it.

"What's this?"

"I have been practicing," Solveig said.

"You carved your name in it too. When have you been practicing? Where have you been practicing?"

"You're not mad, are you?"

"Quite the opposite, actually. But runes can be dangerous."

"I've been careful."

Destin handed the rune stone back to his daughter.

"Your mother would be so proud."

"You are too?" she asked.

"Of course, I am. We are going to start your formal training tomorrow."

A Few Days Later

Destin stood back as Solveig used her rune stone to transform the stump of a tree into iron ore, something he had not learned to do until twice her age. He knelt to be at eye-level with Solveig.

"My parents used to call me a prodigy, but daughter, you are something else entirely," he said.

"Thank you, Father."

"She really is special," said Hrothgar, stepping out from the edge of the tree line.

Hrothgar stood up and positioned himself in front of Solveig.

"How long were you watching us?" he asked.

"Long enough to see this skill runs in the family," Hrothgar said.

"This is a private moment, Hrothgar. You should not be here."

"Isn't that a bit cold for an old friend who is letting you live in his hall while you rebuild your home?"

"Father, it is ok if Uncle Hrothgar watches us practice. I don't mind."

"See, Destin. Your daughter is ok with me observing."

Hrothgar stepped a bit closer. "What are you doing here?"

"Have you given any more thought to what we discussed?"

"The answer remains no."

Hrothgar didn't immediately respond and simply let the quiet fill the void.

Then he nodded and whispered, "Very well."

"Hrothgar, you should consider turning away from this path. You will only destroy yourself and those you love."

"Those I love are gone, my friend."

"You still have Egil and Wealhtheow."

"Solveig, when you are ready to truly master the craft of alchemy let me know. In my travels I have learned of a land where instead of snow there is sand, and the alchemists are so skilled that it is rumored even elves consult with men," said Hrothgar to Solveig.

"Do not talk to her," Destin said sternly.

Hrothgar turned on his heal and began to walk away. Destin reached out and grabbed him by the shoulder.

"Seek peace in your heart and let this go," said Destin.

Hrothgar did not respond. He simply grabbed Destin's hand and removed it from his shoulder. Destin watched his *friend* disappear into the trees.

"What was that about, Father?" asked Solveig.

Destin faced his daughter.

"Your uncle is troubled. Pay him no mind and think not of what he says."

That night as Destin wrapped up working on rebuilding his cottage for the day, he took a moment to look up at the sky and ponder his years in Lejre. He thought about his wife, the time they spent together, and his parents who passed of old age shortly after finally arriving in Lejre years after him. He was happy they got to meet Solveig, though. He thought about his *friend* Hrothgar who, despite his best efforts, had grown angrier and angrier over the years.

The snap of a tree branch drew his attention away from his memories. He put a hand on the hilt of a knife he carried with him.

"Who's there?" he said.

There was no response. Destin looked in all directions but saw no one. He started to ease his grip on the knife, but just as he did, he saw a single man in a grey pelt step before him. He did not recognize the man, but he had his sword drawn.

"What is this?" Destin said. "Who are you?"

The man said nothing. He only stepped closer to Destin. Destin lifted his knife to defend himself. Then from the corner of his eye, he noticed a second man approaching with his sword drawn.

"I'll give you each a chance to rethink this," warned Destin.

There was no reply. Each man raised their sword to strike. Quickly, Destin pulled a rune from his pelt and as the first sword came down to make a killing blow, he deflected with the rune in his hand and the sword crumbled. The second sword fared no better and crumbled upon touching the rune. Each of the aggressors looked extremely confused.

"Give up," threatened Destin.

Destin was outnumbered, but with his alchemy he had the advantage. This was clear to the two men who stood before him. But he should have paid closer attention to all his surroundings.

"I wish we could have become old men together."

TWENTY-FOUR

OLD SCROLLS

Skadi inspected the eight-realm World Tree mural on the ceiling of the room and spotted a tiny latch, hidden behind one of the branches. She scanned the room for a way to reach the latch and decided to flip the bed back upright. Skadi stood on it, reached up, and pulled the mural back, revealing three hinges.

She flicked open the latch and the door opened. Stale air rushed out making Skadi wince. She stood on the tip of her toes and poked her head through the opening. It was dark and the smell of stale air was strong. Quickly, she dropped to the ground and grabbed a torch from the wall before returning to the opening in the ceiling. She lifted the torch first and climbed through the hatch.

It took a moment for her eyes to adjust, but once they did, she saw that it was a sparse, cobweb-infested room. She scanned it and nothing stood out. It was not until her second scan, however, that a glimmer reflecting off the light of the torch caught her eye. She climbed into the room fully and moved towards the glimmer. It was a small chest.

Skadi snapped the lock and opened the chest. A cloud of dust puffed out from within. When the dust cleared, she found scrolls. Skadi picked up the one nearest the top and delicately unrolled it.

"Hrothgar will not let it be. I fear for my safety. I fear for Solveig's safety. He is unhinged and Brokkr is not long for this realm. Sentient transmutation is not to be used this way. I have told him this, but he refuses to listen. Solveig, if you are reading this, know that I love you," Skadi said reading the scroll out loud.

She put the fragile paper down and considered what she read.

Skadi reached beyond the top scrolls and pulled the one at the bottom of the chest, assuming the earlier scrolls were buried. She unrolled it and started to read.

"It was my parent's idea that I come to Lejre. They said I needed to . . ." Skadi said, reading out loud. "They said I needed to see more of Midgard and that I was too sheltered. They thought it was a good idea I travel with my friend Hrothgar and his parents. My parents will never admit this, but I know they are jealous of his parent's wealth. I hope they know alchemy is worth more than gold ever will be."

Skadi sat the scroll down next to her.

"Who wrote these?" she whispered.

She picked up another scroll.

"We just barely made it. Had it not been for those mead merchants we would have been lost forever," she said, reading the scroll. "I'm worried he'll never be ok again. I am not proud of myself for this, but even though Hrothgar lost everything, I still cannot believe we saw Thor. From what I could see, he really does have a red beard."

Skadi skimmed the remainder of the scroll. There was nothing else of note and she sat it down. She grabbed another scroll.

"I hate to admit this, but my parents were right. Moving here has helped quite a bit. My alchemy has never been better. I finally turned wood into iron. I had no one to share the moment with though. Hrothgar could not be bothered. He is about to become the next Earl of this town. I'm sure he is busy. The old guy likes him. I should probably start looking for a wife. I will be of age soon. I can't keep coming back here by myself."

Skadi sat the scroll down.

"This was his room," she whispered.

She quickly grabbed another scroll.

"We had a girl. I cannot thank the gods enough for blessing us with a healthy child. Her name is Solveig. It means *from the house of strength*. I know she will be strong one day. Hrothgar's son, Egil, will now have a friend. Hrothgar does not seem to be as angry as he once was. Perhaps having a child will change me too. I do feel more hopeful."

Skadi put the scroll to her side.

"This is Solveig's father."

She grabbed the next scroll in the chest.

"My beloved passed away today. It is now just Solveig and me. I am worried about her. She is a smart girl, but she has pulled away. I wonder if there is a way, we can reconnect. Hrothgar is never around. He spends much of his time traveling Midgard. He is supposed to be the Earl of this town, but I fear he wants more. I could use a friend now, but I feel so alone. I wish Solveig would just tell me how she is feeling. At least she has Egil."

Skadi put the scroll down. There was nothing left on the page. She reached into the chest and pulled out the next one. She was reaching the bottom of the chest and only a few scrolls remained.

"Hrothgar has gone too far. I thought he would find peace, but he has only grown more detached. He asked me to do something today I have no desire to do. Alchemy is supposed to be a tool to help people. Where did he even find the dwarf? Does he have a means for realm travel or are there dwarves here in Midgard? Why has Hrothgar become such a mystery? And why would he propose such a horrible thing?"

That was all that was written, and Skadi put the final scroll atop the pile to her side. She peaked back in the chest to be sure there was nothing else and there wasn't.

Skadi ran her fingers through her hair and stared at the pile of scrolls she had just read.

"Solveig's father feared Hrothgar was going to do something to Brokkr," whispered Skadi. "The brother of Eitri was here?"

At that moment, she heard footsteps and scrambled to close the hatch. She placed her ear to the floor. The footsteps grew louder as they neared.

"We have to find her," said Beowulf. "That guard said she reentered the tunnels."

"How did she escape you?" said Hovard. "Are you not the killer you claim to be?"

"Hrothgar would not have sent for me if he trusted you to complete this task."

"Why would a king journey to the mainland to take orders from an Earl?"

Skadi heard the two men arguing and kept as still as possible. Hopefully they would pass soon enough.

"You have known him for years. What does he seek to achieve here?" Hovard said. "Tell me honestly. Why would you do his bidding?"

"I do no bidding," Beowulf said quietly.

Skadi heard their footsteps come to a stop right below her. She could feel her heart beating so fast, she was almost convinced they could hear it. The few moments of silence from them felt like a lifetime. But then she heard the magic words.

"She isn't here. Let's keep searching."

Skadi waited a while longer until she was confident the men were gone before moving again. She lifted her torch and scanned the remainder of the secret compartment and spied a second chest. With hopes that there would be more scrolls, providing greater insights into the happenings in Lejre, she opened it. There were no scrolls, but there was a stone with rune carvings and a name.

"Solveig," she whispered.

Solveig patted Egil on the head before turning to Eitri.

"I never would have thought in my wildest dreams that I would see humans possess such power," Eitri said.

"Can he be turned back?" Mimir asked.

Solveig ignored Mimir's question. Instead, she turned to Eitri. "Where are we on Hrothgar's weapons? And what about the armor?"

"I have finished the models. But if we want to make all we need, we'll need to begin transporting a regular supply of ore from Bard Mine. You know this."

"Show me the models."

Eitri disappeared from the room and a moment later returned carrying a shining sword. He placed it on a table in front of Solveig.

"I have named it Hrunting. It shall not fail the hand that hefts it in battle."

Solveig picked up the sword and held it high to inspect it in the full light of the burning torches.

"Your mastery as a blacksmith is unmatched, Eitri."

"It was only possible because of your alchemic refinement of the ore."

"Now show me the armor."

Eitri placed golden chainmail on the table as Solveig sat the sword down. She proceeded to pick up the chainmail and similarly hold it up to the light of the torch.

"This I call the Golden Coat of Chainmail. I took inspiration from chainmail I once witnessed in Fafnir's treasure hall in Nidavellir. It is impenetrable."

"And what of the final piece?"

"Just a moment."

Eitri exited again and seconds later returned with a shield. He sat it next to the chainmail and the sword.

"It is named Svalinn. A shield before the shining god. Mountains and seas would be set in flames if it fell from before the sun."

Solveig touched the shield. It was smooth, save for the ornate runic carvings around it.

"No sword or ax shall break it," added Eitri.

"You have done well, dwarf," Solveig said.

"One man or woman wielding Hrunting and Svalinn while wearing the Golden Coat of Chainman shall be as if they are of the immortal gods. When we have produced enough for an army, the realms will shake."

"Your plan is doomed to fail. Thor destroyed Nyköping for doing just this. Do you not think he will do the same here?" Mimir shouted.

"Let him try," said Solveig.

TWENTY-FIVE

TIME FOR AN EXECUTION

Everything was a blur as her captor sped through the dense forest that populated the furthest reaches of Midgard. She gasped for air, only taking in a portion of what she needed. Hege batted against Hrothgar's grip, but it was to no avail. Not only was he fast, but he had also become impossibly strong.

"Let. Me. Be free," shouted Hege, slamming her fists against Hrothgar's stomach and chest.

He ignored her and picked up the pace. Hege turned her head in the direction they were running. Though everything to the side was a blur, she could make out directly ahead the walls of Lejre in the distance.

"No," she shouted.

Skadi stuck to the shadows of Lejre as she navigated her way towards the cottage with the sign of the Valkyrie. In her hand was the rune with Solveig's name carved into it and tucked under her arm were the scrolls she found. She took care not to be spotted by any guards and to certainly to not be spotted by Beowulf or Hovard.

The town was completely awake. The people were busy going about their routines. It was the first time since she arrived that she fully appreciated, or at least recognized the town for what it was—the most densely populated settlement in mainland Midgard—far different than Fensalir and nothing like the nomadic lifestyle she still considered to be her norm.

Skadi stood with her back to the wall of a storehouse and peaked around the corner. The cottage with the Valkyrie sign was only a few feet away and just beyond that the entrance to the underground forge. She looked around to make sure she was in the clear. No guards, no Beowulf, no Hovard. Skadi was about to move but then . . .

"What are you doing?"

Skadi didn't recognize the voice and turned to face someone who resembled a shopkeeper.

"You're the one they're looking for," said the man.

She was caught but by who?

"Don't move," said the *shopkeeper*.

Then it occurred to Skadi. Stigr had warned her of the guards who dressed as regular people.

Skadi put up a hand.

She whispered. "I am not the person they seek. You are mistaken."

The man did not go for a sword, but rather a small pouch that he tore open and threw on the ground. It combusts and white smoke rose from the ground. Skadi attempted to smother the smoke with her foot, but the scattered powder only spaced out the rising white smoke and as it crested over the nearby cottage, the sounds of footsteps could be heard nearing.

"I don't know what you hoped to achieve here, but this is Hrothgar's town," said the guard.

Skadi put her hand on the hilt of Ridill. The guard placed a hand on his knife.

"We have you surrounded."

Multiple guards turned the corner with swords drawn. Skadi unsheathed Ridill and stood her ground. A stillness washed over them all.

"I am going to warn you all once. Leave me be," Skadi said sternly.

The warning did not land. The guard nearest her attacked. He was fast, skilled, but for Skadi he was no match. She made short work of him, striking him down swiftly. A second guard attempted, but the results were the same. Then again, a third guard tried, but still no ground was made. But it was after the third, that the remaining guards wised up and started attacking in pairs, then as the entire group. But Skadi, even without the power of Yggdrasil was a force to be reckoned with and kept all attackers at bay.

"Try as you might, your efforts make no difference," she said.

"But they do," said Hovard, who appeared alongside Beowulf as Skadi defeated the final guard.

She stepped back and put her sword up in a defensive position.

"Enough," said Hovard raising his one good hand towards her, flame forming in the palm. "What is it you are still fighting for?"

"Uncle, are you blind to what is happening here?" Shouted Skadi.

Hovard kept his hand directed at Skadi.

Beowulf looked at Hovard from the corner of his eyes.

"Kill her," Beowulf said.

"Uncle, listen," Skadi said. "A scheme has been unfolding here for years, going back many decades. We have been drawn into that scheme."

"Why are you entertaining this?" Beowulf said to Hovard. "Is she not the one who killed your boy? Kill her."

"Beowulf, this concerns you too. Your friend, the Earl, has manipulated you. You like to fight. He knows that."

"Hovard, I am giving you an opportunity to do what I came here to do because I know you need this. But if you do not act now then the task will fall upon me. Decide."

Skadi looked at Hovard. She watched his eyes dance between Beowulf and herself. The moment of indecision felt like forever, even if it were just seconds.

"I was reminded recently that I loved you once. Your life is not mine to take," he whispered and lowered his hand.

"Then I shall do what I have set forth to do," Beowulf said.

Skadi looked at Hovard and he turned away from her gaze. She shifted her attention to Beowulf.

"On more than one occasion we have battled and more than once you have evaded defeat by sheer luck. That shall not happen a third time," Beowulf said.

"You're right," she said and sheathed her sword.

Beowulf looked at her curiously.

She held up the runic-covered stone she discovered above Eitri's room.

"What is that?" said Beowulf.

Hovard's attention shifted back to Skadi.

"This is the tool of an alchemist," she said. "A powerful one. Solveig."

"This concerns me why?" Beowulf said. "You're no alchemist."

"But I know how to use this," she lied. "Strength is easy to overcome. Seidr magic, such as this, is different."

Beowulf hesitated. He knew the ramifications of alchemy. He had been around long enough to see its devastating effects in the hands of the skilled and unskilled alike.

"Where did you find that?" he said.

"Uncle, help me stop them," said Skadi.

"You stay where you are," said Beowulf to Hovard.

Skadi noticed Hovard look disapprovingly at Beowulf.

"Speak to me in that tone again and you will regret it," Hovard said plainly.

"Easy," Beowulf said.

"I am not of the Geatland. I do not serve you. I do not serve anyone. I live to be free, and I have been a slave to my anger for too long."

Flames formed in Hovard's palm, and Skadi noticed for the first time, Beowulf shifted towards a more defensive stance, directed at Hovard. She used what she thought was a distraction to step backward.

"Do not go anywhere," said Beowulf, his eyes on Hovard, but his attention still on her. "Nothing has changed."

Skadi froze. There was a stillness all around them with a tension ready to be cut.

"The gift the jötunn granted you is waning, and I am the most skilled warrior you'll ever meet. Do you want to take that risk?" Beowulf said to Hovard.

Skadi's eyes darted back and forth between her uncle Hovard and Beowulf, King of the Geats. She wanted to leave but knew there was nowhere for her to go. Whatever was going to happen, was going to happen with her present.

The flames swirled in Hovard's palm. They were captivating to watch. But Beowulf was unflinching. He had no gifts granted to him by a jötunn or god, and yet he did not appear to be intimidated.

"Either attack me or put that hand down so we can move forward with why we are here," Beowulf said.

Skadi attempted another step backward.

"What did I say?" Beowulf said.

The flames in Hovard's palm erupted so that they consumed his entire arm. Skadi could feel the warmth wash over her even as far away as she was. And then the fire was gone and Hovard dropped his hand to his side.

"There is still some wisdom in you," insisted Beowulf.

Skadi couldn't believe what she just witnessed and shifted entirely towards Beowulf. She held up the rune stone just as before.

"You must be trained as a rune writer or as an alchemist to properly wield runes," said Beowulf. "Otherwise, you risk outcomes you could not anticipate. Have you made peace with the gods you worship?"

"Hrothgar has stolen the power of Yggdrasil for himself and yet you think I am unworthy," said Skadi. "You are a king in your land. Do not do this man's bidding."

Beowulf was quiet for a moment and glanced at the ground.

"You know what she speaks to be true," said Hovard. "You are a great warrior. A proud king. And yet here you are like me, engaged in another man's quest for power that will not benefit you or your people."

"All will serve Hrothgar in the world he seeks to create. The Geatland will not be spared," added Skadi.

"Is that so?" said Solveig, having exited the underground forge. Beside her was the dog Egil had become.

Skadi turned her attention to Solveig.

"Where is Egil?" Skadi asked.

"You have reasoned that it was your uncle who suggested we invite you to Lejre?" Solveig asked.

"I have," answered Skadi looking towards her uncle.

"I was angry. I still am," he said.

Skadi shook her head with disappointment.

"He presented us with a way to test our work, but your presence in Lejre is long overstayed," said Solveig. "Why is she not dead?"

Beowulf repositioned himself to strike. Even Hovard, who seemed to have been waning in drive, stood up straighter. Skadi knew if they attacked, she was done for.

Skadi once again held up the rune stone, but instead of leveraging it as a threat, she held it so Solveig could see the name carved into the side.

"Where did you find that?" said Solveig.

"Within Heorot Hall," she said. "The same place I found these scrolls."

Solveig hesitated for a moment before approaching Skadi. Skadi handed her the scrolls.

"It reads of you as a child," said Skadi.

Solveig started to read each scroll.

"This is my . . . father's handwriting."

Skadi was quiet while Solveig read. She could see the expression on Solveig's face softening.

"These scrolls read of your past . . . of Lejre's past."

Solveig looked up from the scrolls.

"What is not written is just as telling," Skadi said.

"The dwarf is Brokkr," Solveig whispered.

"What of Brokkr?" said Beowulf.

"He was a captive," Skadi answered.

"Does Eitri know this?" Solveig asked rhetorically.

"Beowulf, do you know something?" Skadi asked.

He did not respond but rather looked away from the group.

"What happened to Brokkr?" Solveig insisted.

Just then, a loud boom carried across Lejre, capturing the attention of Skadi, Beowulf, Hovard, and Solveig.

"What now?" Skadi whispered.

She then heard the unmistakable voice of the Earl.

"Gather, Lejre. It has been too long since we had an execution."

TWENTY-SIX

HROTHGAR THE PONTIFICATOR

Hege attempted to resist Hrothgar as he shackled iron chains around her wrists and ankles, locking her in place on her knees. Her attempts at freedom were to no avail. Hrothgar and the iron chains were too strong to resist.

Hege looked in every direction as a crowd formed in the town common around the stage on which she found herself. There was so much chatter that it created a constant buzzing. Sweat formed on her forehead as she anticipated what would happen next.

Hrothgar was to her right and slightly in front of her. He was watching the crowd grow and Hege could see from her angle, the edges of a sinister smile pulling at his lips.

"The funny thing is the road was near completion. You would have all been set free soon."

"No, we would not have."

Hrothgar looked back at her.

"But at least those poor souls would still be alive."

Hege looked behind her as the crowd grew larger and larger. It was as if all had stopped what they were doing to see what was about to happen. Mothers, fathers, sons, and daughters were making their way into the common.

"Gather round," Hrothgar announced. "All shall bear witness."

"You could be helping these people, but instead you enslave them."

"Do you see slaves amongst these people?" Whispered Hrothgar.

"All I see is a small man with an ego."

"That is because your perspective is small."

"My perspective is that of the people."

"The gods see mortals as things in the background—bugs to be crushed under their boots."

"Is that what this about?"

"It is the only thing that matters. I am not a villain. I am just willing to do what must be done at all cost."

"But it is not you who pays this cost. It is us. You are just a tyrant who is capable only of what others have enabled," Hege said.

"You have no idea what I am capable of, but you will know soon."

Skadi watched the people of Lejre flow past her towards the town common. They paid no attention to her, Solveig, Beowulf, or Hovard. Their attention was solely on the commotion in the center of town.

Skadi noticed that Hrothgar's arrival and subsequent announcement caught the attention of Beowulf, Solveig, and Hovard as well. None were looking her way, but rather in the direction of the common.

Hovard was the first to start following the crowd. He broke away from the group without uttering a word and moved towards the common and disappeared around the corner.

The dog that was Egil started to howl.

"Shut your mouth," Solveig snapped.

He quieted immediately.

"Beowulf, what do you know about Brokkr?" said Skadi returning to the conversation right before Hrothgar's arrival.

"I . . ."

She could see something changed in him. His demeanor had shifted.

"Tell us," Skadi said. "What is Hrothgar hiding?"

Beowulf did not answer.

She turned her attention to Solveig.

"This belonged to you," Skadi said tossing the rune stone to Solveig. "Your name is carved into it."

"I made this when I was just a girl," whispered Solveig. "My father was so proud."

"Help me stop Hrothgar," Skadi said.

"I can't," she said.

"You can. Nothing that has been done that cannot be undone."

Solveig looked down at Egil the dog.

"It is too late," whispered Solveig.

"There is no justice here," Hege shouted.

"Quiet yourself," he whispered as he gagged her with a torn piece of pelt that he tied behind her head.

Hege's muffled protests went ignored as Hrothgar turned his attention to the crowd. She tried to pull against her bondage, but her efforts bore no fruit. As she came to terms with the fact that the end of her life was nigh, she thought about Bergljot and hoped that she and the children were making their way to Fensalir safely. She was glad they split the children from the rest of the group. At least they would survive.

"Look at this woman, people of Lejre."

The thoughts of Bergljot and the children faded, and Hege was brought back to the present.

"She would see the peace of this town disrupted. She would see your lives upended for her own selfish reasoning. She would see the walls that protect this town from the undesirables of Midgard torn down."

The chatter amongst the crowd softened as Hrothgar spoke.

"I ask you, when was the last troll attack? Have we suffered the atrocities of a jötunn like those in Fensalir? Do we live in squalor like the raiders who pillage for measly gains in the outskirts of Midgard? No. Because in this battle, we have fought for the peace of Midgard. A peace that you . . . the people of Lejre have achieved. You have sacrificed for Lejre and for Midgard, and those sacrifices have made our town more secure."

The crowd cheered at Hrothgar's words.

"The gains we have made to a secure town for the people of Midgard is a victory in a war that began two hundred years ago in Nyköping. Rogue gods with a hateful ideology gave the people of Midgard a glimpse of their ambitions. By seeking to turn our settlements into killing fields, the gods that attacked that day thought they could break our resolve. But we persevered. This town. You folks. We are proof of that perseverance and the resolve that we humans have."

The crowd cheered even louder. Hege could not believe it. She wondered if these people knew the atrocities that those who worked the road and the mine dealt with regularly.

"Any god or person involved in committing or planning an attack against the people of Lejre becomes a target of our collective swords. The enemies of Lejre and Midgard are not idle, and neither are we. I have taken measures unlike Midgard has ever seen to defend our town and I will hunt down all enemies of Lejre."

The crowd continued to erupt in raucous cheer.

"I do not know the day of final victory, but we have seen the turning of the tide. To those who would do us harm, I say your cause is lost."

Hrothgar looked down at Hege. The crowd was unruly now. People were hooting and hollering at his words. Hege was in disbelief. If only they knew the truth.

"When my dear wife, Wealhtheow, died at the hands of raiders, I made a personal decision that I would not let that happen to anyone else under my watch. My focus has always been you, the people of Lejre and the people of Midgard."

The crowd grew even louder.

"Long live the Earl of Lejre," shouted someone near the stage.

Hege looked out at the people and realized how disconnected they were from the atrocities she and those like her had faced. Perhaps she was wrong—were these folks not slaves?

"But this woman here . . ." said Hrothgar gesturing towards Hege. "Has sought to take from you what we have so painstakingly built. She meant to undermine the safety that these walls provide. This is an injustice that cannot be overlooked."

"No, it cannot," shouted a person in the crowd.

The crowd roared.

Skadi heard the crowd cheering in the common. The energy was worrisome.

"Solveig, think for a moment. I know you have the capacity to see the truth," pleaded Skadi.

Solveig continued to look at the dog by her side.

"I have done a horrible thing," Solveig said.

"I am not my past, and neither are you. We are who we choose to be."

Solveig said nothing.

"I'm going," said Skadi. "Try stopping me if you feel I'm in the wrong."

Skadi took a step back. Neither Beowulf nor Solveig said anything or moved to stop her. She took another step, pivoted, and ran. She caught up to Hovard who was standing at the edge of the crowd. He glanced at her when she stopped next to him.

Skadi, who was taller than most, looked over the crowd at the stage and saw a woman shackled and gagged with Hrothgar standing over her.

"Fortunately for that woman, he likes to pontificate, but I fear he does not intend for her to have an easy death," Hovard said.

"What can we do?" Skadi said.

"You know what must be done. Everything from this point forward is going to happen incredibly fast."

"If you give it your all, you may slow him down, but you will not survive. Even if your power was not waning, it would not be enough."

Hovard turned to face Skadi.

"My boy was my first failure. My second was blaming you for just trying to protect your family. I am proud of the woman you have become."

Skadi reached out and put a hand on Hovard's shoulder. Hovard took her hand and nodded.

"Thank you for taking me in when I lost everything. Even when Fell was at his worst, you made me feel safe," said Skadi. "You saved my life."

Hovard wiped a tear forming in his left eye.

"No Skadi. You saved mine."

Hege's eyes grew wide when she saw Hrothgar pull a knife from within his pelt. She pulled at her shackles, but there was nothing she could do.

"Mmmmmm," she shouted from behind her gag. "Lemmmmeeee gooooo."

"See how the guilty struggles for freedom, knowing full well she intended to deprive you all of yours," shouted Hrothgar. "Well, we have

202

a way of dealing with people like her. I know this town takes no pleasure in the ways of the Vikings, but there is a practice that they would use against their enemies, and I think it suits this moment. According to legend, Ivar the Boneless ritually executed Ælla of Northumbria using the blood eagle. I think it is only fair that she would who bring the evil forces of those beyond the wall upon us, suffer the worst that they would do. Do you all agree?"

Hege heard the crowd launch into its biggest uproar yet. People in the back were cheering and shouting. She tried again, harder than before to free herself but there was no breaking the iron. She looked up at Hrothgar as he neared her with the knife drawn.

Hrothgar exited Hege's view when he moved behind her, but she could feel his hot breath as he got in close.

"You tried, but you see this is what the people want," he whispered.

The outermost layer of her pelt was torn off and the tip of the knife touched her back. Hege closed her eyes and braced for the pain to begin, but just as she was expecting the blade to break skin, the knife left her back and she heard a collective gasp from the crowd. She opened her eyes and saw everyone looking in the same direction. She turned to see a man engulfed in flames, flying towards the stage.

He landed on the stage and the heat emanating from him was almost suffocating.

"Let her go," he said.

"You, my friend, are making a grave mistake," Hrothgar responded.

"Avert your gaze," said Hovard to Hege.

She did as instructed, but as Hovard reached for the chains at her feet, out of the corner of her eyes, she saw Hrothgar push the man off the stage. Hege turned for a better look. Hovard landed many feet away and was slowly trying to collect himself.

The crowd cheered.

"Another would-be usurper," Hrothgar said before leaping from the stage.

Hege tried once more to free herself, knowing the outcome would be the same but trying all the same. The only thing that had changed was the attention of the crowd. No one was looking her way. Sensing an opportunity, she started looking around the stage for anything she could use to leverage an escape and the only thing that stood out was a protruding iron bar used to stake her chains, but it was just out of reach.

"Damn it," she whispered.

As soon as Hovard was thrust from the stage, Skadi shifted her attention to the woman in shackles. The crowd scattered enough as the battle ensued that she had a clear path to the stage and made for the woman with haste. When she was close, she realized she had met the woman before while on Hrothgar's Road.

Skadi heard the woman on stage struggling against her bondage and the frustration in her voice. She approached from behind and tapped the stage. The woman looked back at her. Skadi put a finger to her lips.

An explosion caught everyone's attention. The battle between Hrothgar and Hovard was heating up. Skadi used the distraction to leap on stage. The first thing she noticed was the iron pole staking the woman's chains. She grabbed it, but as she suspected, it would not budge. She turned around and removed the gag from Hege's mouth.

"Don't risk your life for mine."

"What is your name?" Skadi said.

"Hege."

"Hege, I am going to get you out of here."

Reluctantly, Hege nodded.

Skadi jumped off the stage and moved around to an opening so she could see under it. The iron pole was lodged deep into the dirt. She kicked it to loosen it, but it did not budge. She kicked it again and again to dislodge it, but it was for naught. The pole was dug in too deep.

"Do you need help with that?"

Startled, Skadi let go of the pole and stood back for a second. Beowulf was standing behind her. She turned to face him.

"Lift with your legs," he said. "I'll pull from the top of the stage."

Skadi paused for a moment then nodded.

Together with their combined strength, the pole started to budge and within moments it freed from the ground.

Skadi let go and jumped back on stage as Beowulf finished pulling the pole up through the hole in the stage, freeing the chains. Then another explosion caught her attention, and the crowd started to scatter. Hovard hit the ground hard a few feet away from her. He struggled to get his footing.

"Are you ok?" Skadi said.

"I'll make it," he answered.

Skadi turned to help Hege get to her feet.

"Let's go," she said.

"Where do you think you're going?" said Hrothgar landing on the stage behind them.

Skadi quickly stepped between Hrothgar and Hege. Then to her surprise, Beowulf joined her.

"Beowulf, you would turn against a lifelong ally of the Geats?" Hrothgar said.

"Make the honorable decision, old friend, and turn away from this path you are on," said Beowulf.

"Has this Jötunn-Breaker gotten in your head?"

Skadi observed the exchange between the two men and gestured for Hege to climb down from the stage.

"Do you think I do not see you?" Hrothgar said to Skadi.

"I helped you when this town was plagued by Grendel, but I see it is now plagued by you," said Beowulf. "And I do enjoy a challenge."

"Beowulf, I think it is time you return to the Geatland before your people must choose a new king."

Skadi again gestured for Hege to keep moving. Then Hrothgar in an instant slammed into Skadi, sending her flying. She hit the ground and rolled to a stop. She ruminated in the dirt for a moment, shaken by what just happened. She had never been on the receiving end of such power and in that moment, gained a new appreciation for what Yggdrasil had at one time gifted her.

She shook her head as she rose. For a moment Midgard was spinning. Skadi regained focus in time to see Hrothgar still on the stage bypassing Beowulf and approaching Hege.

"Run," whispered Skadi as she still struggled to fully regain her sense of self in her spinning world.

Beowulf stepped in between Hege and Hrothgar.

"We won't win this way," said Solveig, who appeared next to Skadi.

"He is too powerful," Skadi said.

"Hrothgar is no warrior, but that matters little with the power of Yggdrasil coursing through his body."

"Can we use the orb from earlier to drain his power?"

"He consumed it."

Skadi turned her attention away from Hrothgar and Beowulf to Solveig.

"There must be another way to undo what was done."

"There is . . . but . . ."

"What?"

"We were saving it for someone else."

Skadi saw Hovard finally pick himself up and unleash a barrage of fire upon Hrothgar, forcing the Earl to abandon his pursuit of Hege.

"How long do you think your uncle can keep that up?" said Solveig.

Skadi watched Hovard launch himself into the air to avoid retaliation and just barely evade a killing blow.

"Not long," she answered. "And we must free Hege," said Skadi.

The Lejre town common was in complete disarray. The crowd that once cheered on Hrothgar had long since scattered. Cottages and store-houses that decorated the outer rim of the common were burning and collapsing.

Hovard sucked in as much air as he could and proceeded to wipe the sweat from his brow. His heart was racing.

"Look at what you have caused," shouted Hrothgar who was growing frustrated he had yet to kill Hovard.

"This was all your doing, and you can stop this at any moment."

"That moment is fast approaching, and it'll be your last breath."

Hege slid her legs over the edge of the stage and looked down. The drop from where she was to the ground was greater than she realized and still being bound at her ankles and wrists almost assured she would not land with grace. She looked back just once and saw Hovard engaged with

Hrothgar. It was less of a fight and more of a high-stakes game of cat and mouse that left cottages burning.

"You can do this," she whispered to herself.

She heard a building collapse and looked back to see Hrothgar emerging from a storehouse that fell in on itself. Then she felt a yank on the chains around her ankles. Hege jerked her feet away and looked down to see Solveig had grabbed hold.

"Be still," she said.

Hege looked at Skadi who was standing just behind Solveig.

"It's ok," Skadi assured her.

Hege didn't move as Solveig lifted a rune stone to the iron chain. The chain glowed for a moment then crumbled from around Hege's ankles.

"Now your wrists," Solveig said. "Quickly."

Hege did as she was told, and just like the iron chains around her ankles, the ones binding her wrists were turned to dust as well.

"Jump," said Skadi.

Hege hopped to the ground.

Beowulf leapt down right after her to join the group.

"Beowulf, you know what happened to Brokkr. I need you to tell all of us exactly what you know. Especially Eitri. I have a plan, but I need him to make it work," Solveig said.

"What is going on here?" said Hege.

"Should we bring her with us?" Solveig asked, gesturing towards Hege.

Hege looked at Skadi. Skadi nodded.

"The Earl wanted her dead for a reason. Best not to leave her so he might finish the job."

TWENTY-SEVEN

BEOWULF & GRENDEL

"Eitri, do you truly believe Hrothgar will honor any sort of arrangement with you?"

The dwarf kept his back to Mimir as he fiddled with the armor that he had shown Solveig.

"You know this is a fool's errand. The gods are not to be trifled with."

Eitri continued to ignore him.

"If Thor shows up here, this whole town is doomed."

"Silence, Mimir."

"Even if Thor were not a looming threat . . . which he most certainly is . . . Hrothgar sees Midgard atop the World Tree. Not Nidavellir. This will not work out in your favor."

Eitri put down the armor and finally turned around to face Mimir.

"If you, Solveig, and Hrothgar make these weapons, the only thing that will happen is that Thor will slaughter every single person in this town like he did in Nyköping years ago. That I can assure you will happen. No amount of preparation or scheming can help a mortal overcome the sheer might of Thor. He is the one who rides alone, the champion of the Aesir, the God of Thunder."

"You think I do not know what Thor is capable of. We made his hammer, and he killed my brother with it. He will pay for that."

"That's not true," said Beowulf interrupting the conversation.

Mimir looked towards the door as Skadi, Solveig, Beowulf, and Hege entered.

"What did you say?" asked Eitri.

"Listen, and I will tell you a truth that I have struggled to accept for years."

Seven Years Ago

Beowulf observed Hrothgar and his wife, Wealhtheow, leave for bed so that he and his men could guard against Grendel alone. He removed his iron breastplate, his helmet, and gave his blade to one of his fellow Geatish warriors.

"Grendel fights without a sword, and so shall I. Glory will be granted to whichever earns it."

Then from the moor, beneath misty crags, Grendel came loping. The door, braced with iron bands, sprang free at his touch, and Grendel advanced wrathfully. His first victim was one of Beowulf's men by the door. He grabbed him and tore him apart, bit to bone, and consumed him. He committed this violence all the while wailing something near unintelligible—a ghastly scream.

Beowulf rose as Grendel began terrorizing the mead hall. Beowulf roared and beat his chest before engaging the creature. Their bout was great, but glory was given to the warrior from Geatland, and Heorot Hall was cleansed of Grendel's torment and saved from ruin. But the battle had not ceased entirely for Grendel lived and fled minus an arm.

In the morning, Beowulf pursued the blood trails and found Grendel, beaten and doomed, whispering as death came for him. In the water seeped with the creature's gore, Beowulf drew near.

"What is it you speak, foul beast?"

The same unintelligible utterance from the night before escaped Grendel's mouth and Beowulf listened intently.

"Your final words shall be nonsense then."

"Ei . . . tri . . . bro . . . ther."

Death-marked, he died, and Beowulf stood back up with curiosity overshadowing his joy of battle. Beowulf returned to Heorot Hall with Grendel's remains, and that night they feasted as the body burned atop a pyre.

Sitting beside Hrothgar and Wealhtheow Beowulf spoke.

"Grendel's final words were a mystery to me."

"What did the creature speak?" Hrothgar asked.

For a moment Beowulf contemplated not answering and dropping the conversation. He turned to face his men who celebrated in the hall.

"He claims to have been the brother of the dwarf Eitri of Nidavellir."

With those words spoken, Beowulf noticed Hrothgar glance at his wife and the disapproving look she responded with.

"Let us talk at a different time. Tonight, we feast," Hrothgar stated. "You have saved us from the beast in the night who spent twelve years tormenting this hall and my people."

The day following, Beowulf found Hrothgar in Heorot Hall inspecting the damage from the battle.

"You fought well against the ogre," Hrothgar stated.

"He was a mighty creature, but in him, there was a great sadness."

"Tell me, do you sail for the Geatland soon?"

"My men prep the ship as we speak."

"What you have done for this town shall never be forgotten."

"Hrothgar, why did you wait so long to call for me? I could have slain this beast many years ago."

Hrothgar hung his head and then looked woefully up at Beowulf.

"I assure you my friend I wished to but Grendel . . ."

"Grendel was what?"

"Grendel was my greatest shame. I tried all I could to do away with him on my own."

"It said it was Eitri's brother. What do you know of that?"

Hrothgar looked at Beowulf then directed Beowulf to the window along the side of the hall.

"See that town below. I am compelled to see it grow and thrive."

"I understand the pressure to do all you can for your people."

"I dabbled with magic that I was not ready or able to control, my friend."

Beowulf looked away from the window, towards Hrothgar.

"What . . . did you do?"

"I wanted the great blacksmith of the dwarves to use alchemy to forge a weapon for me to protect Lejre. But the alchemy was too great for him and turned him into Grendel. I carried the shame of that disaster for all these years. There was no turning him back. You killing him was an act of mercy."

"Alchemy and seidr magic are chaotic. Best to use your own might. You know that."

"Wealhtheow spoke the same advice. I have learned my lesson."

"Does Eitri know?"

"That is the shame I continue to carry."

"One day you should speak the truth to the dwarf."

Present

"A truth that was never shared," Eitri said.

"A truth that remains evasive," Skadi added. "I read the scrolls that Solveig's father wrote. Hrothgar lied to you and Beowulf about the creation of Grendel."

"She is right," said Solveig. "Brokkr did not accidentally transmute himself. He did it when my father refused to."

The whole room turned their attention to Solveig. "My father had a special rune stone he carved that allowed for sentient transmutation that if you knew how to use could transform anyone into anything."

"Like a dwarf into an ogre."

"Or a human into a dog."

"Hrothgar stole the rune stone your father created and used it without proper knowledge, which resulted in Grendel. That I am confident is true." Skadi moved to the center of the room. The attention of the others all shifted to her.

"Eitri, this is the man you serve. He not only caused your brother's death. He tormented him for years by not killing him sooner. Will you help us make things right?"

There was a moment of pause as they all waited with bated breath for Eitri's response.

"I must avenge my brother," said Eitri.

Hovard kept his distance, flying higher into the sky to evade the Earl while throwing fire in Hrothgar's direction to keep him at bay. Hrothgar zigzagged across the scarred battlefield avoiding all Hovard's attacks from the sky. Each burst of flame exploded around him, but none touched him. Black smoke filled the town common as cottages, mead halls, and storehouses burned.

"You have chosen sides poorly," shouted Hrothgar as he leapt into the air after Hovard.

Hovard released a wave of fire in Hrothgar's direction, with the intent to send the Earl back down to Midgard and him further into the sky. But neither happened. Hrothgar burst through the flames and Hovard did not achieve the heights he was hoping for. At the last second, realizing he was about to be dealt a killing blow, he shot left, and Hrothgar blasted past him.

"You cannot keep this up forever," shouted Hrothgar.

"Make sure to hold the cart steady," said Eitri. "We cannot make mistakes."

Skadi placed both hands on the wooden handles of the cart and looked at Eitri.

"I have it under control," she said flatly.

"Hege," Eitri said, shifting his attention away from Skadi.

"Yes?" she said.

"You should stay behind with Mimir," Eitri stated.

Skadi, Beowulf, and Solveig turned towards Eitri and Hege when he said this. Eitri noticed all the eyes on him and Hege but kept his focus on her.

"We cannot risk mistakes."

"Risk a mistake?"

"I am sorry," Eitri said.

"I fought against this man while you fought for him," said Hege.

"Everything we do in the next few moments will be on a blade's edge."

"My children are dead because of this man. You don't get to take my vengeance away from me," said Hege, her voice seething with frustration.

"There will be much to do after he is defeated," said Solveig. "Your time will come."

Eitri looked her way and nodded.

"We must keep our goal in mind and not our pride," Eitri added.

"I have taken up the blade against my enemies and killed and bled for my people. I should be part of this final battle," she said raising her voice.

"Is there no way she can fight?" said Skadi.

"No," Eitri said. "Now we should be on our way. Surely your uncle has bought us as much time as he could."

"There will be battles to be fought in the future," said Beowulf sympathetically.

Eitri headed for the hallway that led above ground. Beowulf followed and Solveig followed.

"I'm sorry," Skadi said before following the others with the cart.

In moments, Hege was alone with Mimir in the underground forge.

"I have suffered too long at the world's end to not be there when the Earl is broken," she whispered.

"Hrothgar should be brought to justice by the ones he tormented. But those four are hardened warriors and Hrothgar has the power of the World Tree flowing through his veins. The power imbalance is too great," said Mimir.

Hege looked at the bodiless head and let out a small sigh through her nostrils. She turned away from him and looked around the room. The fires of the torches lit the room well enough, and a golden light caught her attention. It emanated from within a chest in the far corner of the room.

She walked over to the chest and pried it open. Her eyes widened at what she saw.

"If you go out there, it will almost certainly mean your death."

"I have already lost everything. Death has no power over me." Hege removed the contents from the chest and headed towards the door exiting the underground forge.

"The blade you wield is called Hrunting. It is meant to represent peace and acceptance. Hrothgar ironically would have mass produced it to wage war. Perhaps you can show us all there is a different way," said Mimir.

Skadi emerged into the town common. Buildings were ablaze and crumbling. Fires raged around her, and the sky was blackened with smoke. All the townspeople who had gathered to watch the execution were gone. Only Hovard and Hrothgar remained.

"We must get the cart into place," said Eitri. "The stage is in the center of the common. Go there."

"You may want to consider using a sword, Beowulf," said Skadi.

"I am no fool, Jötunn-Breaker," he responded while unsheathing his blade.

The stage was directly ahead. Skadi pushed the cart as fast as she could. Beowulf, Eitri, and Solveig escorted her. Overhead, Hrothgar and Hovard battled.

"This is good enough," said Eitri.

Skadi stepped back from the cart as Eitri removed the cloth that covered the front half. It revealed an opaque orb the size of a human head covered in runic symbols.

"You are positive this will work?" Skadi asked.

"If it doesn't then I pray our deaths will be swift," said Solveig.

Eitri proceeded to shift the two halves of the orb so the runic symbols aligned. He then backed away, and Solveig stepped up and placed both her hands on the orb. Skadi watched as Solveig closed her eyes, and the orb started to glow.

"What now?" Skadi whispered.

"We let it work," Solveig answered.

Hrothgar tired of this game he was playing with Hovard. He leapt after the man and just barely missed him. He landed on the ground with a powerful thud that left a crater and toppled a cottage. A beam from the cottage fell at his feet. Looking up, he saw Hovard hovering above, preparing to unleash a torrent of flames upon him.

Hrothgar picked up a fallen beam and threw it at Hovard with all his might. The projectile moved swiftly through the air, but there was enough distance it had to cover that Hovard was able to avoid it. However, he was not able to avoid Hrothgar, who immediately leapt after the beam.

He grabbed Hovard and using his momentum against the man, launched him towards the ground. Hovard hit Midgard with enough force to split the ground. All the flames around his body dissipated upon impact.

Hrothgar landed and stood over top of Hovard. Hovard's breathing was strained. He was gasping for air and unable to move.

"I . . . regret . . . nothing," Hovard said.

Hrothgar drew his sword overhead.

As he prepared to make the killing blow, a sudden strangeness swept through his body, and Hrothgar dropped the sword. It landed just to the left of Hovard's head.

"They would not dare?" he muttered.

He looked around, confused, and saw Beowulf, Skadi, Eitri, and Solveig in the center of the town common with a glowing orb.

"Fools," he shouted.

Hrothgar pulled his sword from the ground and threw the blade in the direction of the orb. Skadi stepped in front of the orb and deflected the blade with Ridill. The force of the impact made her lose her footing, but the blade went flying elsewhere.

"Damn . . . them," Hrothgar said.

He stood up straight and started running towards the orb. He was no longer as fast as he once was, and he felt his strength slipping rapidly. Step after step was harder than the previous. But this was relative to what he once was. He knew if he destroyed the orb in time, he would retain much of the power of the World Tree.

"We have his attention," said Skadi as she took Eitri's hand and pulled herself to her feet.

"You must keep him at bay until the orb can steal back the power of Yggdrasil. Be mindful that he will remain quite powerful for some time," said Eitri.

"Beowulf and I will spearhead the counterattack," Skadi said. "Solveig, use your runes to keep him at a distance. And Eitri make sure the orb does not stop working."

Hrothgar was upon them. Skadi jabbed with Ridill, but he easily evaded her. She pivoted and struck again, but Hrothgar caught the sword and yanked it from her grasp. The sudden jerk pulled her forward, and she stumbled before catching her footing. Hrothgar saw an opportunity, but Skadi jumped backward just in time to avoid her own sword being used against her.

Her heart was racing faster than it ever had before. Beowulf attempted to help, but a well-placed strike from Hrothgar sent the King of the Geats tumbling through the dirt.

Skadi tried to catch her breath but saw Hrothgar approaching the orb. There was no time to recuperate, and she took off running in his direction. But she would not reach him in time.

A lightning strike came down from the sky and blasted Hrothgar mid-charge. The sudden impact sent him flying. He landed many feet away but shook off the impact fast enough. He looked skyward with curiosity and what seemed to Skadi to look like fear. But then his attention shifted back to their level.

Solveig used her rune stone to draw down another lightning strike, but Hrothgar channeled the bolts of electricity through Skadi's own sword and threw the blade at Solveig. Reacting quickly, she managed to dodge the blade, but the energy it was channeling caught her. The surge caused her to collapse on one knee.

Eitri picked up the blade.

"Give it here," said Skadi.

He tossed her Ridill, and she caught the hilt. Skadi pivoted to pursue Hrothgar, who was approaching the orb. Beowulf jumped in front of Hrothgar, swung his sword, but Hrothgar dodged. Then, the Earl ripped the sword from his hands and placed his foot against Beowulf's chest, who went flying.

Skadi caught up to Hrothgar and brought the sword down, but Hrothgar moved to his left and avoided the otherwise killing blow. Skadi struck again, but the result was the same.

"Eitri, get the orb out of here," shouted Skadi.

Beowulf gave chase. Solveig regained her footing and unleashed lightning strike after lightning strike. Eitri grabbed hold of the cart and started to push.

"It's too late," whispered Skadi.

Solveig transmuted the iron pole that had been used to keep Hege's chains in place into a spear.

"Give it to me," Skadi said.

Solveig attempted to pass the spear to Skadi, but Hrothgar appeared between them and caught the weapon. His sudden appearance caught both women by such surprise that they each took half a step backwards. Hrothgar spun to gain momentum and launched the spear at the orb. Eitri tried to move the cart, but the projectile hit the edge of the orb, cracking it.

"Damn him," shouted Solveig.

Hrothgar turned his attention to her.

"You would betray me after all I did for you?"

Skadi noticed Hrothgar's attention shift and ran after him, but he swatted her away as soon she got near. Skadi slowly picked herself up and saw Eitri was just standing and staring.

"Eitri what are you doing?" Skadi shouted. "Go!"

He nodded and started to move. Skadi then got all the way to her feet and again chased after Hrothgar who was approaching Solveig. Beowulf neared as well, but neither he nor Skadi would be there before the tyrant reached Solveig.

Skadi was only a few feet away when Hrothgar grabbed Solveig by the neck. Beowulf was no closer. Solveig swatted at Hrothgar's arms, but it was a futile struggle.

"You have outlived your usefulness," said Hrothgar.

"Don't," shouted Skadi as she continued towards Hrothgar and Solveig.

But she knew she would not reach them in time.

Hrothgar's grip tightened around Solveig's neck, cutting off all oxygen.

At that moment a golden shimmer stole Skadi's attention. She looked left and saw a flashy silhouette of a woman.

Hege lunged for Hrothgar, and he tossed Solveig aside to defend himself. Hrothgar blocked her blade, but she forced him to brace against her attack. Hege stepped back and swung the sword again. He deflected but the impact pushed him backwards and he felt the strike through his forearms. Hege struck again and he evaded, knowing the blow would have been lethal.

"For years we have toiled away at your road and worked in your mine," Hege shouted as she struck with Hrunting.

The strike broke his defense and sliced his chest. He jumped backward and grabbed the wound, but Hege did not let up.

"And when we resisted you tortured us."

She followed with another strike that he deflected, but a third connected on his left shoulder. Blood shot forth from his two open wounds.

"When we tried to free ourselves, you killed us."

Another strike tore into his leg. Hrothgar stumbled and fell to one knee. Hege stood over him and drew her sword back.

"My children were innocent."

Hege brought the sword down towards Hrothgar's neck but was deflected by Skadi.

"He is beaten," she said.

Hege looked at Hrothgar who was breathing heavily and bleeding profusely.

"He deserves this."

"Revenge is a poison."

Hrothgar tried to move but the last of Yggdrasil was drained from him, and Hege had thoroughly broken his body.

Hege pushed for a moment longer but eventually sheathed her sword. She spat in Hrothgar's face and turned her back to him.

TWENTY-EIGHT

AFTERMATH

Skadi saw across the scarred battlefield her uncle lying on his back. She knew before she got to his side that he was gone but knelt to check his breathing anyway. She gently closed his eyelids.

"We shall prepare a pyre."

Hege and Beowulf pulled Hrothgar to his feet.

"Make this right. Kill her, Beowulf," Hrothgar said.

Hege glanced at Beowulf, curious of his response.

"You owe your life to her restraint. I doubt I would have made the same decision."

Hege yanked on the chains to pull Hrothgar along.

"You will be locked away until a decision can be made on how to proceed."

Within his workshop, Eitri repaired the crack in the orb as best he could in the time that he had to do the work. He stood back and looked at it. The glow had dimmed significantly. A knock on the door caught his attention.

"Come forth," he said.

Beowulf entered his forge.

"It is time," he said.

Skadi stood at the end of the pyre, atop of which was the body of Hovard, wrapped in funerary garments.

"My uncle was a complicated man."

Skadi took a torch from Beowulf.

"He lived a warrior's life and died a warrior's death."

She touched the torch to the pyre.

"Lo there do I see my father. Lo there do I see my mother and my sisters and my brothers. Lo there do I see the line of my people back to the beginning. Lo there do they call to me. They bid me take my place among them in the halls of Valhalla, where thine enemies have been vanquished, where the brave shall live forever. Nor shall we mourn but rejoice for those that have died the glorious death."

She stepped backward as the flames took hold.

"Be at peace," Skadi whispered.

One Day Later

Skadi woke up having rested for the first time in days. She slid out of the cot she'd been granted within Heorot Hall and made for the dining hall, where the smell of bread permeated the entire room. Through the windows to her left, she could see the smoldering remains of the town common and the people of the Lejre moving about, cleaning and attempting to repair what remained.

A knock at the door drew her attention away from the town.

"Come in," she said.

Beowulf was standing in the doorway.

"It is Solveig," he said. "Whatever questions you have for her, you had best ask them now."

Moments later, Skadi followed Beowulf into a large room where Solveig lied on a bed against the wall furthest from the door. The dog that was Egil sat at the end of the bed, and Eitri and Hege stood over her. They turned to Skadi when she and Beowulf entered.

"Her breathing has gotten worse. I am afraid Hrothgar damaged her spine and windpipe during the battle," said Eitri. "There is nothing we can do."

Skadi approached Solveig's bedside holding Mimir in one arm. Solveig met her eyes as she stood over her.

"This is not . . . the outcome . . . I was hoping for," Solveig struggled to say. "But here . . . we are."

"Have they not tried your healing solution?" Skadi asked.

"It would take too long to make more," answered Eitri. "The little there was, was used on you."

"You have . . . questions . . . better . . . ask them . . . now," said Solveig.

"I was promised knowledge of the whereabouts of Mimir's body," said Skadi.

"We know now that was a lie to lure us here," added Mimir with a hint of disappointment in his voice.

"However, Lejre is a well-resourced town and a friend of ours has gone missing," said Skadi.

"What is . . . your question?" Solveig said.

"Did you know of the jötunn in Fensalir?"

"Yes," Solveig answered reluctantly.

"Did you know he was Farbauti?" asked Mimir.

"There were whispers Loki's father . . . was in Midgard."

Skadi looked down at Mimir briefly then back at Solveig.

"With the power you amassed here, you could have done something long ago," Skadi said.

Solveig did not respond.

"The three of you sought to bait Thor to Lejre and steal his power. I pieced that together myself. Then what?" Skadi asked.

"We would have made . . . a new Midgard."

"How?" Mimir asked.

"We would take Thor's weapons . . . Mjolnir . . . Megingjörð, and Járngreipr for ourselves. And with the . . .iron ore from Bard Mine, . . . we would raise an army. The gods we did not . . . slay . . . we would . . . transmute to lesser beings."

Skadi breathed in deep and let out a low sigh.

"You thought this all to be possible?" asked Skadi.

"I still do," said Solveig.

"The Aesir gods are a threat. To deny that one would have the mind of a fool. But there are people here who need your help now. One is our friend Eirdóttir."

"Is she . . . the daughter of the Valkyrie . . . Eir . . . and a human?"

Skadi nodded.

"How did she . . . go missing?"

"Loki."

"Oh . . ." responded Solveig.

"What?"

"I do not know what the Trickster . . . would want with her . . . but there is someone I suspect . . . would have interest."

"Who?" Skadi and Mimir asked at the same time.

"The most infamous alchemists . . . of all time . . . a light elf from Alfheim . . . named Volund the Smith. He is known . . . to have been an Aesir ally during the Great War and . . . former husband of the Valkyrie . . . Hervör Alvitr. I have heard Volund is a collector . . . of oddities and . . . a half-Valkyrie like your friend . . . might pique his interest. And Loki being of the Aesir . . . would know Volund."

"How would one find this light elf? Without the power of Yggdrasil to use a Bifrost key, I cannot reach Alfheim," said Skadi.

"There is talk of . . . a dark elf who in Borgarnes . . . displayed a power unique even to her kind and Volund was seen atop a giant eagle. I believe . . . Volund was looking for her . . . but has yet to find her . . . because I have also heard . . . she is presently somewhere in Midgard . . . seeking other dark elves. If you can find this dark elf you . . . may be able to find Volund and then your friend."

"I know this dark elf," Mimir added. "She is a friend."

Solveig gasped for air and started to cough. Skadi reached out and gently rubbed her head. Eitri handed Skadi a cup of water, and she delicately put the cup to Solveig's lips.

"I have one final question," Skadi said when Solveig's coughing subsided.

"What is it?"

"What happened to Egil?"

Hege stood outside of the cell where Hrothgar was locked away. She observed the old man who sat defiantly with his back to her.

"You owe Skadi your life," she said. "I still believe you should hang for the pain you have caused so many."

"I did what I must to make a town that would stand the test of time and be a beacon to all the realms that Midgard has power," said Hrothgar. "My only regret was being forced to rely on those who could not see my vision."

"All you did was hurt the people of your own realm."

"I made sacrifices that others could not."

"*You* sacrificed nothing."

Hrothgar turned around to face Hege.

"You think I'm bad. Trust me, it gets worse. The long winter nears."

"Then your schemes and machinations were misguided. You care only about your legacy and that is how we'll punish you. Every reference to your existence will be stricken so that history will forget you," Hege said. "I will make sure of that."

"Count your children amongst the lucky that they will not face the harsh reality of Fimbulwinter. When the nights are long and the wolves are howling outside your door, remember that I would have been able to save you."

"Thinks highly of himself does he not?" said Mimir, being held by Skadi.

Hege turned towards the two.

"This town needs benevolent leadership. Something it has lacked for too long," said Mimir.

Hege glanced back at Hrothgar and then looked at Mimir and nodded.

Hege had a million thoughts racing through her mind and struggled to find the proper words to express what she was feeling.

"I . . ." she started. "I don't know."

"Mull it over," Mimir said.

"But . . ."

"Midgard does not need any more rulers who are maniacal, corrupt or have delusions of grandeur. We need leaders who are willing to put others ahead of their own interests. Those who have known pain and fought to save others from it," Mimir said.

"But I am not of the mainland. I was born elsewhere. Are you sure it should be me?" Hege asked.

"I will help you," said Mimir.

"What about Skadi? I thought you two are travel companions?" Hege said.

"We agreed that this is more important," Skadi said. "The signs of Fimbulwinter are showing. Lejre can be a haven, but it needs a leader with heart."

"And Solveig?" Hege asked. "She was part of Hrothgar's plan. Where is she going to go? How can I trust she won't betray me?"

"Solveig is not with us anymore," Skadi answered. "A pyre is being prepared for her as we speak."

"That's too bad, because she had a lot to answer for," Hege said.

"Hege, leadership is not always about what is up here," said Skadi pointing to Hege's head. "But rather what is in here." She pointed to her heart.

"There is no one else?"

"How long have you fought against Hrothgar?" Mimir asked.

"Since they rode into our village and demanded we begin work on his road."

"For years your resolve did not break. For years you considered the plight of others. Life is only going to get harder. If the prophecy is true, and Fimbulwinter nears, the people of Midgard will need a place to turn to and someone who can guide them."

"But you cannot simply replace a malevolent leader with one you have deemed to be benevolent. The structure that was used to abuse people still stands," said Hege.

"Then dismantle it," said Skadi. "Create a folkmoot or tribal council that oversees the town. But someone must lead now and that someone should be you."

"What about Egil? Why does he not want to rule Lejre?"

It was then the bark of a dog echoed through the hall. In walked a guard with the dog by his side.

"Solveig's father pioneered a form of alchemy called sentient transmutation. This skill he passed to Solveig. Hrothgar wished to use this power to transmute the gods into mortals. But the most it was ever used for was turning the dwarf Brokkr into Grendel and Egil into . . ." Skadi gestured towards the dog.

Hege jumped to her feet and stumbled backwards.

"We believe it is reversible. There is a dark elf who is a master of transmutation that I am sure can turn him back. The same dark elf Skadi must seek to find our mutual friend, Eirdóttir."

"I will take Egil with me and Mimir will stay with you," said Skadi.

A knock at the door of the hall drew everyone's attention. Eitri stood in the doorway.

"Yes?" Hege said.

"I have tinkered as much as I can, but the orb has nearly lost its glow. Skadi, you should come have a look."

Skadi followed Eitri towards his underground forge. Situated in the middle was the orb they used to absorb the power of Yggdrasil from Hrothgar. The crack was sealed but the orb hardly glowed.

"This was meant to hold great power, but the damage it sustained during the battle meant most of what was absorbed was released. I sealed it but only a tiny portion remains. I can make it so you can reabsorb it and you will regain some of your strength, but you will be nothing like you were before. I'm sorry."

"How much power will I regain?"

"You will certainly be stronger than Beowulf, but still a shadow of your former self."

Skadi reached into the pelt of her pocket and removed the rune stone Egil had given her to access Solveig's secret room within Heorot Hall. She remembered her exchange with Egil.

"The healing potion Solveig created; would it work on them?" whispered Skadi to Egil.

"She did not create nearly enough."

"What would it take to create more?"

"Energy from the World Tree."

"Power is meant to be shared," said Skadi.

A little while later, Skadi opened the door to Stigr's cottage. It was far enough from the town common to avoid any of the destruction. The people were huddled together. Some were walking about, but most remained seated or lying down. Skadi removed the healing solution from a pouch and started distributing it.

Later that day, Skadi joined Beowulf at the pier as he prepared to board his longship home to the Geatland.

"I am sorry about your friend," said Beowulf.

"His name was Stigr. He was a good man."

"I will send back gold to help the people he tended to."

Skadi nodded.

"Until we me again, Jötunn-Breaker. I was wrong about you. You are deserving of all the gifts the World Tree granted you and more."

Skadi watched Beowulf take the helm of his ship. Hege joined her by her side.

"If only he could stay. I would wish for him to regale me of tales of home," said Hege.

"Where are you from?" Skadi asked.

"The same as Beowulf. I, too, am of the Geatland."

HOME

Skadi arrived at the gates of Fensalir on horseback and was greeted by Bjorn.

"Mother," he said. "Welcome home."

She knelt and hugged him.

"Is everything ok?" Bjorn said, suspicious of his mother's affection.

"Let us visit your father."

Under the full moon, Skadi stood next to her son. She rested a hand on his shoulder as the two looked upon the memorial of Bjorn's fallen father and Skadi's fallen husband.

"I love you, Father," Bjorn whispered. "I wish you could be here with us, but know that Mother and I are well."

Skadi smiled at her son.

"He is with us," she whispered.

EPILOGUE

"When will you finish mourning?"

The woman sat with her back to the door, in front of a low burning fire, tending to a stew. She did not respond. She only stirred the contents of the pot and grumbled.

"What the humans took from you cannot be replaced. You deserve your revenge."

She turned her head slightly but did not look upon the man speaking to her.

"Be gone," she said.

She heard the man step further into her cottage.

"What did I say?" she whispered.

"We can right some wrongs. I found someone who can help us."

She turned her head a bit more.

"Who?"

"His name is Elfr. He can calm our son long enough for us to free him."

The woman laughed.

"You just wish to use our son to wage your war with the gods."

"And the humans. My distaste for their kind is just as great as yours. My father is dead."

"He was a nasty creature."

"But he was still my blood."

"Who killed him?"

"She bears the name of your friend the bowhunter."

"Skadi?"

"Frigg guided her so she could consume the power of the World Tree."

The woman turned around fully to face the man.

"My children defended the Ironwood and gave their lives for this sacred place. The humans exploited it for personal gain. But I want to rebuild. I have no interest in your games."

"Fimbulwinter is nearly here. Ragnarök is coming after that. The prophecy says we play a role . . . a significant one."

She sighed.

"I have heard the prophecy. Loki, it mentions your other wife too. Have you spoken with her?"

"If everything goes completely to plan, this will not concern her."

The woman scoffed.

"I have negotiated safe passage from the World Tree so we can survive Surtr's fire."

"What do you need me for then?"

"Angrboda, our daughter does not blame you for what happened to her."

"Getting the family together—that's what this is about, Loki? What about Jörmungandr? The World Serpent, as these Midgardians have come to call him, still roams the seas unaccounted for."

"He's the easy one, my love. We promise him a second bout with Thor."

ABOUT THE AUTHOR

STEVEN GRIER WILLIAMS is an avid traveler, amateur cook, and fantasy author. *Skadi*, *Thyra*, and *Skadi and the Geats* are the first three books in the Prose Edda series. A graduate from Northwestern University, Steven lives in Harrisburg, Pennsylvania, with his wife Danielle. Learn more at StevenGrierWilliams.com.

www.ingramcontent.com/pod-product-compliance
Lightning Source LLC
Chambersburg PA
CBHW011353010726
47494CB00008B/2293